AWAY

MELISSA LANDERS

Disney • HYPERION
Los Angeles New York

First Edition, July 2019
1 3 5 7 9 10 8 6 4 2
FAC-020093-19144
Printed in the United States of America

This book is set in Andale Mono, Janson MT Pro,
Memphis LT Pro/Monotype; Girard/House Industries
Designed by Jamie Alloy

Library of Congress Cataloging-in-Publication Data
Names: Landers, Melissa, author.
Title: Blastaway / by Melissa Landers.
Description: First edition. • Los Angeles ; New York : Disney Hyperion,
2019. • Summary: Teens Ky and Fig become unlikely allies in a stolen
spaceship, eluding space pirates and more as they try to save Earth.
Identifiers: LCCN 2018034547 • ISBN 9781484750230
(hardcover) • ISBN 9781368002349 (ebook)
Subjects: • CYAC: Adventure and adventurers—Fiction. • Brothers—
Fiction. • Orphans—Fiction. • Pirates—Fiction. • Science fiction.
Classification: LCC PZ7.L231717 Bl 2019 • DDC [Fic]—dc23
LC record available at https://lccn.loc.gov/2018034547

Reinforced binding
Visit www.DisneyBooks.com

For Troy and Blake, the original Gooseys

CHAPTER ONE

kyler centaurus

It's not common knowledge or anything, but stealing a spaceship is way easier than it should be. So easy that an innocent kid could do it by accident.

I would know because I was that kid.

And it *was* an accident. Mostly.

It all started on my family's cruiser, the USS *Whirlwind*. We were on our way home from another trip to Nana's planet, taking the same boring route as always, the one without a single nebula or comet, or even any asteroids, to watch through the observatory. Just straight back to Earth in a pitch-black wormhole. Never mind that the Fasti Sun Festival was happening a short hop away. Nooooo, we couldn't spare a few extra days for a once-in-a-lifetime display of man-made stars. That would have been too educational for a family more interested in Astroturf than astrophysics.

But I'm getting off track.

The day it all went down, my mom had her head buried in the gravity drive, tweaking the settings because that was what she did for a living as an engineer. On the other side of the pilothouse, my dad was muttering funny non-swears like *slime-sucking donkey lover* at his tablet while he organized the next anti–Niatrix Corporation protest. As in Quasar Niatrix, the planet flipper. Quasar's company fixed up worlds in other solar systems and sold property to people like my nana, who couldn't afford to live on Earth because of the redonk taxes. Quasar was superrich, with a billboard-worthy face and eleventy dozen charities that helped folks settle on new planets. I imagine he was no saint, but I couldn't deny the man knew how to run a business. A lot of folks thought that was what Earth needed, to be run like a company instead of governed by the United Nations. I wasn't sure about that, but Quasar had offered to absorb Earth into his private corporation and pay every citizen dividends . . . as in free money! I guess my dad was allergic to cash, because he'd been protesting for people to vote no on letting Quasar be the CEO of Earth. That was all my dad did anymore: come home from his nonprofit job and spend all night plotting Quasar's downfall. My father hated Quasar so much that his right eye twitched—actually *twitched*—every time he heard Quasar's name, which was a lot because the dude practically owned the galaxy. Anyway, my point is that my dad was too blinded by his rage-colored glasses to notice what my four brothers were about to do to me in the next room.

Give me a NWARF: a **N**oogie **W**edgie **AR**mpit **F**art.

(It's a thing, look it up. They added it to the slang dictionary.)

And as usual, I didn't do anything to deserve it. I was

minding my own business, kicked back on the sofa, watching a virtual-reality simulation of the Fasti Sun Festival—because, really, man-made stars!—when a set of fists pounded on the door.

"Hey, open up, dork," shouted Duke, my oldest and jerkiest brother.

"Yeah, let us in," called another voice. It sounded like one of the twins, but I couldn't tell whether it was Devin or Rylan. Since they'd turned fourteen and their voices had started cracking, they sounded exactly the same—like a moose in a blender. "We need a fifth man for laser hockey."

"Well . . ." added the other twin. "We need a man, but we'll settle for you, Ky."

A round of chuckles broke out. I heard my kid brother, Bonner, say, "Nice one."

"Butt-kisser," I muttered under my breath. And to think Bonner used to look up to me. For a while there, he'd even copied the way I made my bunk every morning, tucking in the corners to create a tight, crisp edge. That was before he'd sprouted four inches over the summer and decided sports and girls were cooler than tidiness and science. Now that he'd joined forces with my other brothers, I had to look up to *him*—literally—while he helped them terrorize me.

At least I'd remembered to lock the living-room door this time.

With a sigh, I turned up the simulator volume. A canned roar of applause surrounded me as a hologram of my personal hero, Dr. Sally Nesbit, appeared on a hover stage that coasted high above the festival grounds. I clapped along with the crowd until Dr. Nesbit raised one slender brown hand, and the crowd fell silent in admiration. Dr. Nesbit was a pioneer in the field of celestology, the science of creating new solar systems. Last year I'd won an essay competition on why celestology was the wave of the future, and as a reward, Dr. Nesbit had called me—on my own personal comm!—to congratulate me. That call was the highlight of my life. Not only had she grown the first artificial star, she'd invented terraforming, too, making dead planets livable. With Earth so overcrowded, I couldn't imagine anything more important than creating new worlds. Dr. Nesbit was a legend. I didn't just want to meet her. I wanted to *be* her.

I'd settle for meeting her, though.

She would be at the Fasti Sun Festival—the real one—in two days' time. Maybe if I tried hard enough, I could convince my parents to take me there. My mom loved science; she was the one who'd signed me up for my first physics camp when I was five. There had to be a way to sway her.

But how?

Fists pounded on the door again.

"Ugh," I groaned, pausing the simulation. "Take a hint and go away!"

"Come out of your cave, loser," Duke shouted. "We can't play with four people. We need five to make a team."

"That's not my problem," I told him . . . mostly because there was a closed door between us. Duke could make an elephant feel small, but he couldn't break through two inches of solid steel. At least I didn't think so.

"Not cool, bro," Bonner hollered. "Why you gotta be like that?"

Before I could think of a good comeback, I heard a series of beeps echoing from the keypad, and I froze. The twins were overriding the lock. A moment later, the door slid into the wall with a *hiss*, and all four of my brothers strolled into the room, slow and easy, like sharks circling their prey.

Duke shook his head at me. "You should've come peacefully, Ky. Now you have to pay for ditching your team."

"Yeah, there's no *I* in *team*," Bonner said with his arms folded. The little traitor.

"No," I told him. "But there's a *u* in *bug off*."

Bonner jutted his pimply chin at Dr. Nesbit's frozen hologram. "Laser hockey's more important than some lame sim. Bros before shows, man."

"It's not a show." I switched off the sim before Bonner could make fun of my obsession with celestology. It stung more, coming from him. Maybe because he was the closest I'd come to having an ally in this family. "It's a playback of last year's Fasti Sun Festival."

"Doesn't matter," Bonner said. "We're sick of you locking us out."

"Or *trying* to lock us out." Rylan smirked. "There's not a switch on this ship that we can't hack."

His twin, Devin, nodded in agreement. "You'd think Ky would've learned by now. Kind of slow for a genius, isn't he?"

"True," Rylan said. Then he glanced at his bare wrist. "Hey, random question. Anyone know what time it is?"

"Oh, I think I know what time it is," Duke said with a smile I didn't like at all.

"Me too." Devin licked an index finger and held it up as if testing the wind. "Judging by the angle of the breeze and the position of the nearest sun, I'd say it's . . . NWARF time!"

I leaped off the sofa. "No!"

Duke pounded a fist into his opposite palm. "Yes."

I bolted for the exit, but I wasn't fast enough. Duke caught me in a headlock under his smelly armpit and told me, "Don't fight it. You know there's no use."

"Gross!" I yelled, trying to breathe through my mouth instead of my nose. Duke seriously needed to use his water rations for a shower. I pushed against him, but there was no escaping his quarterback arm. "Knock it off," I told him, still struggling. "You didn't let Ricky Sheiver beat me up at school, so why is it okay for you to—"

"That's because Ricky Sheiver is a little butt-chinned punk," Duke interrupted. "Ricky doesn't get to mess with my kid brother." An evil chuckle shook Duke's chest. "Only *I* get to mess with my kid brother."

"Mooooom!" I hollered, right before Duke clapped a palm over my mouth and forced me to inhale through my nostrils.

Oh man, the *stank*.

If I thought that was bad, it was nothing compared with the moment Bonner stuck his butt in my face and ripped one. Bonner had exactly one superpower, and it was converting food into toxic gas.

"Quit whining, dork," he told me, squeezing out another

SBD (Silent But Deadly). Emphasis on the *deadly*. I'm not lying when I say that Bonner's farts could gag a maggot.

"Yeah, take it like a man," added Rylan while he scrubbed his knuckles over my scalp. Then Devin said, "We're putting hair on your chest," and he yanked my underwear so far up my crack that I tasted cotton.

That was when I snapped.

I bit the fleshy area between Duke's thumb and pointer finger—hard. He screeched like a howler monkey and let go of my neck, which allowed me to snap back my head and clock Devin in the face. Next I made a fist and aimed for Rylan's shoulder, but before I could land a punch, my feet drifted up from the floor, and I windmilled my arms for balance as the ceiling rushed toward me.

Gasping, I braced for impact.

We were about to crash.

CHAPTER TWO

kyler centaurus

Okay, never mind.

We didn't crash. My mom just turned off the ship's gravity drive to break up our fight. (You see, there's no gravity in space, so without a special gadget drawing us to the floor, we would float around all the time. And it's a lot harder to throw punches when we're drifting in midair.) Mom disabled the gravity every once in a while, but it was a total mind freak and always made me feel like I was free-falling to my death.

In the air above the living room, random objects floated past my head: sofa cushions, shoes, dirty socks, bagged snacks, an *Encyclopedia Universica* volume, and the sim projector I'd been watching when my brothers had attacked me. I waved aside a dusty sock and reached for a fixed object to hold on to, some way to right myself, but all I could do was drift upside down and wait for my mom to appear on the scene and ground me into next year. Because no matter what my brothers did, they always made sure the blame landed on yours truly.

Brothers are the worst.

My mom sailed into the living room like a blond torpedo. She narrowed her eyes, glaring first at the other blonds in the room and then at me. Of all five kids, I was the only one who didn't resemble our parents. Duke, Rylan, Bonner, and Devin looked so similar that you could barely pick them out of a lineup. They were jocks with Mom's light hair and Dad's chocolate-brown eyes and tanned skin. I was the odd-ball of the family, with dark hair and light eyes that could pass for blue or gray. Plus, I was super-pale, like full-on pasty, with orange freckles that blended together on my cheeks to form blotches resembling radiation scars. That was why my brothers liked telling everyone I was adopted from a group of radioactive mutants called Wanderers.

Did I mention that brothers are the worst?

Mom's gaze jumped from one kid to the next until she noticed the red blood droplets floating out from Devin's nose. Then her cheeks darkened, and I swear I saw steam escape from her ears. Mom hated it when we fought. It was the only thing that really flipped her switch.

"What the cuss is going on here?" she demanded.

Four index fingers pointed at me.

"It was Ky," said Bonner.

Rylan rubbed the shoulder I hadn't hit. "He slugged me for no reason."

"Well, he head-butted *me!*" Devin said in a nasally tone. He was floating sideways, one hand cupped over his face. "I think my nose is broken!"

Good, I thought. But I knew better than to say it out loud.

"The little jerk bit me!" Duke cradled his palm to his chest.

9

"Actually *bit* me, right on the tendon!" Duke weakly tried to make a fist, playing up his injury to milk sympathy from our mom. For such a big guy, he could be a total wuss sometimes. "I can't grip a ball now. Scouts are coming to Friday night's game . . . Astro League scouts!" He glared at me while his nostrils flared. "If I lose my scholarship because of you, I swear I'll—"

He cut off as the ship entered Earth's gravitational field, and we slowly drifted down until our feet made contact with the steely floor. In the living room—and in every room beyond—the clutter that had risen into the air now pelted down like hailstones. As soon as my boots hit metal, I scurried behind my mom. I didn't want to act like a baby or anything, but Duke had some serious murder in his eyes, and I sort of enjoyed being, you know, alive.

"You guys can dish it out," I told my brothers, especially Duke, "but you can't take it. Remember that the next time you think you're so tough."

"Kyler," Mom ground out through her teeth. She closed her eyes and pinched the bridge of her nose. "Why do you always have to . . . Why can't you just . . ." She sputtered for a while, until she sighed and said, "I don't even know what to do with you anymore."

Something in Mom's words made my ribs feel heavy. I had disappointed her. More than usual, I mean. And why hadn't she asked for my side of the story? Most of the time she at least pretended to give me a chance before she brought down the hammer of justice. My eyes started to prickle, but I couldn't cry in front of my brothers. So to stop the tears, I doubled down on my anger and blurted the first thing that jumped off my tongue.

"Maybe you don't know what to do with me because I don't belong here! I've never belonged here! I hate this family!"

Everyone drew a gasp, and the room went silent. No one moved or blinked. I saw my brothers trading sideways glances, but they seemed to have stopped breathing. Bonner was the first to unfreeze his face. He made a little circle with his lips as if to say *Oooooh, Ky's gonna get it!*

My mom's voice turned flat in a way that sent my stomach dipping into my shorts—which were still lodged in my butt crack, by the way. "Go help your father dock the ship," she said to my brothers while using her eyes to tell me to stay put. Her gaze was so misty that I could only stand it for a moment before I had to look down at my boots. "And make sure you send him in when he's done."

I knew what that meant: *Just wait until your father hears about this.* And thanks to the protest, my dad was already wearing his rage-colored glasses.

Bonner was right. I was *so* gonna get it.

CHAPTER THREE

kyler centaurus

You know that sick, tingly sensation that spreads down your legs when you realize you're busted? Or maybe you feel it in your spine. Whatever. That part doesn't matter. The point is everyone has an uh-oh feeling, and mine went into hyperdrive the instant my dad walked into the living room and found it looking like a crime scene.

I knew my brothers had already told him their warped version of the truth, because Dad was grinding his teeth, something he started doing a few months ago when the anti-Niatrix protests started. Aside from Dad's right eye twitching, his grinding teeth was a surefire sign that he was about to blow his top.

I grinned to break the ice. "Keep doing that and you'll crack a molar, Dad."

He didn't smile. Neither did my mom. Tough crowd, my parents.

"Aw, come on." I spread my arms wide. "I was just defending myself."

Dad raised an eyebrow. "That's not how I heard it from your brothers."

"Well, duh," I said. "Obviously, they lied."

"Really?" he asked. "Funny thing about bruises and bloody noses: They don't lie. But there's not a scratch on you. Makes me wonder what you were defending yourself from."

My mom flung her hand in the air and yelled, "Kyler, we don't use our fists to settle arguments. Especially with your brothers. You know that!"

"Whatever!" I shouted back. "They use their fists on me all the time!"

Mom folded both arms and lifted her chin. "So your brothers were punching you?" She nodded at the mess. "Today, when all of this happened?"

I frowned and pulled my wedgie loose. "Not exactly."

"You hurt your brothers, Ky," she said, and for the first time, she sounded more sad than frustrated. The heaviness in my ribs gained another pound. "You're not a little boy anymore. You're thirteen now, strong enough to do real damage to people."

I huffed a dry laugh. Duke could bench-press me with one arm, and Devin and Rylan probably outweighed me by a cow. Even Bonner was taller than me, and he was the youngest. "Not when they gang up on me like they always do."

My mom sighed. "Did it ever occur to you that they're trying to get your attention? That they want to include you?" She pointed at the *Encyclopedia Universica* lying open on the floor. "You barely look up from your books long enough to notice the rest of us."

13

That wasn't fair, or true. I noticed my family plenty. It was impossible not to when they were all around me every single day, talking and bonding over stupid sportsball, or whatever, while I sat at the dinner table with nothing to say. Nothing to contribute. Aching for someone to talk to about things that actually mattered to me. My family had taught me that I didn't have to be alone to feel lonely. Books and sims were my only escape from the ordinary world. I'd go nuts without them.

"But I don't like sports," I said. "I like reading and sims. That's not my fault. Why should I have to play laser hockey if I don't want to?"

"Because that's part of being a family," my dad told me. "We do things for each other, not just for ourselves. Do you think I enjoyed running math drills with you when you couldn't figure out multiplication?"

I narrowed my eyes at him. "Low blow, Dad. First of all, the teacher didn't explain it right. Plus, I was, like, four years old back then."

"The point is I didn't want to spend my free time on math drills. I did it for you."

"But that's different," I argued back. "You're a parent. Stuff like that is your job. My only job is my education—you said so yourself last summer when I asked if I could work part-time."

My dad tipped back his head and groaned at the ceiling.

"Listen, Kyler," my mom said, clearly taking over for Dad, who was grinding his teeth again. "What we're trying to make you see is that your brothers want a relationship with you. They just don't know how to ask for it."

Yeah, right.

My mom was bonkers if she thought my brothers wanted anything from me except to physically split me in half using my own underwear. But her delusion about brotherly love gave me an idea. If I could convince her that the Fasti Sun Festival would be a bonding experience for the whole family, maybe she would take me there. I would have to play it just right, though. My mom had a built-in lie detector that would trip at the slightest sign of fakery.

I twirled the hair at my temple and feigned deep thought, pretending she had reached me with her lecture. "So . . ." I paused, biting my lip for effect. "You really think Duke and Bonner and Rylan and Devin want to spend time with me? That they . . . *love* me for who I am?"

"Of course, Ky," she said, pressing a hand to her heart. "We all do."

"So I should probably try to include them in the things I like." I raised an eyebrow. "Don't you think?"

My dad's eyes softened. "I think that's a great idea."

"Good. Then I have the perfect plan." I picked up the simulator box from where it had fallen and turned it back on. Dr. Nesbit's hologram appeared. I showcased her with both hands, like the superstar she was. "Let's change our course and go to Fasti. All of us, together. It would be fun—like a family vacation but educational. I'll bet we could even get school credit for it."

In perfect sync, my parents' smiles went flat, and they shared a sideways glance. My stomach dipped. They'd seen through my act. I was busted.

"Seriously?" my dad asked, jerking a thumb at Dr. Nesbit.

"This again? I told you we wouldn't be a part of anything that involves Quasar Niatrix."

I scrunched my face so hard I almost sprained a muscle. My dad was next-level paranoid. "Quasar has nothing to do with the Fasti Sun Festival. He gives money to the scientists for research, and sometimes he buys a sun for a solar system he's building. But that's it. He won't even be at the festival."

"I don't care," my dad said. "That man is pure poison. It's bad enough that Quasar wants to turn Earth into a business; it's even worse that he's dividing us to do it. He keeps saying the United Nations shouldn't give equal rights to Wanderers. That's because he wants voters to think Wanderers are a threat, that mutants will take away our jobs and our land. It's a smoke screen to hide what he's really doing, which is stealing our planet. Why do you think I organize all these protests?"

"To stop voters from giving him control," I droned.

"Not just that," he said. "I also want to show my support for Wanderers. The UN *should* give them the right to live on Earth. Anyway, the bottom line is this: If Quasar Niatrix has his fingers in a pie, you can bet it's dirty. I won't support the Fasti festival, not with my money or with my attendance."

"But even if we *would*," my mom added, "we wouldn't reward your bad behavior with a trip. The only place you're going is to your room. You're grounded for two weeks, or until Devin's nose heals, whichever comes first."

"*What?*" I demanded. "But that wasn't my fault. I was defending myself."

My parents rolled their eyes at me—actually rolled their eyes!

The longer I stood there, the hotter my face grew. All of my parents' talk about families sharing each other's interests was garbage. My brothers didn't care about the things I liked, and neither did my mom and dad. They just wanted the fighting to stop so they could focus more on protesting and work. And whose job was it to stop the fighting? Mine. Because even though my brothers made it a sport to tag team me, somehow it was *my* fault. *My* responsibility to play their stupid games and bend to their will to avoid getting NWARF'd.

Oh, heck no.

I planted both hands on my hips and looked my parents dead in the eyes. "I wish I really *was* adopted from mutants," I spat. "Then I might have someone out there who actually cares about me."

I spun around and started cleaning up the clutter from the floor before they could order me to do it. Neither of them said a word after that. The last sound I heard from my parents was the heavy stomping of their shoes as they walked away.

The *Whirlwind* landed on our docking lot, situated on the roof of the high-rise building where we lived. I stayed on board the ship long after my family went inside our apartment to unpack. The sun had set by the time I finished putting everything back in its place. My eyes burned, and my head felt like an invisible hand was juicing it. I walked into the pilothouse and peeked out the window at our building, wondering what was happening on the other side of the thick concrete roof.

Dinner, maybe.

My stomach growled, but I didn't want to go inside. I

doubted my family wanted me there, anyway. The only time anyone noticed my existence was when they needed an extra player for laser hockey or something lame like that. My family didn't care about me. No one had offered to help me clean up the ship, or even bothered to check on me. So the odds of them apologizing were about the same as the moon coming alive and tap-dancing on the stars.

Stars, I thought with a sigh. I plopped down onto the pilot's seat and pictured what a man-made star might look like when Dr. Nesbit presented it in the night sky. I could barely wrap my head around the fact that we could create stars at all, let alone imagine them moving from one place to the next. New suns meant more planets to colonize. More life. How could my family not be amazed by that?

Because they were cretins, that was why.

I would give anything to go to the festival.

A quiet voice inside my head whispered, *Who says you can't?*

That was when it occurred to me that I had a sedan-class spaceship all to myself . . . and my parents hadn't removed the security key. A devilish idea bloomed in my mind. What if I ran, or rather *flew,* away from home? I didn't belong here, not with this "family" of jocks and bullies and protesters. Nothing would change if I stayed.

But if I left . . .

If I left, the galaxy would be open to me. I could start over somewhere new with the press of a button. The ship would pilot itself. All I had to do was set the course.

So I did.

But when the time came to fire up the thrusters, I sat there with my fingertip frozen an inch above the EXECUTE button.

Who was I kidding?

I didn't have any money. Or food, for that matter, except for the leftovers in the galley. I wouldn't last a week before I had to come crawling back home, and that would be even worse than not leaving at all. Then there was the issue of my parents killing me, restarting my heart, and killing me again. So instead of running away, I slumped over in my chair and daydreamed about the Fasti stars I would never see.

At some point, I must have fallen asleep.

I say that for two reasons. First, my chin was wet with drool, and I hardly ever slobber on myself when I'm awake. And second, I was no longer on Earth.

I sat bolt upright and stared out the window as distant stars whizzed past in a blur. There were no planets in sight, and judging by the swirling purple nebula ahead of me, this wasn't the way to Nana's house. I checked the navigation screen and felt my mouth drop open. The flashing beacon that represented my ship was halfway between Earth and Fasti.

(So you see, it *is* totally possible to steal a spaceship by accident.)

I guess my hand hit the EXECUTE button when I fell asleep. And because it would take just as long for me to turn around and go home as it would to finish my journey, it made sense to keep going, right? Either way, my parents would ground me into the afterlife, so I might as well earn the sentence, right?

Right.

An electric thrill rushed through my veins when I thought about the possibilities that lay ahead of me. Anything could happen on this trip. Literally *anything*. I could discover a brand-new element. Or meet a secret race of aliens. Or invent a new energy source. Or eat so much chocolate that I puked. Either way, I had complete freedom to make this journey into whatever I wanted, and once I realized that, there was no freaking way I could turn back. It was like the universe had dropped a gift in my lap, a gift I had no intention of returning.

I wiped the drool off my chin and smiled.

"Hold on to your stars, Fasti. Here I come."

CHAPTER FOUR

figerella jammeslot

Mutants get no respect. Especially mutant girls like me.

Which is stupid, really, because the word *mutate* basically means *to change*, which I consider a good thing. I mean, who wouldn't want to grow and change, to adapt to their surroundings and be a megaboss in the game of life? Who wouldn't want to be better at survival?

Humans, I guess.

That's the problem. Humans want everything to stay the same: boring and safe. They don't like to take risks. They would rather sit on Earth, just like their ancestors did, because they're afraid of losing their spot on the globe. The only people allowed to live on the "Original Planet" are humans with proof of ancestors born there within the last two generations. So in other words, if your parents and grandparents were born somewhere else—on a spaceship, on a colony planet, on a satellite hub—you're flat out of luck. There are a few exceptions, like for diplomats or Galaxy Guards whose families have to work in remote places. But for the most part, Earth belongs to the descendants of people who were either too scared or too lazy to break out of their comfort zones and go exploring.

My people packed up and left the solar system ages ago, so we're not allowed to come back. Technically speaking, we're still human, but people don't treat us that way. They would rather look down their noses at Wanderers like me, just because we don't stay in one place and we weren't born on their precious planet. I mean, what's so special about Earth, anyway?

But whatever. I had bigger things on my mind than the Original Planet.

Someone wanted to hire me. For a real, paying demolition job—my first since the accident that took out my blaster and my ship.

And my whole life, I thought with an ache.

I shook my head, swallowing the emotion inside me until it dissolved like an asteroid caught in a T-5 laser beam. It had been two years since the wreck, and I wasn't a kid anymore. I was thirteen years old, tall enough to pass for sixteen, and tired of hitching rides from one sketchy outpost to the next, begging for work and picking pockets when the pay didn't stretch far enough. My parents wouldn't want that for me. They would want me to pull myself up and get back on top. To do what I was born to do:

Blow things to smithereens.

From the day I picked up my first laser blaster at age three and clipped a flying space scorpion from a hundred paces, we all knew I had a gift for destruction. Word spread among the asteroid crews, and soon I was scoring more demolition work than Wanderers twice my age. Not to brag, but I was the best shot in the galaxy. If it weren't for my missing blaster—well, and the fact that freelance demo was kind of illegal—I would be swimming in credits right now.

But I wasn't, as my rumbling stomach reminded me.

The smell of roasting meat made my mouth water as I pushed open the pub door and headed to my meeting place in the back, where the tables were empty and cloaked in shadows. Of all the run-down mining stations in the galaxy, this one was the seediest, which made it perfect for dealing outside the law. The only downside was the miners—serious jerks. At the bar, every pair of eyes turned to slits when I walked by. Lips curled in offense, whispers spreading faster than disease.

Like I said, mutants get no respect.

Someone hissed the word *ghost*, and I tensed for a moment before lifting my chin and walking faster. *Ghost* was a slur for Wanderers. We had spent so many generations traveling in ships, deprived of natural sunlight, that we lost most of our pigment. So now we look like ghosts. Get it? Not the most original insult. As a bonus, our bodies had adapted to the radiation in space, which was good in that we didn't get cancer, but bad because the mutation left blotchy red birthmarks on our cheeks. I could blend in if I wanted to. All it would take was skin concealer, a bottle of hair dye, and some tanning pills. But why bother? I wasn't ashamed of who I was, and if anyone had a problem with me, they could kiss my blaster.

Well, as soon as I bought a new one.

"Hey, kid," a deep male voice called from the shadows.

"Yeah, you," a woman said. "Ghostie girl with the crazy eyes. Over here."

Ghostie girl with the crazy eyes?

I forced myself to unclench my fists. Whoever my mysterious bosses were, they probably wouldn't hire me if I threw a mug at their heads. So I sat on the edge of their table to give myself the height advantage. Maybe they would take me more seriously if they had to look up at my "crazy eyes" instead of down at them.

There were only two people at the table, a brown-haired man who was wildly bouncing his leg under the table, and a redheaded woman who sat as still as the grave. Looking closer, I could see that each of them had tattoos of bones inked across their cheeks and down the lengths of their noses, making them resemble living skeletons. The ink must have been holographic, because it covered their skin in a 3-D way, so realistic I wanted to touch the bones to see if they would feel solid under my hand. But I didn't, of course. These people were creepier than a balloon-toting clown in a sewer.

"Too much for you, huh?" the guy said. He snapped his fingers, and his tats vanished, revealing a pretty-boy face that only an idiot would cover up. "You probably thought I was a monster. Monsters ain't real, kid."

Okay, yeah. He *was* an idiot.

But even so, the collection of weapons and gadgets strapped to his chest told me not to underestimate him. This guy might be a few threads short of a sweater, but he had some slick tech, and I was betting he knew how to use it. What he didn't seem to know how to use was a shower. The pits of his T-shirt were dark with sweat stains, seriously gross.

Ugh. *Boys.*

The woman's tats had disappeared, too, but the way she tipped her red head at me and smiled caused the hairs on the back of my neck to stand on end. There was something cold and dangerous in her gaze that warned me not to mess with her. Not that I would have, anyway, because she was fit—like *seriously* shredded. I couldn't help admiring her long, corded muscles. I wanted to be fierce like that . . . but, you know, still keep my soul.

"I'm Corpse," she said, and thumbed at her partner. "This is my brother, Cadaver."

"We're twins," he announced. Then he felt the need to explain, "But not the identical kind. The fraternal kind."

"Yeah, I picked up on that," I said. I wondered if Corpse and Cadaver were the actual names their parents had given them. More likely nicknames they'd given themselves to justify getting creepy death-themed tattoos. "I'm Figerella. You can call me Fig."

Corpse frowned at me. "I thought you'd be bigger."

"Yeah," Cadaver added with a laugh, now shuffling his feet on the floor in a seated tap dance. He couldn't seem to sit still, which explained the sweat stains. "I've made *smells* stronger than you, kid."

I believed him. Even from an arm's length away, the guy stank like low tide. A fly had already buzzed over to circle his head.

"Maybe," I told him. "But I don't need arms of steel to do

this. . . ." And before he could blink, I dipped my finger in his drink and flicked a bead of liquid at the fly, knocking it from the air. The fly landed on an empty section of tabletop, where it lay stunned for a moment, then eventually got to its feet and zigzagged away in a clumsy path to the bar.

Corpse raised one red eyebrow. "Good aim."

"The best," I corrected.

"All right," she said while rubbing her jaw. "Maybe we'll hire you."

I smiled, but I hid my mouth behind one hand to cover up my excitement. I would make more money if I didn't seem too eager. "What's the job?"

"Ever heard of the Fasti stars?" she asked.

Of course I'd heard of them. Man-made stars were a pretty big deal.

Corpse leaned forward and grinned. "We want you to blow one up."

Even as I blinked in confusion, the idea of blowing up a star sent a thrill dancing along my spine. I could almost picture it: a flash of blinding light followed by a force so huge it shook the galaxy. It would be my greatest achievement, my personal masterpiece. I cupped my ear in case I'd heard wrong. "As in demolish an actual sun? Is that even possible?"

Cadaver bounced in his seat, practically vibrating with excitement. "It is if you have dark matter. Which we scored from—"

Corpse jammed an elbow in his side. "A little louder, you idiot," she hissed. "The Galaxy Guards in the next sector didn't hear you."

Whoa, dark matter.

That stuff was hard core—and super-illegal. I'd heard dark matter was some kind of mystery substance that made up the universe. I didn't understand the science behind it, but I knew it was powerful enough to destroy planets, which explained the "super-illegal" part. I wondered where Corpse and Cadaver had gotten it.

More than that, I was curious why anyone would want to destroy a perfectly good star. Asteroids, sure. They wrecked ships and rained down on planets like car-size hail. The only good asteroid was a blasted one. But a custom-built yellow sun, perfect for making colony planets livable? Seemed like a waste to me. . . . Not that I wouldn't enjoy blowing it to smithereens.

"Why a star?" I asked. "What's in it for you?"

Corpse gave me a look that could melt steel. "Do you care?"

Inwardly I shrugged. No, I didn't really care. But if I had to work with dark matter, that would be dangerous, not to mention next-level criminal. Maybe I could use that to my advantage. The shadier the job, the greater the risk, which translated into more money for me.

I pretended to think it over. "Depends on how much you're paying."

Corpse crooked a finger at me. When I leaned in close, she whispered a number so high I almost choked on my own tongue.

"Nope," I told her. "I definitely don't care."

"That's what I thought," she said.

"I'll need a blaster and a ship."

She slid a credit chip across the table. "This should cover

a blaster and a one-way ticket to Fasti. That's all you need for now."

I frowned at the chip before I tucked it in my pocket. I had hoped to score a ship out of the deal. As much money as Corpse had offered me, it wasn't close to enough to buy a proper blasting cruiser, the kind with a triple-reinforced hull to protect me from asteroids. Maybe I could afford a small fixer-upper when the job was done. I would have to watch every penny—make do with my cramped boots and my short pants—but it would be worth it to have my own ship and my own private space, where no one could tell me what to do, or how to act, or when to go to bed at night. I wanted to earn a living, all by myself. To be completely free . . . and all alone.

That was the dream. This job might help me reach it.

"Here, take this, too," Cadaver said. He handed me a comm link that resembled a glossy black button. "Call us when you land on Fasti. Then we'll tell you what to do next."

"What about my money?" I asked.

"You'll get it when the job's finished," he said.

I shook my head. I liked getting part of my payment up front, just in case a client decided not to pay. "I want half now."

"Why?" he asked. "It's not like we're gonna stiff you. Not unless we want to spend the rest of our lives with targets on our backs."

I couldn't argue with that. He was right.

Kind of.

My people had our own government that fought for our rights on Earth, not that it did any good. They were called the Council of Wanderers, and everyone knew that if a client refused to pay, we could add their name to the Council's burn list, making them a target for every Wanderer in the galaxy. But what Cadaver didn't know was that the Council handed out punishments for mutants, too, not just for humans. And *my* name was at the top of a different list . . . a Most Wanted list. I was a criminal to my own people, so I couldn't very well ask the Council to hunt down someone who crossed me. In fact, if I wasn't careful, I would end up at the mercy of mutants who didn't know the meaning of the word.

But I couldn't tell Corpse and Cadaver that. So instead, I said, "It's an act of good faith to pay some money up front."

Corpse pointed at the credit chip in my pocket. "Consider that your down payment."

"But—"

"Or I can take back my credits and find another ghost to do the job," she interrupted. "It's not like there's a shortage of you mutants begging for work in every port. I don't need the best shot in the galaxy. Second best will do."

"Or third." Cadaver snorted. "Or fourth, or tenth, or whatever. A star's an easy target. It's impossible to miss. Heck, I could do the job myself if I wanted to."

I scoffed at his bragging. He couldn't handle the job, and we both knew it. Demolition was tricky work with a lot of science involved. It wasn't enough to hit a target. You had to hit it in just the right place with the right amount of force, otherwise it would splinter into more targets instead of exploding into harmless bits. And destroying a sun was even more complicated, because stars were made up of gases and radiation instead of solid matter. Nothing about this job was easy.

But still, other Wanderers *would* do the work for less.

My rumbling stomach told me not to risk it. "Fine. But I might need more—"

"Make do," Corpse interrupted again. Then she stood up and charged out of the pub without a backward glance, pumping her muscled arms while Cadaver danced after her.

I blew out a sigh and glanced through the open doorway. In the distance, a boxy shuttle lifted off from the transport station, flying its passengers to larger ships floating above the atmosphere. There were only two shuttles per day, so I should probably hurry if I wanted to catch the next one.

Looked like I was going to Fasti to blow up a star.

My parents would be so proud.

CHAPTER FIVE

kyler centaurus

Banana shenanigans.

That was what my mom used to call the science experiments I wanted to do in zero gravity, to pass the time during all those boring trips to Nana's planet. "The gravity drive isn't a toy," my mom had always said in that finger-wagging tone of hers. "It's there for our safety, not for your banana shenanigans."

Well, guess what? My mom was a billion miles away.

And so began the banana shenanigans! (Say that ten times fast.)

I learned some interesting stuff by the end of my first day alone on the ship. Fun fact: In zero gravity, a fire extinguisher becomes a wizard's broomstick. Just saddle up, point the spray nozzle behind you, squeeze the trigger, and _zoom_! You're Harry Potter . . . in space! Slightly less fun fact: Farts will _not_ propel you across the room, something I wish I had known before I fueled up on two cans of beans from the pantry.

But despite my epic gas, I was in science-nerd heaven. I tried things my parents would have killed me for even thinking about. Like using a laser and a magnifying glass to ignite a bowl of sugar. (That experiment worked a little too well, hence my need for the fire extinguisher.) But once I learned how flammable sugar was, I applied my findings to a new project: making pasta rockets out of gummy bears and dried macaroni noodles. It took a few tries to find the right proportion of candy to noodles, but I finally succeeded in setting off my own fireworks show.

Then later on after a bathroom break, I got curious about the ship's plumbing and decided to follow the toilet pipe to a tank in the lower level. It was interesting to learn where our waste products ended up, but I shouldn't have opened that tank. It was seriously gross. And as someone who lives with four brothers—not ordinary boys, but chest-beating, knuckle-dragging Neanderthals who regularly "forgot" to flush the toilet as a means of terrorism—I know a thing or two about nastiness.

Aside from that, my day was perfect. I even discovered my parents had linked their credit account to the ship, so I could download all the games and apps I wanted. As a bonus, I found my mom's secret stash of chocolate bars in the drawer under her bed.

Best vacation ever!

The only downside was the high-pitched ringing coming from the ship's speakers, followed by a computerized voice repeating, "Incoming message. Centaurus residence, Earth." It seemed my parents were calling again. They had finally figured out I was gone—six hours later.

That's right, six hours.

They'd slept halfway through the night before they noticed they were missing a ship worth more than their apartment. Oh, and a son, of course, but I guess they had plenty of those to spare. Too bad I wasn't born a girl. We all knew Mom had always wanted a daughter, just not enough to keep rolling the dice and getting more boys.

To make the ringing stop, I rode my fire extinguisher to the comm station and held my finger above the DENY button. But then I paused to take a deep breath, which cooled my anger enough to make me wonder if I was judging my parents too harshly.

Was it really a big deal that they hadn't noticed me gone for so long? Was I being dramatic or oversensitive? Maybe my parents had a good reason for sleeping through my accidental blastoff. Maybe they'd been tired from the trip to Nana's planet or stressed out because of our fight. They had to be worried about me. After all, I *was* their kid.

I should probably answer the call and tell them I was okay. That was the right thing to do. Besides, they might go easier on me if they knew I was safe. . . .

Or they might yell my eardrums inside out and order me to come home. Then I would never see a Fasti star.

Six hours.

An image popped into my head of my mom and dad snoozing on their pillows while I zoomed through deep space, defenseless and alone. There was no way my parents had simply collapsed onto their mattress from stress or exhaustion. We had a bedtime routine in our home that never changed. Before turning out the lights, my dad always made sure the high-rise windows were locked so no one could break in using a hovercraft. And while he ran a security check, my mom collected everyone's tablets and comms so we couldn't stay up all night playing games. My folks must have checked on my brothers before going to bed.

They just hadn't checked on me.

With a frown, I punched the DENY key and floated out of the pilothouse on my fire extinguisher. I would call my parents on the way home from Fasti. In the meantime, let them worry about me for a change.

Today *I* would call the shots.

I was on my way to raid the pantry when I heard a knock coming from below the floor, and I paused, turning my ear toward the sound. The thump happened again, this time louder, and with a raspy *hiss* at the end. There were only two levels on the ship. The living areas were all upstairs: the family room, galley, bedrooms, and pilothouse. The boring mechanical stuff like engines and pipes were on the bottom level. Judging by the *thump*'s position on the floor, it seemed to be coming from the downstairs utility closet.

Knock, hissssss.

I stared at the floor as chills danced down my spine. Probably a piece of equipment had come loose and bumped the ceiling. That happened in zero gravity. But what about the hissing sound at the end? That had sounded . . . alive.

Snakes could get inside ships. So could rats and roaches and all kinds of mutated creepy-crawlies. They could squish their bodies through the tiniest cracks and then spring on people when they least expected it. And sometimes the radiation in space made bugs grow to monster size. I had heard stories about it. Like this one time, Duke told me about a kid who woke up in his ship's bed, wrapped in spider silk, human burrito–style. The spider had sucked the kid half dry before his parents had killed it with a golf club. (Though I'm not sure why anyone would bring a golf club to space. That's kind of weird.)

"Computer," I called to the ship's automated system. "Restore gravity to Earth-standard level."

"Restoring gravity," she chimed.

After my feet drifted to the floor, I set aside the fire extinguisher and glanced around the living room for something handier that I could use as a weapon. Everything good was bolted down: lamps, chairs, wastebaskets, side tables. I picked up a ship's manual and tested its weight in my palm. There was a nice heft to it. It was no golf club, but a book upside the head might stun a mutated spider if I hit it hard enough.

The air was thick with dust and engine grease as I crept down the stairs to the dim lower level. I thought about that classic scene in every horror movie, when someone's about to go into a dark basement and never come out again. Part of me yelled, *Don't do it!*

I paused, feeling a cold sweat break out on my upper lip. I couldn't make my feet move. I wished I were brave like Duke, or clever with electronics like the twins, or even reckless like Bonner, who would probably just laugh and stick his butt in the closet and kill the spider with his toxic gas.

I wasn't brave or skilled or reckless. The only thing I had going for me was smarts, and I couldn't quiz a spider to death. But as I stood there on the steps, the logical side of me knew

I would never be able to rest until I found out what was in the closet. There was simply no avoiding it. I would rather face my fears now than go to sleep tonight and wake up as a human burrito.

So I kept going.

The hissing sound turned into a rattle that raised goose bumps on my arms. Swallowing hard, I curled one hand around the closet door while I gripped my book in the other trembling hand. I gulped a breath and held it. Then before I could change my mind, I yanked back on the lever and threw open the door.

A tentacle snaked out at me, and I shrieked high enough to shatter glass. Stumbling backward, I dropped my book and landed right on my butt. Helplessly, I glanced up at the monster's arm, its curves glinting metallic in the overhead light. Something about the metal arms seemed familiar, but my freaked-out brain wouldn't let my eyes process any information. It took a few moments before I could squint and bring the creature's arms into focus.

Then I released the longest breath of my life.

The "monster" was only Cabe, our utility robot. We hadn't used him in so long that I'd forgotten he was on board. Cabe, short for Cable Aid 010, could fix things with the thin metal ropes coiled inside his body. He was good for tying things down or fishing for remote objects in space, but that was about it. He tended to glitch a lot and overreact. One time on a trip home from Nana's house, Dad burned his hand while cooking dinner. Cabe heard the yelling and thought Dad was in mortal danger, so he rolled into the galley with cables spewing from both armholes and covered the stove in rope. Only the stove hadn't switched off yet. You know how metal conducts heat? Well, the heat from the stove traveled through Cabe to the steel floor panels, which turned our trip into a real-life game of the Floor Is Lava. After that, Dad shut down Cabe and stowed him in the closet.

I stood up and brushed off the back of my pants, glancing at yards of loose cable spilling across the floor. With his cylinder-shape head, barrel chest, and bendy legs on wheels, Cabe resembled a living trash can. He was cute, in a goofy sort of way. I knew he had always meant well, even if he'd screwed up a lot. Plus, he'd been nice to me—sometimes nicer than my own family. He'd kept me company during a few trips, quizzing me on science facts when I'd had no one else to talk to. My heart felt heavy to see him like this, slumped against the wall, forgotten and alone . . . kind of like me.

I decided to switch him on.

One flick of the button behind his neck, and his body hummed with power. Light shone behind his eyes. He jerked upright and blurted in a tinny voice, "Moon of My Life, how can I serve you?"

I snickered at the funny nickname my mom had programmed Cabe to call her. I had almost forgotten about it. *Moon of My Life* was a reference to some five-hundred-year-old fantasy novel series where pretty much everyone died at the end. My mom was obsessed with twenty-first-century literature. She called it the Juicy Age of Storytelling. She'd passed on that love to me, too. But no matter how much she raved about her favorite fantasy novels, I knew no book series could stand the test of time like Harry Potter.

"I'm Ky," I said. "Mom's not here. It's just you and me, buddy."

Cabe swiveled his head in my direction and droned, "Hello, Goosey."

I frowned, remembering Mom had also programmed Cabe to call me by a totally embarrassing nickname from my diaper days. No one had called me Goosey since my last growth spurt.

Cabe scanned me from head to toe. When he spoke, his voice raised a pitch. "Goosey, your body mass has increased by twenty-seven percent. Are you in mortal danger?"

See what I meant about overreacting?

"I'm fine," I assured him. "I've grown since you were deactivated, that's all."

"Please stand by," he said. He went silent for a few beats while he synched with the ship's computer. "Two years, one month, six days, and twenty hours have passed since my last session. Was I in disrepair?" He retracted the loose cable on the floor like a kid slurping up spaghetti noodles. "I detect no new parts."

"No, there's nothing wrong with you. You were in storage."

His voice lowered in a way that made him seem sad. "Was my service unsatisfactory?"

"Nah." I clapped him on the shoulder. "They just don't appreciate us, bud."

A beep rang through the speakers as another call came in. I covered my ears and began leading Cabe to the pilothouse. "Come on. I want you to turn off the comm."

"Disabling communication is not advisable, Goosey."

"But you have to do what I say, right?"

"Only within my programming guidelines."

"Does that include turning off the comm?"

"Yes."

"Okay, then. Let's—"

The beeping interrupted me, but this time the computer announced, "Incoming message. Raptor vessel."

"Raptor vessel?" I said. What kind of ship was that? And why was it calling me?

"Pirates," Cabe hollered as the cable reel inside him began whirring. "Mortal danger! We must defend the ship!"

"Whoa, whoa, whoa." I reached out a hand to stop him before he covered the pilothouse in cable. "You're glitching again. Mom and Dad probably sent this ship to—"

"Message override," the ship's computer announced. Then a woman's voice came over the speakers, so cold and raspy that it made my scalp prickle. "Prepare to be boarded," she said. "And surrender your ship . . . if you want to live."

"Oh, fudge," I breathed.

They really were pirates.

Space pirates were no joke. Forget the yo-ho-ho-and-a-bottle-of-rum nonsense you've read about in storybooks. Real pirates weren't jolly at all. They slunk around the galaxy stealing stuff—engine parts, tools, metal, fuel—whatever was easy to carry and worth a few credits on the black market. If a ship was nice enough, the pirates would jack the whole thing and leave the crew floating in space with nothing but the air in their emergency helmets. My ship definitely qualified as "nice enough." It was no yacht, but my parents had sprung for some serious upgrades, including a triple-reinforced hull to protect against asteroids.

Cabe was right. We had to defend the ship.

"Computer, disable the main speakers," I ordered, making sure the pirates couldn't listen in on me.

"Speakers disabled," she chimed.

I turned to Cabe. "Can we outrun a Raptor-class vessel?"

"Negative, Goosey."

"Okay," I said. "So we need a plan B."

I glanced at Cabe's chest, still whirring with indestructible rope. If he covered all of the ship's doors with cable, the pirates would never get inside. I had just opened my mouth to tell him so when a *clang* rang out, and the ship lurched, sending me to the floor. The engine revved once and shut down. The pirates had already latched on to our hull. Next they would ram the doors until they found a way inside.

My fingertips tingled as panic set in. Hammering noises from below told me the pirates were trying to force open the main boarding dock, the one near the utility closet where I had just found Cabe.

I closed my eyes and tried to remember the ship's best hiding places. But then I realized hiding wouldn't work. Ships didn't fly themselves, at least not without a pilot to set the course, so the pirates had to know there was at least one person on board. If they stormed the ship and found it empty, they would just tear the place apart until they found me.

I thought harder.

I had heard rumors that pirates didn't like taking risks, that they were cowards who would turn tail and run at the first sign of a fair fight. If I couldn't keep them out, maybe I could wreak enough havoc to send them packing.

I acted fast and grabbed an armload of supplies. "Come on, Cabe," I called as I jogged down the stairs. "You're gonna help me make some mayhem."

Ten minutes later, the loading-bay door gave way.

I held my breath, afraid to make a sound as I stretched out, facedown, on a plumbing pipe near the ceiling. Below me, a tall redheaded woman wearing a glass helmet strutted on board my ship like she owned it. She didn't carry a blaster in her hands, and I didn't see any weapons hooked to her thermal suit. That was a good sign. But just as I released a sigh of relief, she pulled off her helmet and gave me a glimpse of her skeleton face.

What was up with *that*?

Then I saw the monstrous muscles straining her shirt sleeve, and my sigh turned to a lump in my throat. This lady didn't need a blaster. She could put me in a headlock and crush my noggin with an armpit fart.

"Yes," she purred, gazing around the loading bay. "This will do nicely."

A tall man skipped up behind her, making me rethink the whole pirates-not-being-jolly thing. When he pulled off his helmet, all I saw was a handsome face. No freaky skull hologram like the lady's. He wore a chest strap full of gadgets that clanked and jangled with his movements, which seemed to annoy the redheaded woman.

She frowned at him. "Can't you stand still for one second?"

He froze in place and counted, "One one-thousand." Then he bounced on his toes as a grin broke out on his mouth. His chest belt jangled again. "Nailed it!"

"Ugh." The woman waved at his face. "And why aren't you wearing your mask? You're supposed to put it on before every mission."

She snapped her fingers twice, and the image of a skull covered the man's face. The two of them must've had holographic chips implanted in their skin. Pretty clever for anyone who wanted to hide their identity at a moment's notice.

The guy jutted out his bottom lip, which looked weird poking through the bones. Like a skeleton sticking out its tongue. "I can't see as good with this thing on."

"Well, too bad," she said. "Your face is easy to identify."

She was right about that. The guy could rock a career in modeling if the space-pirate gig didn't work out for him.

"No easier than your hair," he argued. But then he flinched away at the look she gave him. "It's nice hair," he added with a weak smile. "Color of nosebleeds. Really brings out your eyes."

"Oh, shut up and seal the door," she said, pointing behind him. "We can't let the crew get away. You heard what the boss said. No witnesses."

No witnesses.

I gulped. That meant the pirates wouldn't leave me floating in space with the air in my emergency helmet. They would just leave me . . . floating. I had to get them off my ship, preferably before the dancy man closed the door. The pirates would leave a lot easier if the exit wasn't blocked.

As quietly as I could, I fastened my glass helmet over my head and whispered a message to Cabe, who was hiding at the top of the stairs and linked to my mic.

"It's *go* time," I told him.

"Warning," Cabe blasted loud enough to make the pirates jump. "This ship is under quarantine for the vortex stomach influenza. Leave at once or suffer deadly force."

Now it was my turn to act. I had read about quarantined ships in the *Encyclopedia Universica*. If a space traveler picked up an unknown virus, the whole ship had to go on lockdown to stop the virus from spreading to other planets. There was no such thing as the vortex stomach flu, but if there were, I imagined the crew would get sick from both ends, creating an epic stink. So I twisted the release valve on the sewer pipe, just enough to let off some of the gas trapped inside. Safe within my helmet, I couldn't smell anything except my own gummy bear–scented breath, but the look on the pirates' faces told me their noses were fully operational.

"Aaaaaah!" The man recoiled, slinging an arm over his nostrils. "It smells like a hundred skunks threw up in a broccoli sewer!"

I nodded in respect for his analogy. That was a pretty good description for the poop of five Centaurus boys.

The redheaded woman dry-heaved a few times before choking out, "I've never heard of the vortex flu. Use your air inspector to check"—she paused to retch—"for viruses."

Her partner nodded while squeezing his head into his space helmet. He switched on his oxygen supply and drew a long breath of relief. "Oh my Google," he said through his suit comm. "That's so much better." He pulled a device resembling a Magic Marker from his chest and waved it around a few times. It must have read the microparticles in the air, because he glanced at the object and told the woman, "No trace of any known viruses. The crew could be lying. Or they might have a new kind of flu that my inspector doesn't recognize."

The woman had refastened her helmet, too. She thought for a moment, tapping a finger against her face shield, before she called up the stairs, "We're here to help you. The Galaxy Guard sent us with medicine. Let us up, and we'll give it to you."

"Bull hockey," I whispered to Cabe. "Repeat the warning."

He did as I asked.

"What if it's real?" the guy pirate asked his partner. "I don't wanna get sick."

The lady shook her head. "Even if there *is* a new kind of flu, we can still take the ship. We'll float the crew and set off a germ fogger." She pointed toward the upper level. "Come on. Let's get rid of them."

Uh-oh. The stink had lost its bite. Time to deploy phase two.

"Light 'em up, buddy," I whispered to Cabe.

"Final warning," Cabe called. "Use of deadly force in three . . . two . . . one."

And then from the stairs, "bullets" rained down on the pirates in a firestorm that sent them covering their helmeted heads and running in circles. Pasta rockets zoomed through the air, each one popping like gunfire as its candy-core fuel exploded.

Both pirates ran for the exit, where they collided in the doorway and got stuck. I expected the redheaded woman to shove the man behind her and race out of sight, but instead, she reached for his chest strap and pulled free two flat metal disks the size of hamburgers.

"Use your shield," she told the man, handing him one of the discs. The device expanded into some kind of super-thin umbrella that covered her upper body. The pasta rockets zinged off the metallic barrier, protecting her from impact. She used the shield to guard her partner while he expanded his own device. Then they advanced together toward the stairs and began a slow but steady climb.

I bit back a curse. Whatever happened to pirates being cowards?

"Looks like we're going to have to deploy phase three," I whispered while shaking my head in regret. I had hoped to avoid phase three, because the cleanup was going to be a total bear. But scrubbing the stairs for a week was better than certain death, so I gave Cabe the go-ahead and told him, "Use the Mega Über Lube."

(In case you didn't know, Mega Über Lube is the most slippery substance known to man. It's used on ships to keep engine parts moving freely in subzero temperatures. And if one drop of it gets on your shoes, you'll feel like you're skiing down the side of an ice-covered mountain with a jet pack strapped to your back. . . . Something I discovered a few years ago when my twin brothers, Devin and Rylan, coated my boots in the lube as a practical joke. The joke wasn't funny. I ended up with a broken arm, and the twins got off with a warning from our parents. Typical neglect. Thanks for nothing, Mom and Dad.)

Anyway, Cabe replied in the affirmative and squirted two jets of neon-purple goo onto the stairs. That goo reacted to the oxygen in the air, just as it was supposed to, and instantly thinned into a pink-hued oil that spread out all over the steps. What happened next was so hilarious that I wished I'd recorded it.

The redheaded woman's boot made contact with the next step, and she went horizontal so fast she kicked the other pirate in the gut. No sooner had the man doubled over with an *oof* than the woman tried to right herself, and her other boot shot out and landed right in the poor guy's beanbags.

I cringed in sympathy while my shoulders shook with laughter. Watching the two of them slip and slide was like something out of a goofy game show. The pirates scrambled to stay upright as their feet disappeared from beneath them, over and over again, eventually landing them at the base of the stairs.

But the stubborn buggers still didn't quit.

"Use your grappling hook," the woman shouted.

The guy snagged another gadget from his vest, this time a metallic ball that turned into a massive hook when he threw it. The hook caught the railing at the top of the stairs and then produced a silvery rope, which came sailing toward the man. He caught it in one hand and wrapped it twice around his wrist for a better grip.

"Hold on to me," he told his partner. "We'll scale the steps together."

It took three tries before the woman could climb onto his back without sliding off. She finally managed it by wrapping her long arms around his neck and hooking them at the elbows.

"Can't . . . breathe," the guy sputtered.

"Quit whining! You can breathe when we reach the top!"

After a cough, he croaked, "Retract," and the hook reeled in the pirates like a pair of giant slimy fish.

Seriously? I had to admire their dedication, but this was getting old.

"Cabe," I said, "we need to dislodge that hook. Can you do it?"

"Affirmative, Goosey," he answered.

From out of sight, one of his metal cables snaked into view. It caught the pointed end of the hook and bent the whole thing into a straight line. At once, both pirates went careening down the stairs again, where the guy landed on top of his partner, crushing her like a bug.

"Cabe, hold on to something," I said while I wrapped my arms and legs tighter around the plumbing pipe in the ceiling. Then I gave the ship a direct command. "Computer, remove artificial gravity."

A sense of weightlessness settled over me as I watched the pirates drift up from the floor, covered in pink goo and windmilling their arms for balance. I waited for them to rise another few feet into the air before I grinned and said, "Computer, restore Earth gravity levels."

The pirates clattered to the floor.

"Computer, remove artificial gravity," I said, barely able to hold in my laughter while the pirates floated up again. "Now restore Earth gravity levels."

They clunked to the floor with an *oof!* and an *ow!*

That was when I realized how wrong my mom had been. The gravity drive totally *was* there for my banana shenanigans. I repeated my commands to the ship . . . three more times . . . just for the fun of it. (Don't judge me. It really was hilarious, especially when the pirate dude turned a cartwheel and landed on his helmet.) But eventually I knew playtime was over, and I deployed the final phase of my plan.

"Computer," I said, "tilt the ship thirty degrees to the starboard side."

The *Whirlwind* tipped hard to the right.

"Now open the door to the lower-level garbage chute," I ordered.

The pirates slid across the loading-bay floor at the exact time the garbage door opened in the lower wall. One after the other, the redheaded woman and her partner skidded into the trash chute and out of sight.

"Computer," I said, "close the garbage door and empty the chute."

The ship carried out my command, closing the inside hatch. Then, from somewhere on the outer hull, another door opened, and the pirates were ejected into space, along with a week's worth of melon rinds, snotty tissues, and banana peels.

I jumped down from my pipe and closed the loading-bay door so the pirates couldn't make their way back inside. Using an electromagnetic surge device from my mom's tool kit, I sent a bolt of energy through the *Whirlwind*'s hull to forcibly detach the pirates' ship from mine. A loud *buzz-click* told me when the ships separated. Seconds later, I ordered the computer to rev up the engines, and just like that, I left the pirates behind, floating with the rest of the stinky garbage.

I stood in the loading bay for a beat or two, too stunned to move. A soft laugh escaped my lips, and then all of the breath whooshed out of my lungs in a chortle so deep it fogged my helmet. I had done it! I'd actually pulled it off! I had saved the *Whirlwind* all by myself, using nothing but the science that my jock brothers had always said was useless and dorky.

"Who's the dork now?" I said, puffing out my chest.

"Goosey," Cabe called. He poked his head through the upper doorway. "Are you free from mortal danger?"

I smiled at my robotic partner in crime. Okay, maybe I hadn't defeated the pirates *all* by myself. "I'm safe, thanks to you," I told him. "We made a great team, Cabe. Now all that's left is to clean up the mess."

He beeped happily, his version of a giggle.

"Computer," I called to the ship. "Resume our course to Fasti. That's the last we'll see of those pirates."

"Course resumed," she chimed.

As the ship changed direction, I gripped my hips, superhero-style, and imagined a cape flapping behind me. "Cabe," I said, "I'm issuing you a program override. Instead of Goosey, I want you to call me Ky the Magnificent, Champion of Science, Master of the Galaxy, and Destroyer of Scalawags."

"Error, Goosey. Unauthorized request."

I shrugged. "Oh, well. Can't win 'em all."

CHAPTER SIX

figerella jammeslot

If you blast an asteroid correctly, which I always do, there's one short, beautiful moment when you can actually see it come apart from the inside, like a ruby bursting from cold gray stone. The rock ignites at its core and glows white hot, right before it explodes into dust particles. I call it the birth of destruction. It's almost as satisfying as getting paid.

Almost.

Anyway, my parents had always told me not to look directly at the laser—it's bad for the eyes—but I could never resist peeking through my fingers after firing a shot, because it gave me such a thrill. And if blowing up an asteroid could make my blood rush like a geyser, I wondered how destroying a star would feel.

My heart might actually explode.

I tingled with anticipation as I stepped off the shuttle and shielded my eyes from the man-made sun looming on the horizon. The big reveal hadn't happened yet, so the star was hidden behind a planet-size ship, which seemed backward considering suns were supposed to be something like a thousand times larger than planets. I'd heard that Fasti scientists had ways of keeping a star tiny until delivery to its new home was complete. Then the engineers would activate something with the press of a button, and *kablow!* Full-size sun, just like that.

But even in its shrunken state, the sun refused to hide its warmth. Radiance leaked around the ship's edges like a solar eclipse, heating the blotches on my face until my skin went tight and tingly. The sun was wrapped in an invisible force field that contained most of its radiation, but not all of it. Luckily, my body was equipped for that sort of thing. I could feel my cells absorbing and neutralizing the radiation that touched me, almost as if my mutated DNA were armed with tiny lasers. Like microscopic versions of myself. Maybe that was why I loved blasting things so much—it was practically in my blood.

Speaking of blasting, my trigger finger twitched, reminding me it had been too long since I'd had a good demolition. I reached into my pocket for the fob I kept there. It was a handheld target game that projected little 3-D bubbles for me to fire at with my fingertip. The tech was nothing special, just a kid's throwaway that I'd found in a trash can. But when the bubbles burst, they made a satisfying *pop* that calmed me down when I was feeling edgy.

I raised my pointer finger toward the sun and imagined popping it.

"Hey! Don't look directly at the star," a blond man snapped at me, tearing my attention away from my game. I recognized the man as the shuttle attendant. He hadn't smiled during our flight, and he wasn't smiling now. His eyebrows formed a slash above the same dark sunglasses I was supposed to be wearing. "I told you about the safety lenses when we landed," he said, handing me an extra pair. "Were you even listening?"

Muttering a quick *sorry*, I tucked my game fob back into my pocket, then slid on the sunglasses and scanned the festival grounds. There had been no windows on the shuttle, so this was my first glance at Fasti. I have to say I wasn't impressed. I'd read about the planet during the flight, but I hadn't expected it to look so . . . brown.

The entire landscape was made of mud, miles and miles of drab tan goop stretching in all directions, with piers and platforms built above it for walking. The setup reminded me of an ocean planet I'd visited once, except not as pretty. There was no natural color here. Nothing grew on Fasti—no trees, no grass, no flowers, not even weeds. The planet didn't have its own sun, so it spent most of the year frozen. Then when the solar engineers created a new star, the heat from the miniature sun would melt the ice into muck until someone purchased the star and towed it away, and the planet would freeze all over again.

A cycle of sludge.

At least from the ground up, the festival organizers had done a decent job of transforming the place. Restaurant booths and hover-chair rentals lined the pier, all of it covered by a clear sunscreen canopy that protected the tourists from getting too toasty. If I stood on tiptoe, I could see beyond the festival to the marketplace, where I had a lead on finding a new blaster. To get there, however, I would have to wade through an ocean of visitors.

Sweaty visitors.

Because even hidden, the sun was hot enough to melt my teeth, and people were everywhere. I mean *everywhere*. They clogged the path to the marketplace, not walking with a purpose but milling around sipping drinks and taking selfies.

Ugh. Seriously annoying.

"And I hope you brought a hat," the shuttle attendant said. I had almost forgotten he was there. "Because the force field isn't strong enough to protect someone like you from getting a sunburn." He frowned at the translucent skin on my forearms, already turning blotchy and pink. Clearly he didn't realize the color change was part of my mutation, and that it was impossible for "someone like me" to get a sunburn. "Where are your parents?" he added. "You said they were coming to meet you."

My stomach dipped. I recognized that tone. He wanted to call security.

"Right over there," I said, pointing at a general spot near the restrooms. Then I hightailed it off the landing pad and into the festival before he could ask any more questions about the parents I didn't have.

For good measure, I avoided the open areas and let the crowd swallow me.

That was my first mistake.

You see, Wanderers don't really do the whole *people* thing. We keep to ourselves on our ships, mostly because there are no asteroids to blast on the ground (duh), and also because the stares and whispers and "ghost" jokes get old pretty fast. When people used to gawk at me, I had gawked back and given them my I'm-a-mutant-deal-with-it! glare. But that had ended up earning me a few reports to security for suspicious behavior. So now I kept my head down in crowded places and focused on getting where I needed to go. It was easier that way. Plus, I'm an introvert, like next-level antisocial. In fact, while I inched through the mass of bodies, I couldn't help daydreaming about plowing ahead and knocking people down like bowling pins.

It made me grin.

"You there," called an old woman selling holographic tattoos of a dancing cartoon sun. I thought she might try to harass me or sell me something, but she just tipped her head in my direction. Her skin was brown and paper-thin, crinkling as her mouth curved up. "You have a sweet smile, young one," she said. "You should use it more often."

I didn't expect her to say that, and it knocked me off my game, as kindness usually did. I hesitated for a beat, unsure of how to respond. It rubbed me the wrong way when people, even other Wanderers, told me to smile. My face belonged to me, and if I wanted to smile, I would friggin' smile. But the woman had kind eyes, and that was rare, so I decided to thank her and take a closer look at what she had to sell.

I noticed something unusual lying among the souvenirs, an object that didn't seem to belong with the others. It had a thin handle, roughly the length of my palm, and protruding from the handle were three "branches" with clips at the end. I couldn't figure out what the object was used for. I was starting to think someone had left it there by accident, when the elderly woman picked it up and held it out for me to examine.

"Popular item," she said. "This is my last one." She pointed at the clips. "It's an automatic braider. You divide your hair into three sections, snap these over the ends, and choose what kind of braid you want. Then, voilà." She waved a hand like a magician. "A perfect plait, without the hassle of bending over backward to do it yourself."

An instant ache opened up in the pit of my stomach. My mother used to braid my hair at night to keep it from tangling. It was part of our bedtime ritual. Back then, I'd complained about how long it had taken to brush and separate my thick locks, but secretly I had enjoyed the way her gentle fingers had raised chills over my scalp. There had been love in my mama's touch. The kind of love a machine can't duplicate. But even if it could, I didn't need a gadget to do my hair for me. I could learn how to braid for myself if I wanted to. But I didn't want to. Just the idea of trying it made my chest feel tight.

I reached up and touched my rat's nest of a hairdo, so snarled I couldn't even work my fingers through it. I eyed the braiding machine while I bit my lip in hesitation. Maybe it would be nice to get rid of the knots in my hair. Mama had always said it was a sign of respect to look my best each day. She wouldn't be proud to see me like this. If she were here, no doubt she would tell me to buy the gadget. I could probably afford it if I skipped a couple of meals or picked up an odd job at the festival.

I had just begun to reach for the braider when a surge of panic rose in my chest, and I pulled back my hand. What was I thinking? I didn't have the credits to waste on something so silly as a styler. What did it matter if my hair was in knots? All my clients cared about was my aim, and that was on point.

I shook my head at the old woman. "No, thanks. I have better things to spend my money on."

Then I turned and walked away.

My mood soured after that, and by the time I made it to the other side of the pier to the marketplace, my shoulders were tensed halfway to my ears. The crowd was thinner at the outer booths, probably because the vendors there were selling useful (aka: boring) things like engine parts and tools instead of flashy souvenirs of a cartoon sun. I let out a long breath and tried to relax, but my muscles were still locked when I walked up to the laser booth to negotiate for a blaster.

That was my second mistake.

Never haggle on a bad day or on an empty stomach—my father used to say that. Money was important to people (double duh) and getting someone to take less of it was a tricky dance with a lot of steps to follow. You had to pretend to be a little bit interested but not too interested. You had to pretend to think hard about a price, even when you knew you could pay it. And most important, you had to be willing to walk away from a deal. Because if the seller knew you needed what he had to offer, you lost the control. Game over.

Even more complicated was negotiating for something illegal. So the last thing you wanted to do was march up to a seller and blurt, "I need an asteroid blaster." Which was exactly what I did.

The guy behind the booth already looked kind of sketchy, bald and tattooed and picking his fingernails with a rusted knife that had seen better days. But when a slow grin crept across his lips, I swear he could have made the devil wet his pants. In fact, I was glad I'd peed before leaving the shuttle.

"Is that so?" he asked, looking me up and down. "And what would a sweet little girl like you want with a big, nasty laser blaster?"

The gleam in his eyes told me he knew exactly what I wanted with the laser blaster. Everyone knew that Wanderers blew stuff up for a living. It was also common knowledge that blasting for hire was criminal. Only Earth-trained demo experts were supposed to destroy asteroids. But certified experts were pricey, and Wanderers weren't. That was why we got the work.

Since I had already lost my bargaining power, I didn't see any point in playing nice. So I heaved a sigh and snarked, "I think it'll look pretty next to my doll collection." Then I scanned the counter and the racks on the rear-booth wall, seeing only personal weapons. "Where's the T-five cannon? I heard you've got one for sale."

"Shhh!" He darted a nervous glance around the booth. "Keep your voice down, kid. I don't keep the big guns on display. And even if I did, a T-class laser is nothing to play around with. I'd hate to see you blow your feet off. If your old man wants the blaster, he should come see me himself. I've dealt with your kind before, but I don't sell to kids."

There were those words again: *your kind*. I nearly rolled my eyes out of my head. "I think my feet will be okay."

"For real," he said. The edge in his voice told me his patience was wearing thin. "Let the grown-ups handle it. Go get your dad and tell him to come deal with me." He pointed at a minilaser that looked like a squirt gun. It was the sort of thing an old lady might use to make her cats chase a red dot across the floor. "This is more your size."

I didn't know what made me angrier, that he had mentioned my dad, or that he assumed I played with toys. But either way, I snapped. I picked up a hefty laser pistol and aimed it at a few discarded plastic cups sitting on the pier railing. With a series of quick trigger pulls, I melted each one before the man could open his mouth.

I blew a wisp of smoke from the pistol tip. "Still think I'll shoot my feet off?"

His jaw dropped. It took a few tries for him to sputter, "Put that down. Now."

I did as he asked.

"What's your problem?" he asked.

"Problem?" I repeated. "I don't see any problems here. Only solutions. You have a laser cannon to sell. I want to buy it. Seems simple enough to me, so let's talk price."

His beady eyes focused on me, this time taking in my patched clothes and scuffed boots. He scoffed. "It's more than you can afford."

"Try me."

"All right," he said, lifting a beefy shoulder. "Ten thousand credits."

Ten thousand credits?

That was twice the amount a blaster should have cost, and it was everything I had—the exact amount of the credit chip Corpse had given me. And because Corpse hadn't answered her comm since I'd landed on Fasti, I had no idea if the job was still a go or when I would get paid again. Sure, I could maybe use the laser cannon to score some other jobs if I hustled my mining connections, but I couldn't eat a laser cannon or sleep in it . . . or fly it off this stinking mud planet if Corpse left me stranded here. I needed to save some money to give myself a safety net.

"Seven," I countered.

"Ten."

"Eight."

"Ten."

"Nine," I said, and when the word *ten* formed on the man's lips, I added, "Come on! I could buy a new blaster for that!"

He swept a go-ahead hand. "Then do it. I'm not stopping you."

We both knew I couldn't. Only licensed professionals were allowed to buy hard-core laser weapons. "You're a jerk," I spat.

He leaned down until his eyes were level with mine. "Yeah, you're right. I'm the jerk who's gonna turn you in for illegal blasting if you don't shut your annoying mouth and pay me ten thousand credits."

I snorted. He was bluffing—he had to be. "You won't turn me in, because you'd get busted, too," I pointed out. "For illegal weapon sales."

"I'd get off with a warning, because I have the right kind of DNA," he said. He used both hands to showcase his face before pointing at my mutated skin. "But you? I think we both know you wouldn't be so lucky. You'd get a one-way ticket to the farm."

The farm. A prison work camp.

I pressed my lips together while my pulse thumped with

fear. He was right. The farms were full of my kind. Some Earth-born sleaze owned the prison-camp system. He used prisoners like slave labor to build stuff for him to sell for a huge profit. And when Wanderers went into the system, they rarely came back out again. The camp owner found ways to keep prisoners around, making up new charges and adding years to their sentences until he used up their lives and discarded them like dead batteries.

Suddenly, I missed my parents so hard it almost buckled my knees. I wished my dad were here to close this deal so I wouldn't have to do it. I wished my mom were here to braid my hair so I didn't look like a rabid animal. I wished I knew where I was going to sleep that night, or whether I'd be able to afford dinner.

I wished I weren't all alone in the galaxy.

But then I came to my senses and remembered that wishes didn't come true for people like me. And since whining about my life wouldn't change anything, I stood up straighter and faced the man who was trying to bully me.

Like it or not, I was alone.

And like it or not, I was taking this deal on the chin.

But I would not be bullied.

"Fine." I held up my credit chip, but I yanked it back when the man reached for it. "*After* I see the blaster."

He frowned, eventually giving a reluctant nod. "Meet me in the docking lot an hour before the show starts. Look for a red ship with a white stripe down the middle." He jabbed a warning finger toward me. "And no funny business. If I catch one whiff of trouble off you, I'll—"

"Whatever," I interrupted. On a normal day, *trouble* wafted off me like perfume dabbed behind my ears. If you stood too close to me on a day like this, you were bound to catch more than just a whiff. "I'll be there."

I turned my back on him but immediately stopped short at the sight of a dark-haired boy blocking my path. It was obvious the boy had heard at least part of my conversation, because he stood there watching me like a spectator at the zoo. He seemed roughly my age, though a few inches shorter than me, and with the kind of clean haircut and shiny boots that said his family had money.

Must be nice.

I expected the boy to move, but instead he pulled down his sunglasses—actually lowered them all the way to the tip of his nose—to get a better look at me. It was a bold move that would have gotten his butt kicked if we were in a less crowded place. As I gripped my hips, I met his eyes, and then the little jerk pruned his mouth like he'd stepped in something gross.

That was all I could take.

"What're you staring at?" I snapped. "Never seen a mutant before?"

He didn't answer. His eyes flew wide with fear, and then he backed away and made tracks so fast I expected to see skid marks on the pier.

"Yeah, that's what I thought," I muttered with a laugh. "Keep running, brat."

CHAPTER SEVEN

kyler centaurus

Brat?

What had I done to deserve that? All I'd wanted to do was look at the girl, maybe find out what she was like. So I had gawked a little bit—sue me. I'd never seen a Wanderer before, and I'd always thought it was interesting how their bodies had mutated to adapt to life in space. Not only could Wanderers' blood cells fight radiation, but their bones and muscles stayed strong, even after years in zero gravity. And their skin made its own vitamin D, so they could get by with less sunlight than the rest of us.

Forgive me for thinking that was wicked cool.

My parents had taught me Wanderers and humans were equals. Now I knew that was true in more ways than one. Today I learned that Wanderers can be equally as mean as humans, too. That girl was a serious jerk.

I didn't know what her problem was, but I took her advice and kept on walking. No way would she ruin this day for me.

I had waited my whole life to see a Fasti star, and considering my life would be over as soon as I got home, I planned to jam twice the fun into every moment.

I set out to explore the festival.

In the marketplace, I used some credit chips I'd found on my ship to try the kinds of foods we can't get on Earth. I bought frozen citri-berries (a hybrid fruit that tasted like strawberry lemonade), fried protein on a stick (which was every bit as boring as it sounds), and cloned corn on the cob (which tasted like . . . corn on the cob). My favorite dish was called slorghetti, a pasta made from grain that expanded and contracted when it cooked, so the noodles moved around like buttery worms in my bowl. Bonner would have lost his mind over the stuff, so I took a video to capture what he'd missed. Not gonna lie, the idea of bragging about the noodles tasted better than the actual slorghetti. When my stomach was full, I browsed the souvenir booths and spent my last few credits on a holographic sun bracelet that rose and set around my wrist, so I would never forget the day my life peaked.

As I walked, I raised my sunglass-covered face to the sky and spread my arms wide, soaking up the man-made rays that filtered through the invisible canopy above the pier. I couldn't see the sun, but I could feel it in the blanket of heat that surrounded me, warming me from head to toe. The sensation was amazing, like a hug from the sky. I didn't know what the difference was between a Fasti star and a natural one, but this radiance seemed completely real to me, and I couldn't wait to find out more.

My next stop was the learning center, a wide floating stage

where my personal hero, *the* Dr. Sally Nesbit, would give a welcome speech in about thirty minutes. In the meantime, the rest of the astral physics team used a slideshow to explain how natural stars were formed. I already knew the answer—giant clouds of dust and gas rotating and colliding to form a dense core, blah, blah, blah—so I tuned out the lesson until it was over. Then an announcement came over the speakers: "Ladies and gentlemen, please put your hands together for the woman who started it all, the one, the only, the inventor of the Fasti stars . . . Doctor Sally Nesbit!"

I bounced in excitement as a hole opened up in the stage floor and Dr. Nesbit's brown head appeared. She rose higher onto the platform, and I waved, hoping to catch her eye. But oddly, she wasn't looking at me—or at anyone else in the crowd. Her gaze was fixed on some random point in the distance. I glanced over my shoulder to see what had caught her attention, but there was nothing back there except a horizon of mud.

That was strange.

I squinted at Dr. Nesbit's face. Was it my imagination, or did she look a little pale? The longer I watched her, the more I wondered if she was nervous, or sick, or just having a bad day. Because her forehead was glistening with sweat. (More sweat than the rest of us, anyway.) And instead of her usual "chill" stance, with one hip cocked to the side and both hands clasped in front of her, she was wringing her fingers like she was worried. She didn't even wave to the crowd. If I didn't know better, I would think Fasti was the last place she wanted to be.

"Welcome," she told us. "And, um, thank you for . . . for

coming." Her gaze wandered to the horizon again, and she began scratching the back of her neck. "I ... uh ... I'm glad ... to ... uh ..."

I leaned forward, willing her to finish the sentence, but she never did.

One of the other physicists, a short blond man with a pony-tail, stepped forward. "You'll have to forgive Doctor Nesbit. She's a bit under the weather today." At that, Dr. Nesbit gave the man an awkward smile as if to say *Yep, it's true.* The blond man introduced himself. "I'm her assistant, Doctor Reed. I know you've come here to listen to a speech, but why don't we skip straight to the Q and A, since that's the best part. If you have questions for Doctor Nesbit, I'll take them now."

My hand shot instantly into the air, and I made the kind of intense eye contact that my teachers called "uncomfortable."

Dr. Reed pointed at me. "Yes, young man. What's your name?"

I cupped my hands around my mouth and hollered, "Kyler. Kyler Centaurus."

"Nice to meet you," he said. "What's your question, Tyler?"

"It's actually *Kyler*," I corrected. "I was the student who won the essay contest last year. Remember, Doctor Nesbit? You called me and we talked about ..." I trailed off because I'd been too nervous to remember the call. "Never mind, not important. You explained how stars are formed in nature, but what about man-made stars? How do you create enough pressure to form a protostar core? What materials and equipment do you use? And how long does the process take from start to finish?"

Dr. Nesbit glanced at me, but she didn't seem to remember who I was. I fought off a wave of disappointment, telling myself she had more important things on her mind than a short conversation she'd had last year with one boy.

"I'm sorry," she said to me. "Those are very intelligent questions, but the answers are proprietary."

"Proprietary," added her assistant, "means *a secret*, Tyler."

"Yeah, I know what it means," I said. And my name wasn't Tyler. But whatever. "Can you tell us how you keep the man-made star in a shrunken state until it reaches its new home?"

Dr. Nesbit shook her head. "Sorry. That's also proprietary."

I sighed. Whatever happened to working together, to sharing research and helping the next generation of young scientists, like me? *"Okay,"* I said, trying to stay positive. "Can I take a tour of the lab? I'd love to see where you build the stars, even if you can't tell me your secrets."

"As much as I'd like to do that, I'm afraid our lab facilities are—"

"Let me guess," I muttered. "Proprietary."

"—proprietary."

Yep, I called it.

"But thank you for your participation, Tyler," the blond assistant said.

OMG, MY NAME WAS NOT TYLER.

After that, Dr. Reed chose a different person from the crowd to ask a question. I glanced around to see if anyone else shared my disappointment in not learning anything new, but all of the tourists seemed more interested in the next subject:

whether Fasti stocks were a good money-making investment.

For the life of me, I couldn't understand why anyone would travel all the way to Fasti to ask about anything other than man-made stars. This festival was supposed to be a celebration of celestology, so where were all of my people? Where were the other wannabe celestologists? I had come here to find my tribe, to meet others who wanted to talk about stars instead of stocks. People who would make me feel like I belonged. But looking around, the only people I saw were the kind of folks I had left behind on Earth.

My shoulders sank. Maybe the problem wasn't them. Maybe it was me.

Maybe I didn't have a tribe.

I dragged my feet out of the so-called learning center and hung out on the fringes of the festival for the rest of the day, doing my best to convince myself that this trip hadn't been a total waste of my time and freedom. When night fell and the sky turned to a purple haze, a timer appeared in the air above the festival, counting down the minutes until the big reveal.

I peered around for the best place to watch the presentation. It wasn't like anyone's head could block my view—there was no hiding a star, even in miniature form—but I wanted to get away from the crowd and witness the miracle of science all by myself, to protect the moment from those who would ruin it for me.

I decided to go back to my ship. The docking lot was mostly deserted, so no one would bother me there. I climbed on top of the *Whirlwind*'s hull and leaned back against the windshield with both arms folded behind my head. And then with nothing around me but the breeze in my hair, I watched the timer count down the seconds from five to zero.

Four ... three ... two ... one.

I held my breath.

Silence fell. It was like the planet was holding its breath, too.

I turned my eyes to the heavens. Soft music played from distant speakers, a tinkling tune that swelled as fireworks rained sparkles across the sky. The music grew louder and more urgent. My heart raced, my gaze widening behind dark glasses. And there in the blackness of space, an enormous towing ship drifted away from the sun, creating a crescent of pure, blinding light. The sun pulsed like a beating heart, growing brighter with each throb, practically alive. It was the most beautiful thing I'd ever seen. And when the star glowed full and uncovered, the music in the background hit a crescendo that raised chills all over my body. Gazing up in awe, I had to remind myself to breathe.

Oh yes, the trip had been worth it.

We made that star, I thought. Humans actually *made* that. Five hundred years ago we couldn't travel beyond the moon, and now we were breathing new life into the cosmos by creating our own solar systems. How could anyone not tear up at the thought of it? I sure did. Emotion leaked from my eyes until the sun became a wet blur. I blotted my watery gaze and blinked up once more.

I was so caught up in the moment that I didn't notice I had

company until I heard a sigh coming from the ship next to mine. I turned to find a girl sitting cross-legged atop a red ship with a white stripe painted down the middle. She was playing a holographic game, using her hand like a gun to shoot at three shimmery bubbles. Without even looking, she burst two of them with a musical *pop*. In the blazing light of day, I recognized the girl as the Wanderer who had yelled at me in the marketplace. But she seemed different now. Instead of a scowl, she wore a dreamy look on her face.

"Mind-blowing, right?" she asked, still gazing at the star as she popped the last bubble. It was clear she'd known I was there the whole time, and I wondered why she didn't say anything before. Or why she was being nice to me now. Maybe the heat from the sun had thawed her frozen heart.

"Yeah." I faked a shrug, embarrassed by the moisture in my eyes. "I guess so."

"That your ship?" she said, nodding at the *Whirlwind*.

"Yeah. Well, my family's ship."

"Nice." She inched her glasses down the bridge of her nose and studied the hull. "Is that double reinforced?"

"Triple," I corrected. "You can't take chances with asteroids."

"Don't I know it," she muttered under her breath.

"Oh, that's right." I mentally smacked my own forehead. Her people destroyed asteroids for a living. "Sorry. I forgot you're an expert on asteroids."

"No worries." A hint of a smile played at her lips. "I'm the one who should be sorry. I didn't mean to go off on you back there." She thumbed toward the marketplace. "I get a lot of stares, usually not friendly. Makes me snippy sometimes. I shouldn't have taken it out on you."

I hadn't thought of it that way. Wanderers weren't popular people. No wonder my gawking had put her on edge.

"I didn't mean to stare," I told her. "I've just never seen"—I searched for the right words—"a genetic mutation as cool as yours. I think it's awesome how your body changed to make you better at surviving in space. You're like science in action—a living, breathing example of the miracles nature can do." My cheeks heated again. I hadn't meant to go full dork on her. "I have a thing for science, if you can't tell."

After that she looked at me for the longest time, wrinkling her forehead as though she couldn't decide how she felt about what I'd said. She went quiet for so many beats that I thought I'd ticked her off again. But then she stood up, took off toward me at a run, and leaped onto my ship with a celebratory *whoop*. In seconds, she was sitting cross-legged beside me.

"Figerella," she said, extending a hand for me to shake. "Call me Fig."

I couldn't help but laugh. This girl had style, I'd give her that. I took her hand and squeezed it. "Kyler Centaurus," I said. "Ky, for short."

"Nice to meet you, Ky."

"Same."

"So where's your family?" she asked.

I groaned. "It's a long story."

"It's a long night." She jutted her chin at the sun. "Or day, I guess, since the sun technically rose. Anyway, I'm in no hurry to go home."

Neither was I, so I kicked back and told Fig about my last day on Earth.

"Wait a minute," she said, holding up an index finger after I had described my accidental blastoff. "So you stole a spaceship . . . in your sleep?"

I laughed at the way she put it. "That sounds so much cooler than how it really went down. But yeah, I guess I did." I scratched my chin, smiling. "Pretty sure that makes me the galaxy's youngest master thief."

"You could be a pirate legend." She giggled. "A modern-day Blackbeard."

"Hard pass," I said. "Not a fan of pirates." I was about to tell her the story of my own brush with ship thieves when I heard a familiar pair of voices talking right below the *Whirlwind*. I froze to listen, holding a finger over my lips in a signal for Fig to be quiet.

"Look!" a woman whisper-yelled. "Right there at the scratches on the loading-bay door! That's from where we forced it open. It's the same ship."

My stomach dropped into my pants. I knew that voice—it was the redheaded pirate with the skull face.

"Huh," a man said. "Why would the crew come here to be quarantined?"

I knew that voice, too—the fidgety good-looking guy with the gadgets strapped to his chest.

There was a meaty *thud* of fist against flesh, and the woman hissed, "Because there was no quarantine, you idiot. They lied to try to scare us away."

"Ooooooh," the man said.

Fig pointed down and mouthed, *Friends of yours?*

I shook my head and scanned the docking lot for Galaxy Guards ... or private guards ... or buff guys ... or buff kids ... or anyone at all who could help me. But no such luck. I had come here to be alone, and I'd gotten exactly what I'd wanted. I had even shut down Cabe and stowed him in the utility closet so he wouldn't freak out about the festival and try to plaster me to the ship. I might be able to activate him from my key fob, but could he open the hatch with his ropy hands?

I wasn't sure.

Fig elbowed me, whispering, "What's going on?"

I leaned in close to her ear. "Those are pirates," I breathed, pointing down. "They tried to take my ship. I got rid of them and escaped, but they found me again."

Fig bit her lip, deep in thought for a moment, before she glanced over her shoulder to the ship where she had sat a few minutes earlier. I followed the direction of her gaze and spotted a long, skinny box she must have left on the hull. Whatever was inside the box seemed to spark an idea for her.

"I'll make you a deal," she whispered.

I nodded for her to go on.

"If I can get rid of the pirates, you give me a ride to Earth."

"Deal," I said. I would've given her a ride anyway.

"Okay. Be right back."

I didn't know what I expected Fig to do, but it wasn't to leap onto the next ship and pull something resembling a rocket launcher out of the long, skinny box she'd left there. In one easy motion, she hoisted the canister over one shoulder and shouted, "Yo ho, scalawags! Want to hear a joke? Why couldn't the pirate sit down?"

"Whoa, whoa, what're you doing?" yelled the redheaded woman.

"Stop messing around with that laser, kid," hollered the man.

Fig told them, "Because he lost his booty!"

While the pirates kept clamoring for her to put down the cannon, Fig winked at me and said, "Get it? Booty? As in stolen treasure?" When I didn't answer right away, because, you know, I was completely in shock, she added, "Pirate booty. See what I did there?"

"Yeah," I muttered. "I see what you did there."

"I thought it was funny." She shrugged. "Oh, well."

She peeked through a round scope mounted to the side of the cannon and took aim. A beam of red light shot from the barrel, forcing me to shield my eyes. I heard a sizzle and a bunch of pops. When I peeked between my fingers, smoke was rising from a hole in the docking lot, and the pirates were gone.

Holy mother of Einstein. Had she . . . vaporized them?

"Hope you can swim," Fig hollered at the hole.

I craned my neck and found the pirates bobbing up and down like corks in the watery mud below the dock. A smile sprang to my lips. "That was amazing!"

Fig patted the weapon as if to say *Good job*. "That was only level one. This baby's got ninety-nine more where that came from."

"Whoa," I breathed. If that was level one, I would hate to see what it could do on full power.

"We should get airborne," she said, tucking the cannon back in its box. "Before someone calls security to report the—"

A siren interrupted her. I whirled toward the high-pitched wailing and recognized a Galaxy Guard air bike speeding toward us from the other end of the docking lot. The smoke from Fig's laser cannon must have caught his attention, and now he was coming to investigate.

"It's about time," I said to Fig, but she wasn't listening. Her face had gone white. "What's wrong?" I asked her. "This is a good thing. Now the pirates will go to jail."

Fig shook her head, her eyes flashing as they met mine. "This is *not* a good thing. Who's the Galaxy Guard going to believe? Two adults—two *human* adults—floating in the mud, or the mutant kid who fired on them with an illegal blaster?"

"But I'm human," I argued. "I can back up your story about the pirates."

She flung a hand toward the laser cannon. "And what about that?"

"Oh, right. The illegal blaster." I'd forgotten that part. "Yeah, we should motor."

"Forget what I said before," she told me. "You'd make an awful pirate."

"The worst," I agreed. "I think I'll stick with celestology."

I jumped down from the windshield and keyed the entrance code into the loading-bay door. It lowered with a mechanical whine until it touched the landing pad, covering the hole the pirates had fallen into and muffling their shouted curses. Fig handed me the blaster case so she could climb down from the other ship. Meanwhile, the Galaxy Guard air bike had closed half the distance of the docking lot, near enough for me to make out the lettering on the rider's chrome helmet. It read *OFC Zen.*

"Halt," Officer Zen called through his helmet speaker. "Close your vehicle door and stand aside with both hands in the air."

"Not likely, buddy," Fig said as she passed me up the docking ramp. She helped me haul the laser cannon into the loading bay, then she punched the button to close and seal the door before jogging up the stairs to the main level. "The pilothouse is on the top floor, right?"

I chased after her. "Yeah. But it'll take me a minute to set the auto—"

"Forget the autopilot," she told me. "I'll fly her myself."

"You can fly a cruiser?"

"In my sleep," she said, skidding to a stop in front of the pilot's seat. "My people don't live on the ground, remember? I was born on a cruiser." She took a moment to glance at the controls as she sat down. "This ship has fingerprint recognition. You'll have to give me flight privileges."

She was right. The *Whirlwind*'s security package made it nearly impossible to steal . . . unless you were a Centaurus who fell asleep at the wheel. Anyone in my family could use the ship because our fingerprints and voices had been uploaded into the system. In order for an outsider to pilot the ship, one of us had to turn off the security lock. That would give the guest one hour of flight time before a crew member had to give approval again.

"Computer," I said to the ship while I strapped into the copilot's seat. "Disable the flight lock."

"Flight lock disabled."

Fig didn't waste a moment. She fired up the engines with one hand and gripped the wheel with the other. Next thing I knew, we were rocketing off the ground so fast my stomach tried to make an exit through my butt. Then she hooked the wheel to the left and sent us spiraling like a top as we rose higher into the atmosphere.

The spinning made me vurp (vomit-burp). I gritted my teeth and tried to say, "I'm gonna hurl," but it came out "Grrrrrr," like a drunken bear.

"Hold on," Fig told me. "I'm just trying to make sure Officer Whosey-Whatsit can't read our ship's name on the bottom of the hull. The last thing we want is for him to send out a BOL for the *Whirlwind*."

"Wh-what's a BOL?"

"Be On the Lookout," she explained.

That made sense, but it brought a bigger problem to mind. Our ship could easily outrun an air bike, but there was no escaping the Galaxy Guard's comm network. The officer on the ground must have reported us by now, which meant other Guard ships were on their way . . . faster ships, armed with electric nets and surge guns to disable our engines. So unless Fig could spin us into another dimension, we were as good as busted.

I was about to get arrested. At age thirteen.

My parents would ground me into the afterlife.

I noticed movement from the navigation screen and glanced down to find two beacons zooming toward our position. A whimper rose in my throat. The Guard ships were here.

"Hey, plug this in, will you?" Fig asked. She handed me a cord, which was attached to something that looked like a tube of my mom's lipstick. "Today, please," she pressed when I didn't move fast enough.

The cord was old tech, so it took me a second to find a charging port. I plugged it in. Only then did it occur to me that we had stopped spinning. In fact, we'd stopped moving altogether. We were just floating on the other side of the planet, waiting for the Guard to scoop us up.

Too bad my stomach didn't get the message. I clapped a palm over my mouth and willed myself not to puke. "Why aren't we running?" I asked from between my fingers. I nodded at the lipstick. "And what is that thing?"

Fig pointed out the front windshield. "Watch and see."

I followed her gaze into the distance, where two Galaxy Guard cruisers were speeding toward each other from opposite directions. It was clear they meant to trap us in between them. But just as I held my breath and prepared for the worst, the cruisers flew past us and kept going.

I tipped my head. "Huh?"

Fig chuckled. "Keep watching."

So I did. The Guard cruisers flew all the way around planet Fasti—three times—before they descended into the atmosphere and eventually landed on the ground. I still didn't understand. Here we were, sitting (well, *floating*), in plain sight. Why hadn't the Guard disabled our engines and boarded us?

Fig lifted the tube for show, then gave it a kiss. "Personal cloaking device. Nifty little contraption. Last of its kind."

A smile broke out on my face. "You mean they couldn't see us?"

"They still can't." She frowned at the tube, which had begun to crackle and fizz. "Well, not yet, anyway. But it looks like our invisibility cloak is about to wear out. We should get as far away from here as we can."

I wasn't about to argue. "Computer, set a course for Earth. Top speed."

"Confirmed," the ship responded.

I had just started to ask if Fig wanted a tour of the ship when I paused. Something she'd said had caught my attention. "Wait. Did you say *invisibility cloak*?"

"Yeah. Like in the Harry Potter series."

My eyes went so wide they almost fell out of my head. "You've read the Harry Potter books?"

"Psh," she said, as if the answer should be obvious. Never mind that hardly anyone read old books, let alone *ancient* books. Meeting a fellow Potterhead was like finding a diamond on the sidewalk. Except more valuable. "All seven of them, at least a dozen times. Anyone who doesn't love that series can't be trusted."

"Good answer," I told her. "Fifty points to Ravenclaw."

"Ravenclaw?" She laughed, shaking her head. "Make that Slytherin. And I think I deserve a hundred points for the magic I just pulled off."

"Uh-oh, a Slytherin," I teased. "Everyone knows they can't be trusted. But I guess I can overlook it, seeing as how you saved my bacon and all."

"Yeah, well, Ravenclaws are stuffy brainiacs, but I guess you're welcome, seeing as how you're giving me a ride to Earth and all."

We eyed each other for a moment or two, until we couldn't keep a straight face anymore. Then we both snickered and said, "Better than Hufflepuff."

All I could do was smile. This girl was cool.

Maybe I *did* have a tribe.

CHAPTER EIGHT

figerella jammeslot

Have you ever been someplace so perfect it fit you like a warm sweater, and all of a sudden you just knew you were home? It's a rare thing for me. My people don't stay in one spot for long, hence the name *Wanderers,* but I can honestly say I've felt at home in two places—first on my parents' ship, because it *was* my home, and again when Kyler led me on a tour of the *Whirlwind.*

Mine, I thought.

Even though Kyler didn't know it, this magnificent beauty was all mine. Of course, first I would have to trick him into giving me the ship. That was something I'd never done before, and I didn't feel particularly good about it. But if a kid like Kyler could steal a ship in his sleep, then how hard could it be?

I would worry about the details later.

Right now I wanted to study the loading bay. I gazed at the titanium hardware that bound the seams of the interior walls. The bolts might not look impressive to the untrained eye, but most ships were welded at the seams, not welded *and* double bound with eighteen-inch titanium screws. Hardware like that was only used on ships with reinforced hulls, a sign of quality craftsmanship that I didn't take for granted. This ship was built like a tank. The engine had plenty of giddyup as well; I could tell from the whirring of the turbines as they propelled us through space.

I poked my head into the engine room and admired the poetry of moving parts. I didn't know much about engines, but I wanted to learn. That way I could do my own repairs and not have to rely on anyone. I had just knelt down to study how the chrome pieces fit together into a frenzied puzzle when Kyler crouched down by my side. He tilted his head and watched me watching the engine.

"Not much to look at," he said.

I snorted a dry laugh. Oh, how wrong he was.

I could work and scrimp and save for my entire lifetime and never afford a ship like this. Most Wanderers had to band together into multifamily groups and pool their money to buy a blasting cruiser. The *Whirlwind* was a passenger vessel, but I could fix that by attaching my cannon to the hull with a good welding kit. And after Corpse and Cadaver paid me for the rest of the job, I would have enough money to afford a decade of fuel and supplies. This ship was my ticket to an easy life, all on my own, without anybody telling me what to do.

And I had the chump next to me to thank for it.

Don't get me wrong—Kyler was a nice kid. But "nice" only took you so far in space. To survive out here in the cold, surrounded by asteroids and black holes and pirates and *worse* than pirates, "nice" was about as useful as a chocolate teapot. But even though I could tell that Ky was a pampered prince, I didn't hate him for it. He wasn't a jerk. He didn't hold his nose in the air as he led me up the stairs to give me a tour of the ship. And he didn't talk down to me. He was just sort of . . . clueless.

"I still can't believe what you did back there," Ky told me as he strode into the common room. He had a bounce in his step, his eyes still bright from the thrill of escape. I knew that feeling. There was nothing better than blowing up stuff and living to brag about it. He waggled his eyebrows. "If I believed in fate, I'd say the universe put us together."

"Hey, maybe it did," I told him.

But that was a lie.

Because what my new friend didn't know was the whole pirate-showdown thing had been staged like a traveling theater show.

As if I would double-cross my bosses . . . before they paid me.

I had finally heard from Corpse and Cadaver after I'd left the marketplace on Fasti. They'd told me to steal a ship and fly it to Earth, which had been a stupid idea because it would've had the Galaxy Guard chasing me through multiple solar systems. And I had no intention of spending the rest of my life on a prison farm, thank you very much. So when I noticed the *Whirlwind* in the docking lot, I ran her registration numbers and researched who she belonged to, along with a picture of the owner's family. As it turned out, Corpse and Cadaver had already tried to take the ship by force—small galaxy, right?—and Ky had fooled them into thinking it was quarantined, then dumped them out the garbage chute.

I had to give him credit for that. The way he'd punked the pirates was brilliant—and hilarious. It also told me not to underestimate him. Kyler was clueless, but he was crafty, too.

Anyway, after I figured out Ky was traveling alone, the plan couldn't have been any easier. My dad used to say a lie was only as strong as a person's will to believe it. And Kyler *really* wanted to believe I was his hero.

So I let him.

And whenever little pangs of guilt tugged at my ribs, I reminded myself that the lie was good for both of us. We had a symbiotic relationship, like those tiny fish that ate the algae off shark butts. Ky would get a safe ride home, and I'd score a ship.

Win-win.

Heck, maybe the universe really *had* put us together.

"Cozy," I said to myself, admiring an L-shaped sofa large enough to sleep two grown-ups. The fabric was velvet, not leather, and it felt warm and soft when I skimmed my hand over the cushions. I noticed a set of bookshelves built into the wall, with clear sliding doors to hold the volumes in place if the flight became bumpy. There were even real books inside! My heart fluttered. I hadn't seen a paperbound book since the accident that took out my family's ship. Printed books were rare, even among Wanderers. While our ancestors had taken their home libraries into space, five hundred years was a long time for paper to survive.

I slid aside the shelf door and skimmed my fingertips over the spines, reading the titles laid out before me. *The Hunger Games, Comets of Glass, The Hobbit, Magna Fury, Starflight, The Lightning Thief* . . .

I gasped and pulled out the last title. I'd been dying to read *The Lightning Thief* ever since my father told me it was his favorite. Basically, the story was about a kid named Percy Jackson who learned he was the son of a Greek god. Then Percy had to go to a special camp to fit in with other Olympians and fight monsters and rescue his mom and stuff like that. The book had sounded like so much fun that I'd decided to save it for last. I wish I hadn't done that. Because now it was too late. I'd waited too long, and I would never get to talk to my dad about our favorite parts, or argue over which character we liked best. I had missed out on sharing that with him.

A small voice inside my head whispered, *Maybe it's not too late.* Maybe this book could make me feel close to my father, like he was still with me. I could easily imagine which characters he would love and which ones he would love to hate. Maybe we could still share this.

I opened the book and buried my nose inside for a deep whiff. "Oh yeah, that's the stuff," I said, tipping back my head. "I miss that smell."

I glanced at Kyler and found him watching me with the same curiosity as before, like he couldn't understand what I was thinking. Since I was in a good mood, I explained, "I used to have a lot of books, growing up. Tons of them, enough to start a small library. This smell is one of the first things I remember."

"Used to?" he repeated. "Where are your books now?"

Somewhere in space, scorched and blasted to bits, I thought. An image flashed in my mind of orange flames. The ghost of smoke filled my nostrils. I blinked and saw the panic on my mother's face as she shoved me into the escape pod and ejected it right before the explosion that blew apart our ship.

I cleared my throat and told Kyler, "They're gone."

Everything was gone. I had lost more than my parents that day. I had lost all of our heirlooms from Earth—the books, photographs, and music my ancestors had taken with them when they'd set off to explore the galaxy. The only thing that had survived the wreck was the necklace I'd worn when I escaped. It was a ruby pendant on a silver chain, both mined from Earth. One of my ancestors had brought it with her to space as a reminder of where she'd come from. Then my mom had given it to me on my tenth birthday. I touched my throat out of habit, but I knew the pendant wasn't there. It had been taken from me, too.

"Well," Kyler said, pointing at the book in my hands. "You should read it, if you haven't already. It's good. One of my favorites."

I grinned at him. Hearing that made me feel better. "Thanks. I will."

"By the way, how did you end up with so many books?" he asked. "They're not easy to find. The only reason we have so many is because my grandpa left his collection to my dad after he died." He shrugged. "My dad could've sold them for a fortune, but instead he gave them to my mom. She's a freak for classic lit. It would have broken her heart if he'd gotten rid of a single copy. Anyway, I wouldn't expect there to be a whole lot of antiques in space."

"To us, they're not antiques," I pointed out. "They're our culture."

"Huh?"

"Think about it. When the first Wanderers left Earth five hundred years ago, they took their favorite things with them, right?"

"Oh." Kyler's eyes brightened with understanding. "And then they weren't allowed to come back."

"Exactly. We were cut off from the rest of mankind. So even though music and movies and fashion changed on Earth, for us, things mostly stayed the same. I mean, once in a while I hear a new song in a space station, or watch a new movie on a shuttle, but for the most part my life is a time capsule." I lifted a shoulder. "Anyway, they stopped making good music after 2020."

"That's what my mom says about stories."

"At least you and I have one thing in common. We love old books."

"Two things, actually," he said, and pointed to a small black box on the floor. "We both like holographic games." He used his hand like a pistol. "I saw you popping those sparkly bubbles back on Fasti."

I nodded. "It's an old game, but it's fun."

"Well, if you like that, then this is going to blow your mind."

He put on a glove studded with tiny silver electrodes and handed me one. As soon as I slid it over my hand, the fabric hummed against my skin. Kyler explained that the electrodes would read my muscle movements—even the slightest twitch—and react for me, so there was no delay between my thoughts and my actions in the game. He turned off the lights and switched on the virtual-reality box. In an instant, the room was transformed into an asteroid field set against the backdrop of a swirling purple nebula. I gazed all around me with my mouth hanging open. The view seemed so real, each asteroid so textured and vivid I had to resist the urge to reach out and touch them.

Kyler was right. It blew my mind.

"I assume we're gonna blast rocks?" I asked.

"Nope," he said. A sinister noise *bwoop*ed from the projector box, and dozens of disk-shaped spaceships appeared in between the asteroids. "We're gonna blast evil aliens."

"Awesome."

The game began in demo mode to teach me the object of level one. But the alien ships and their laser beam rockets were so lifelike that my heart raced, and my trigger finger begged to be set free. I got the basic gist of the game. My job was to blast aliens, and Ky's job was to guide our ship through the asteroid field. That was all I needed to know.

"Hit play," I told him, bouncing on my toes. "Hurry, hurry, hurry."

I was ready when level one began, firing lasers so fast that all the aliens in the first round exploded practically at the same time. Our points soared. The next fleet of ships appeared, and I destroyed them even faster than before. A rush surged through my veins. I noticed that Kyler was trying to tell me something, but I couldn't hear him over the loud *booms* erupting all around us. Probably he was amazed by my score, so I said, "Thanks," and prepared for the next wave.

I crushed that one, too.

But when I glanced at our score, it had dropped to nearly nothing. "What the . . ."

"That's what I've been trying to tell you," Ky said as he paused the game. "We lose points if the alien ships hit us after they explode. You have to give me time to move out of the way before you blast—"

"Oh, okay, got it," I said. "Hit play."

He started level two, and more alien craft flew into view, plus a giant mother ship that spat out two flying saucers for every one I destroyed. I tried to talk to Kyler as I took aim, but my trigger finger didn't want to obey. It fired in a glorious blur of movement. I took out the entire fleet, but our score went into the red and announced GAME OVER.

"Sorry." I grimaced. "I'm not used to working with a partner."

Ky didn't seem upset. He grinned while pulling off his glove. "No worries. You'll get there. But that was fun, right?"

"The best!"

"Then you should keep playing," he said. "I'll set it to single-player mode so you can blast your heart out."

And I did. I crushed one alien fleet after another while Kyler cheered for me in the background. For hours we laughed and shouted and victory-danced until both of us collapsed onto the sofa, too tired to move.

"That was a blast," I said.

"Literally and figuratively," Ky added. He turned on the lights, and we both squinted at the brightness.

"I had no idea gaming tech had come so far. I've been missing out."

"Maybe once we get back to Earth, you can hang out for a while," Kyler said. "You know, catch up with the times and all that."

His voice was full of hope, but he didn't know what he was talking about. Not that I blamed him. He was a human, sheltered since birth. He hadn't lived my life. He couldn't understand what it felt like to be an outsider. Hearing him talk reminded me that even though we both liked video games and old books, we had nothing in common. Nothing real, anyway.

"I heard your Council of Wanderers is meeting with the United Nations this week," he went on. "They want the right to live on Earth. No more travel visas."

I huffed a laugh. A travel visa was basically a permission slip to land on Earth and stay for a while, usually long enough to do business with some corporation or another. But anyone with a visa had to pay for every hour they spent on the ground. I doubted the government would give up that money. As for the Council, I wanted nothing to do with them. They would lock me away for life (or worse) if they could.

"Wanting and getting are two different things," I said. A yawn took over. I hadn't realized how sleepy I was. "Hey, can you show me which cabin is mine? I need to crash for a while. Blasting pirates and outrunning the law really takes it out of me, you know?"

"Yeah, I can imagine." He stood up and pointed to a short

hall on the other side of the room. "This way. After I find you a bed, I'll work on finding us something to eat."

As I followed him across the living room, I noticed a few homey touches I'd missed before. Fuzzy blankets were draped over seat backs. A potted plant with pink flowers in bloom stood brightly in the corner beneath the light of a single nourishing UV bulb. There was even a magnetic chessboard built into the coffee table. Someone had put a lot of care into making the room a place where people would want to hang out.

"Who decorated?" I asked. "Your mom?"

"I dunno," Ky said with a shrug. "I never asked."

For some reason, his answer made my face hot. What was his deal? He couldn't be bothered to notice how nice his ship was? *Or that he has parents to decorate it,* I said to myself before I could block the thought. All of a sudden my pulse throbbed, and I found myself kicking the back of Ky's booted heel.

I couldn't believe I'd done that.

He stumbled and caught himself against the wall. When he turned to me with a frown, I had my apology ready. "Oops, sorry," I said. "I get clumsy when I'm tired."

"Yeah. No worries." He side-eyed me for a second before thumbing at a closed metal door on the left. "You can sleep in my parents' cabin. It's the biggest room, plus it has its own bathroom."

My anger dissolved at once, and I eagerly rubbed my palms together. I had spent so long sleeping in transport chairs or curled up in the corners of buildings that I'd almost forgotten what a real mattress felt like. And the master suite, too! I would sleep like royalty tonight.

But my shoulders sank when the cabin door slid open and the air from inside washed over me. There wasn't anything wrong with the room. It was actually much nicer than I had expected, decked out with floor-to-ceiling storage drawers and a wall-size entertainment screen that faced a plush double bed. The problem was the smell of lavender face cream lingering in the air. Kyler's mom must have used the lotion during her last trip—probably the Eterna Beauty brand, the kind that came in a tiny white jar with a silver lid.

I knew because my mom had used it, too.

An invisible fist tightened around my heart. Soon it was hard to breathe. I slammed the door shut so fast that Ky barely had time to yank his fingers out of the way. "I don't want this room," I snapped. "You take it."

He blinked at me as if I'd grown horns and a tail. *"Oooooooookay . . ."*

I was in no mood to explain, so I shoved past him and charged toward the only other bedroom on the ship. It was half the size of the master suite with six bunks protruding from the walls. It looked like a prison cell and smelled like gym shoes and sweaty butt cracks.

"Perfect," I said. "I'll sleep here."

Then I shut the door and tossed myself onto the nearest bunk, where I punched a pillow until the hot pressure of tears backed off my eyelids.

I don't know how long I slept, but I must have really needed a nap, because I woke up with a pillowcase crease stamped in my cheek, soaked in a puddle of my own drool. That only happens when I sleep hard, like *coma* hard.

I yawned and stretched and sat up to look around, taking in some details I hadn't noticed before. A poster hung on the ceiling of my bunk, a glossy photo of some roided-out athlete squashing a football between his hands as if he meant to pop it. If I leaned to the side, I could see posters tacked to the other bunk ceilings, too. Sports was a common theme. There was a zero-gravity soccer player turned upside down to kick a ball over the other team's heads, a laser sharpshooter on Earth hitting a target on the moon, and a helmeted rodeo rider astride a mechanical bear.

A lot of jocks in this family.

Kyler didn't strike me as the sporty type, so I kept scanning the posters to figure out which bunk was his. I narrowed it down to two beds: one bearing the image of a dog squeezing out a poo, and another bed that was neatly made, with holographic glow-in-the-dark stars and galaxies stuck to the ceiling in perfect arrangement.

Science geek, I reminded myself. The star bunk had to be Ky's. It was all the way at the top with barely six inches of wiggle room between the mattress and the dome—clearly the least desirable spot, so either he'd drawn the short straw, or he was the weakest of the pack and his brothers had forced him up there. My money was on scenario number two. He seemed like a neat freak, too, which didn't surprise me.

I stood up and peeked in the closet, where the smell of gym shoes was coming from. Someone had used a mechanic's grease pencil to write *Aystay outyay ofyay onner'sbay uffstay oryay ieday* on the back wall near the storage drawers. That was weird, so I made a mental note to ask Ky what it meant. Four pairs of sneakers were tucked into elastic pockets on the wall, each of them large enough to house an ox. Based on that, I figured Kyler must be the baby of the family. I'd seen his boots. No way were any of these shoes his.

I poked around the storage drawers and found a picture of a shapely cheerleader, along with some holey underwear and unwashed socks—seriously, boys are so gross—but nothing to tell me anything I didn't already know. And there was no evidence of a girl in the family. Mrs. Centaurus must feel so outnumbered.

The ghost of lavender crossed my nose, so I pushed Mrs. Centaurus out of my mind and quit snooping. I didn't know why I'd bothered looking around in the first place. It wasn't like I cared about these people.

My grumbling stomach forced me to leave the man-boy cave. But no sooner had I opened the door than I stopped short and took a backward step. A goofy-looking robot stood facing me, spooling and unspooling metal rope from his armholes as if he were nervous.

I clung to the doorway, unsure of what to do. I didn't have a lot of experience with robots, but I knew enough not to trust them. The last time I'd let my guard down around a robot, it had held me prisoner for a month. (Long story.) But something in the way this model behaved, fidgeting and rocking from side to side, made him seem more afraid of me than I was of him. So I relaxed and took a forward step.

"Hi," I told him. "What's up?"

His digital eyes blinked at me, and he droned, "Hello, *weirdo girl, oh crap, don't call her that, Cabe, that's not her real name!*"

I scowled. It seemed Kyler had been telling tales about me.

"*Weirdo girl, oh crap, don't call her that, Cabe, that's not her real name!*" the robot repeated. "Your title is unusually long. Would you prefer an abbreviated—"

"Call me Fig."

"Fig is not an abbreviation of your formal title."

Rolling my eyes, I said, "Fine. Call me Weirdo."

"Confirmed," said the robot, Cabe, I assumed. He seemed relieved to have that formality out of the way, because he quit fidgeting with his cable. "I was instructed to watch your door until you awoke, and then escort you to Goosey."

"Goosey?" My forehead wrinkled until I realized he meant Kyler, and then I let out a chuckle. I was *sooooo* going to give him heck for that nickname. Sweeping a hand toward the common room, I said, "Lead the way, Cable dude."

As Cabe rolled ahead of me to the galley, I picked up the scents of garlic and tomato sauce in the air, and my stomach rumbled again. Pasta with marinara sauce was one of my favorites. It was a staple in space, along with chili, beans, rice, and protein cubes, all of which could be canned or dry-stored for years. There were no delivery restaurants in space, no corner markets where you could pop in and grab a frozen pizza if you forgot to cook dinner. Out here in the void, you either meal-planned before a voyage or you went hungry.

When I reached the galley, I found Kyler standing in front of a small two-burner stove, where a pot of boiling water sent steam swirling into the air. If nothing else, at least his parents had taught him how to cook. He didn't seem to notice me, so I took in the galley, which only required a single glance. It was small, but it had all the essentials I would expect: an oven, a cooler, a metal sink, a picnic-style table with two long benches on either side for seating, a few cabinets, and some steel pans magnetized to the walls. There were no upgrades, but that was all right. I would rather have a battering-ram hull than a fancy kitchen any day.

"Hey, Goosey," I said, smirking when Kyler flinched. "What's cookin'?"

He didn't turn around. Instead, he took a sudden interest in stirring the pot. "Penne and sauce. And don't call me that."

"Oh, I think it's only fair, *Goosey*, considering the nickname I'm stuck with."

He cringed. "Yeah, about that . . ."

I leaned against the doorway with my arms folded. I couldn't wait to hear him explain his way out of this one.

"You did kind of freak out on me," he said into the steam. Apparently that was as close to an apology as I was going to get. He pointed a ladle at Cabe and explained, "He's quirky. I don't have admin permission to change his settings."

I shrugged. I supposed it wasn't fair to hold a grudge against Kyler, considering I planned on swindling him out of his family's ship. "Goosey and Weirdo," I said, testing our names. They didn't sound so bad. "At least we're not boring."

"Nothing about this trip has been boring."

"Oh, that reminds me," I said. "What's with *Aystay onner'sbay oryay blahtay*, or whatever all that nonsense on your closet wall says?" I flapped a hand because I knew I wasn't getting it right. "It means something, doesn't it?"

Ky snickered. "It's pig Latin. My little brother, Bonner, is a super freak when it comes to secret codes. He's into all kinds of ciphers, but he taught us pig Latin because it's the easiest. To change a word, you take the first set of consonants and move them to the end, then add *ay*. So *happy* would be *appyhay*. If a word starts with a vowel, you leave it the way it is and add *yay* at the end. So *eat omelets* would be *eatyay omletsyay*." He lifted a shoulder. "Mostly we use it to talk smack around our parents."

"What does the writing in the closet mean?"

"Stay out of Bonner's stuff or die," Kyler told me. "He doesn't want us to know he keeps a picture of Lori Ann McCallum in his underwear drawer. As if we haven't seen him making googly eyes at it ten times a day."

"Ah," I said, nodding. That explained the cheerleader. "Sounds like he's got it bad for the girl."

"Yep, and no shot whatsoever." Ky lifted his ladle thoughtfully. "Unless she likes the smell of methane. In which case, they're a match made in heaven."

"What about your other brothers?" I asked. "What are they like?"

"Duke is the oldest," Kyler told me. "He eats, drinks, and breathes football. Then there are the twins, Devin and Rylan. They specialize in hacking and wisecracks."

"Hacking?" I asked. That could be useful. "What kinds of things can they hack?"

"The usual stuff, like computer programs and electronics. And comms, too. Supposedly, if you link the yellow and purple wires before you send a transmission, you can listen in on the caller after you hang up."

"How's that possible?"

"I don't know," he said. "It has something to do with controlling the other person's mic, kind of how you can hack camera feeds and stuff like that."

"Huh." I tucked away that information for later. "So the twins have skills. What can Bonner do?"

"He's the youngest," Ky said. "Mostly he's good at making trouble . . . and gas."

"Wow. Sounds like a party."

"If by *party* you mean *torture*, then yeah, it's a party every day."

"Goosey," the robot Cabe piped up. "Galactic law requires the logging of all new passengers. Shall I add Weirdo as a guest, or as a permanent crew member?"

"Add her to the crew," Kyler said.

"With which level of ship privileges?" Cabe asked.

"Uh, level two, I guess."

Level two meant I could use the comm station and access every part of the ship except the navigation equipment and the pilot's controls. "I won't be able to fly the ship unless you give me level three or higher," I pointed out. "I come in handy as a pilot."

"Oh yeah," Ky said. "Cabe, add her to the crew at level three."

"Confirmed," Cabe droned. "Weirdo is added with advanced crew privileges."

What I chose not to mention—and what Kyler probably didn't know—was that level-three crew privileges would also allow me to change the name on the ship's registration. Which I planned to do the first chance I got. A small swelling of guilt needled my rib cage, but I pushed it away, reminding myself that Kyler's family had plenty of money. Plus, the ship was probably insured for theft. They didn't need it for survival. They would barely even miss it.

I didn't want to make Ky suspicious, so I played it cool. At least until the robot wheeled around to face me with eyes that glowed red. Then I jumped back against the wall to put some distance between us.

"Scanning crew member Weirdo," Cabe said, and after a pause, his tone went berserk. "Advanced radiation levels! Possible contamination detected!" His motor whirred, and a cable spewed toward me from his body. Instinctively, I covered my head, and the next thing I knew, I was trapped inside a dark bubble of metal rope.

I pounded my fists against the "wall" he'd created around me and yelled, "Let me out!" There was no way he heard me, though, because he was too busy shouting, "MORTAL DANGER!" over and over.

"Calm down," I heard Kyler tell the robot. "She's not contaminated. She developed a genetic mutation to adapt to radiation in space. That's what you're sensing."

I couldn't tell what was happening out there, but my heart went into overdrive, and I felt a burst of nervous energy that made me want to run. The space around me seemed like it was closing in, crushing me. I had to get out. Nothing else mattered.

With one shaky hand, I felt along the inside of my boot for the laser knife I kept hidden there. It was a P-class weapon, small but mighty, and more than powerful enough to slice through metal cables like butter. It wouldn't hurt Cabe, at least not permanently. And it seemed like he had plenty more rope inside him to replace whatever I hacked off. So I flicked the laser's switch to maximum strength and unleashed the dragon.

What I didn't count on was Cabe backing away from me at the exact same time.

Everything happened in a rush after that. The wall of cable dropped as my laser fired a beam of amplified heat across the room. With nothing to block it, the beam hit the stove, where it cut the pot of noodles in half and sent steaming pasta exploding into the air. I cringed, shielding myself from scalding water droplets, which must have caused my laser to cut a path through the ceiling. When I opened my eyes and finally released the trigger, air and steam from the ship's oxygen system came spewing at me like an upside-down geyser.

But that wasn't the worst of it.

"The stove," Kyler yelled, pointing and backing away from the bisected oven, which crackled and popped and spat sparks at us like a rabid animal threatening to attack. "I think it's going to—"

I didn't wait for him to finish. I knew what was happening. The laser had ignited the oven's heating core, the second-most-likely cause of ship explosions, right behind igniting the fuel tank. Fed by oxygen leaking from the overhead pipes, the sparks bloomed into instant flames. I lunged for Kyler's shirt and grabbed him as my feet took control and backed us the heck out of there.

My heart lurched as my boots stumbled to put more distance between us and the rising fire in the galley. Orange flames roared, licking their way up to the ventilation ducts and casting heat through the doorway. Smoke tinted the air, burning my eyes and blurring my vision. Alarms blared through the ceiling speakers, a piercing siren that muddled my head.

Instinct told me that no matter how far we retreated, it wouldn't be far enough. I'd just begun to panic when Cabe's outline appeared in the haze. He faced us for one brief moment, only long enough to seal the doorway with a wall of metal rope and trap himself inside the galley.

"Cabe!" shouted Kyler, but the robot couldn't possibly hear him over the chaos.

I tugged Ky's elbow toward the stairs and yelled, "Come on." The safest place for us was near the exit hatch with our emergency helmets and thermal suits on. That way if the ship blew, we'd have a chance—however slim—of surviving long enough for someone to rescue us.

We made it halfway down the stairs when the ship shook with a single lurch, almost like a sneeze, and we gripped the stair rail for balance. All movement stopped as the engines shut down. A loud vacuum noise roared overhead, and then there was nothing. No alarms. No popping flames. No whirring machinery. Only the ringing of dead silence in my ears.

I shared a glance with Ky. Neither of us spoke, but the question *What happened?* passed between us in the universal language of wide-eyed fear.

I had just unlocked my knees to go the rest of the way down the stairs when a thump sounded from above, followed by the sound of rolling wheels, and then Cabe's tinny voice called, "Crisis averted, Goosey and Weirdo. Are you free from mortal danger?"

A smile bounced to my lips. I turned to find Kyler laughing in relief. Our gazes locked, and for a few short heartbeats, we weren't so different. We were no longer human and mutant, boy and girl, rich and poor, chump and swindler. We were survivors, each of us the same. As cheesy as it sounds, I felt like I knew him, and for a sliver of a second, I didn't feel so alone.

The moment lasted until we scaled the stairs and took in the damage to the second floor. Scorch marks were everywhere—the floors, the walls, the ceiling—all of it so thickly covered in black streaks that the lights seemed dim. I could see into the galley now, although *galley* was a loose definition for what remained of the room. All of the appliances and furniture were gone. The wall where the stove used to be was covered in a thick layer of metal cable in the shape of a patch. It seemed the explosion had breached a hole in the ship, large enough to blow everything out into space. Overhead, the pierced air ducts were also patched. Cabe must have fastened himself to the wall after sealing himself inside the room, and then allowed the lack of oxygen from space to choke out the fire before he repaired the hull and air pipes. Maybe he wasn't so bad . . . for a robot.

I was about to say so when Kyler whirled on me.

He spread his arms wide and demanded, "What *was* that?"

"What do you mean?"

"I mean one minute you're this really cool superhero, and the next minute you lose your mind and you blow up my ship. What's your deal?"

"What's *my* deal?" I repeated while jabbing a finger toward Cabe. "He's the one who flipped his lid and tried to smother me with rope! What did you expect me to do, just stand there and wait for you to rescue me?"

"No, but you could've waited for, oh, I dunno, like, *half a second*, before you tried carving up my robot like a loaf of bread."

"I was scared," I told him. "Is that so hard to understand?"

"So you fired a laser at a combustible power source?" Ky splayed both hands at his temples to mimic an exploding head. "That seemed like a good idea to you at the time?"

I drew a calming breath. "I wasn't thinking."

"Yeah, that's obvious."

"I'm sorry. Are we cool?"

He grumbled something I couldn't understand and held out a palm. "I want your laser. Then we'll be cool. You can have it back when we get to Earth."

I jutted my chin at the galley. "I dropped it in there."

Kyler quirked his mouth to one side, clearly deciding whether or not to believe my story.

"I did," I said with a shrug. "It's long gone. You don't have to worry."

"Fine. I'm going to run a damage report." Ky opened his

mouth as if to say something else, but he must have thought better of it, because he left me with a firm nod and walked away to the pilothouse.

After he was out of sight, I pushed my laser deeper into my side pocket.

He could have it when I was dead.

CHAPTER NINE

kyler centaurus

I sat in the smoky pilothouse, scrolling—and scrolling some more—through the ship's damage log while I shivered inside a blanket I had snatched from my parents' bed. The galley was a total loss, no surprise there. It would have to be gutted and reinstalled. But a ruined kitchen was the least of my worries. The heat from the fire had damaged the thermal sensors on the second floor, tricking the ship into thinking we needed an arctic blast of air-conditioning, which explained why I was wrapped in a blanket.

The air filters weren't working, either, as evidenced by the haze of smoke in the room. And the metal Cabe had used to seal off the fire had created some kind of byproduct that the ship detected as potentially toxic. Oh, and the best part: The explosion had torn through all three layers of the reinforced hull bordering the galley. So in a nutshell, we had no heat, no way to cook our food, no food *to* cook, a possibly poisoned air supply, and a weak spot in the hull capable of popping the ship like a soap bubble with a single tap of an asteroid.

Trouble everywhere. And I hadn't started any of it.

No, I had a certain trigger-happy Wanderer to thank for that.

Right on cue with my thoughts, Fig shuffled into the pilot-house with her own blanket pulled around her shoulders. She plopped down beside me in the copilot's seat as if she hadn't just wrecked my life ten minutes earlier.

"It's cold in here," she said.

I slid her a glare. "You don't say."

"So turn off the thermal regulators and set the temperature manually," she suggested, as if that wouldn't have occurred to me. She nodded at the nasty look I gave her. "Yeah, okay, I'm guessing you already tried that."

"That and more."

"Where's Cabe?"

"Charging."

"Good," she said. "He earned a break. He's kind of smart, for a robot."

At least we agreed on one thing.

With a sigh, I closed out the damage report. Rereading it wouldn't accomplish anything except maybe giving me a headache. "We need to stop for repairs," I said. My stomach growled, reminding me that the pasta I had cooked was now floating somewhere in deep space. "And food. It's two more days to Earth, maybe three depending on how long it takes a mechanic to fix the air-filtration system."

"I know a place." Fig tugged the blanket over her head until only her nose was visible. "Travel depots are everywhere, especially along the route to Earth. It won't be a problem to get the ship fixed and pick up a few supplies."

"Yeah," I said. "But there's the matter of money."

"As in . . ." she prompted.

"As in we don't have any."

"So ask your parents to transfer some credits," she said. "They can afford it."

Maybe it was fate, or just my lousy luck, but my parents chose that exact moment to call the ship for the first time since I'd left Fasti.

"Incoming transmission," the ship announced. "Centaurus residence, Earth."

When I didn't tap the ACCEPT button after the first few beeps, Fig nodded her blanketed head at the comm station. "You going to get that?"

I swiped the screen, dismissing the call.

"Guess not," she muttered.

Guilt gnawed at my empty stomach. I should have answered. I knew my parents were worried about me, and honestly, I had planned to call them after the festival. But what was I supposed to say? *Hey, Mom and Dad. Sorry I've been ignoring your calls, but I'm on my way home now. Oh, and I'm bringing a guest. Don't freak out or anything, but after I stole your ship, pirates attacked me—twice—so I promised to give a ride to a girl who just blew up the galley. That's cool, right?*

Yeah, no. They were going to kill me. I was practically dead already. In fact, I wouldn't be surprised if the Man Upstairs was already arguing with the devil for custody of my soul . . . and losing. I could almost feel that pitchfork in my butt.

"Recorded message," the computer announced. And before I could stop her, Fig reached for the screen and tapped PLAY.

My mom's face appeared on the screen, giving me an instant ache in my chest. She looked terrible, worse than the time she had caught pinkeye from Bonner when she'd chaperoned his third grade field trip to the petting zoo. Her skin was almost as pale as the girl sitting next to me, and that was saying a lot. My mom's typically glossy blond hair was dishwater dull, scrunched at the temples like she'd been running her hands through it over and over again.

She probably had. Because of me.

My dad leaned in to press his face next to hers. His eyes were clear and his jaw was freshly shaven, but I could see new creases around his mouth and across his forehead. I didn't know if I was the reason for his frown lines, though, because I recognized the T-shirt he was wearing, and I knew that right below the camera cutoff, the word RESIST glowed in holographic lettering. It was the shirt he wore to all of his protests. I frowned at the tight set of his jaw. He had probably just returned from an anti-Niatrix demonstration. Not even a missing son could come between my dad and his hate affair with Quasar Niatrix.

"Kyler Gregory Centaurus," my mom said in a soft, scratchy voice that negated the threatening use of my middle name. "I know you're seeing these messages because I've been getting read receipts from the ship."

"Tsk, tsk, tsk," Fig said to me. "Busted."

"We also know," Dad chimed in, "that you set a course for Fasti. And judging by the charges to my account before the bank froze my money, you were safe enough to play a hundred credits worth of video games on the way there." He paused to grind his teeth and suck a loud breath through his nose. "What we don't know is why you disabled the ship's tracker two days ago."

"*What?*" I said. I hadn't disabled the ship's tracker. I didn't even know how to do that. The pirates must have done it the first time they'd attacked the ship.

"Kyler, you need to tell us where you are," my mom said. "We can't send help for you if we don't know your coordinates. And after what happened on Fasti . . ." Her voice faltered, and she cleared her throat. "We're not mad at you. Just tell us where you are."

"We *are* mad at you," my dad said with a lifted finger. "But we're more worried. Bottom line: Call home, right now. Whatever trouble you think you're in, I promise it'll be worse for every minute you make us wait to hear—"

I paused the playback, intrigued by something my mom had said. I glanced at Fig and asked, "What happened on Fasti? Aside from us ditching the Guard, I mean, because that wouldn't have made the news."

Fig didn't seem to be listening. Her eyes were still fixed on my parents' frozen faces. She jutted her chin at the screen. "Are you going to call them back?"

"Yeah, I guess," I said, though I didn't know why she cared. Maybe she was just nosy. If so, she would have to live with disappointment, because I wasn't going to call home while she was in the room. I didn't want an audience when my parents yelled me into next year.

I pulled up the computer's search bar and typed *Fasti Sun Festival*, then waited for the results. "First I want to find out what my mom was talking about."

Fig jerked her gaze to mine. The blanket on her head fell

back far enough for me to see the anger in her eyes. It caught me off guard, because I hadn't done anything wrong. This girl had serious mood swings.

"What?" I demanded.

She shook her head at me and muttered something I couldn't hear.

The computer displayed my search results, and all thoughts of Fig's weirdness vanished. Now I understood why my mom had been so freaked out. Right there in bold headlines, a dozen news sources reported "Fasti Star Stolen!"

"No way," I muttered, expanding one of the stories for more information. How could anyone steal a sun? Even in miniature form, a ball of radioactive gas wasn't the sort of thing you could simply tuck in your back pocket and sneak home with a five-finger discount.

My reaction made Fig curious enough to lean in over my shoulder, and together we skimmed the article.

GALAXY ROCKED BY SUN THEFT

Festivalgoers at this year's Fasti Presentation of Man-made Stars got front-row seats to the heist of a lifetime— the theft of an artificial yellow dwarf sun from its route to the Dingo system, which had purchased the star to complete its terraform process, making the orbiting planets habitable for human colonists. Security specialists

are tight-lipped regarding the details of the crime, but sources have reported mutiny on board the solar barge tasked with towing the star to Dingo, and multiple witnesses have claimed it was the act of mutants, who many believe are protesting "unfair treatment" on Earth.

"We urge everyone to remain calm," said Fasti spokesman Joshua Ulti. "The culprits won't get far. Each man-made sun is kept in a state of miniature and suspended activity until it reaches its new home. While the process is incomplete, the star poses no greater threat to nearby planets than a hundred nuclear bombs—"

"A hundred nukes?" Fig gave a sarcastic snort. "Yeah, there's no reason to panic or anything."

"—likely not enough to destroy an entire planet."

Now heading in the wrong direction, the star-toting barge is causing panic, riots, and mass evacuations for colonies in its path. In response to the threat, interplanetary travel in the affected quadrant has been restricted to government ships and authorized evacuation vessels. The Galaxy Guard insists that the motive for the theft is unknown, as is the star's ultimate destination, but if reports of mutant terrorism are correct, Earth could be a likely target. Until more details are available, citizens are urged to remain at home and report suspicious activity to the Galaxy Guard hotline.

"Oh, sure, blame the mutants," Fig said. "Story of my life."

I glanced at the navigation equipment to see how close we were to the restricted area. Just my luck, we were smack-dab in the middle of it. "The restricted area is the same quadrant we're in. Now we really have to find a place to land."

Fig shivered in her blanket, shifting me a worried glance. "If we get caught flying during a landside curfew . . ."

"Then we'll explain that we tried to land as soon as we could. Worst-case scenario is they give us a ticket. It's no big deal."

"No big deal for *you*," she stressed. "You'll get a warning or a lecture or, at the very worst, a ticket. *You've* got the right kind of DNA."

"The right kind of DNA? This isn't a human versus mutant thing."

"Everything is a human versus mutant thing."

I fought the urge to roll my eyes. This girl had a Milky Way–size chip on her shoulder when it came to humans. "Oh, come on."

"Don't 'oh, come on' me," she said, using her fingers to make quotes. "Didn't you read the article? Your people are blaming my people for stealing the star. Which is ridiculous. First of all, why would we do that? And second, did you even see any mutants at the festival?"

"Besides you?"

"Well, obviously."

I thought about it and came up with nothing. I hadn't been looking for Wanderers at the festival, but I was pretty sure I would have noticed if one of them had crossed my path. Wanderers tended to stand out in a crowd.

"No," I admitted. "Not unless they were in disguise."

"Okay, for argument's sake, let's say they were in disguise.

Why would Wanderers steal a sun? What are they going to do with it?"

I nodded at the article. "They could crash the star into Earth and—"

"And kill billions of innocent people," Fig interrupted. "Just because we're salty about not being allowed to live there? Does that make sense to you?"

Honestly, no, it didn't. I came up with another motive. "If I were a Wanderer, maybe I'd use the star to create a solar system for my people. So we'd have a planet of our own, and we wouldn't have to keep moving and living on ships."

"Okay, but there's a huge hole in that theory," she said. "Think about it."

I did, and right away I saw a snag in my logic. "A star is impossible to hide. Everyone would know where it was, and that it was stolen. No one would let the Wanderers get away with it. The people who bought the sun would want their merchandise back—either that or a refund—so they would try to take back the star."

"Or hire paid fighters to round up all the mutants on that planet and send them to farms, to pay for the cost of ten stars."

"Farms?" I asked, confused. "Like with cows and crops and stuff? I thought all the farms were run by machines. Why would anyone send Wanderers to work there?"

She shook her head. "Not that kind of farm. I'm talking about the prison camps where my people get sent to do slave labor for life." She huffed bitterly. "We're not even allowed on Earth to go to *jail*. How messed up is that?"

"What prison camps?"

"Huh? You've seriously never heard of them?"

"No," I said. And I really hadn't. On Earth, people who broke the law went to huge floating prison complexes in the middle of the oceans. The system was seriously flawed, but it didn't sound anything like these labor camps.

"They're run by an oily slimeball from Earth," Fig explained. "He builds new planets for people to live on. Or rather his *slaves* build the planets while he sits back and collects the profits."

I sat bolt upright in my chair. There was only one person who terraformed planets and sold them to settlers. "Do you mean Quasar Niatrix?"

"The name sounds familiar. Does he have a pretty face and a smile that belongs in a toothpaste commercial?"

I nodded.

"Yeah, that's him," she said. "That guy is living proof that looks can be deceiving. Do you know him?"

"Not personally," I said. "But I know *of* him. Everyone does. He's probably the most famous man on Earth right now because of the vote."

"What vote?" she asked.

"Wow. You really *are* cut off, aren't you?"

"Dude," she said, giving me the stink eye. "Thirty seconds ago, you didn't know prison camps were a thing."

That was a fair point. So I told her about what was happening on Earth, mainly that Quasar wanted to absorb the planet into his private company and run it like a business. "He said we'll get free money out of it, something called dividends.

And he promised to take over the planet's security, since the Galaxy Guard budget is the reason taxes are so high."

"There's no such thing as free money," Fig said. "If he's offering to pay you, it's because he's getting something out of it. Besides, I've heard he already has a bunch of Galaxy Guards in his pocket. He pays them on the down-low, and they do shady stuff for him like make up charges against mutants to get them convicted and sent to his work camps. That's why mutants don't trust the Guard."

"You sound like my dad," I told her. "He thinks Quasar controls the media, too. He says the news outlets don't tell the whole truth about Niatrix Industries because a bunch of reporters are paid to 'spin' the stories in Quasar's favor."

"Your dad sounds smart. I think he's right."

I sniffed a humorless laugh.

"Seriously," she said. "How would you feel if people looked down on you because of your DNA, or because of where you were born? As if you could control either of those things, even if you wanted to."

"I know," I assured her. My parents had talked to me about human-Wanderer equality since I was old enough to listen to the news and ask what *ghost* meant. (Side note: *Ghost* was the ultimate dirty word in our house. When I'd said it, my dad's eyeballs had almost exploded.) "I get it."

"No, I don't think you do."

"Then explain what I'm missing," I said. "Because I'm doing my best here. I think mutants are super cool. I'm on your side."

"I believe you. But being on my side doesn't mean you understand what life is like for me." She puckered her lips in thought for a moment. "You've gone on vacations to other planets, right?"

"Yeah. We just got back from my nana's place a few days ago."

"Okay, so tell me what happened when you landed on Earth."

I wrinkled my forehead. I didn't understand the question. Nothing had happened when we'd landed. We had just . . . landed.

"Let me guess," she offered. "Your ship entered the atmosphere, and your parents flew to your house and parked on your landing pad. Then everyone got out of the ship and went inside the house to unpack their bags or grab a snack or whatever. Easy peasy, right?"

"Pretty much."

"That's because your ship is registered to a human family. The satellite scanners above Earth's atmosphere know this, and they let you pass. But that's not how it would happen for me. If I wanted to visit Earth, I would have to buy a travel visa first. Then I'd have to show that visa to the flight crew before I was even allowed on the ship. When we landed on Earth, I wouldn't be able to get off at a travel depot with the humans. I would have to wait for a second stop, to a special Galaxy Guard station where I would have to show my visa *again*, then have my picture taken, get my fingerprints scanned, and explain the reason for my visit. After that, they would insert a chip behind my ear to let me know when my time was up—and do you know how the chip would tell me?"

I shook my head.

"It would start beeping," she said. "*Constantly*. And it wouldn't stop until I left Earth's atmosphere. Now let's talk about what my day would look like on the ground. The minute I walked out of the Galaxy Guard station, a dozen people would stop and stare at me, or throw themselves out of my way on the sidewalk because they think I'm going to give them radiation poisoning or something stupid like that. Forget about shopping. If I went inside a store, the owner would give me the side-eye and assume I don't have money to spend. Just to buy a hot dog from a street vendor, I'd have to pay first, to prove that I *can* pay."

My gaze dropped to my lap. I had always known that Wanderers were treated unfairly, but until now, I hadn't thought much about it. I wanted to say something meaningful, but when I spoke, all that came out was "You can't buy a hot dog from a street vendor anymore. Hot dogs were outlawed a long time ago because the ingredients caused—"

"That's not the point," she cut in. "The point is you can't understand what it's like to be a mutant if you haven't been in my shoes. You say you're on my side, but are you, really?"

"Of course I am," I argued.

"A few minutes ago, I told you that Quasar Niatrix uses mutants for slave labor. But when you talked about the vote on Earth, you seemed pretty impressed by the 'free money' you stand to get out of it. Anyone who was truly on my side would have nothing to do with that man, no matter how much money he promised them. Anyone on my side would do the right thing and wouldn't care about the cost."

I opened my mouth to defend myself, but I closed it again. I didn't know what to say. The shame burning in my chest told me Fig was right—that I hadn't understood what life was really like for her—but something inside me wouldn't let me admit it. So I just sat there, feeling like a jerk. . . .

Until she flapped a hand and said, "Never mind. It doesn't matter."

I glanced at Fig to find her staring into her own lap, chewing the inside of her cheek as if *she'd* done something wrong. She seemed to feel as guilty as I did. That didn't add up, but it gave me a perfect chance to change the subject.

"I'd better call home and ask for some credits so we can get out of this sector," I said. "I hope the bank unfroze my parents' money."

"Yeah," Fig agreed with an eager nod. Clearly she was glad to put the old topic behind us, too. She pointed to a beacon on the navigation screen. "We're right on top of a planet." She leaned closer to the screen and read aloud, "It's called New Dakota. Should be plenty of service stations facing this side of the world. Tell your folks to transfer money to us there."

I set the autopilot to land on New Dakota. Then as the *Whirlwind* motored toward our new destination, I took a deep breath and prepared to face my mom and dad. But no sooner had I entered their transmission code than the overhead lights flickered once, then twice, and the next thing I knew, we were sitting in the dark. We're talking full dark. No backlit screens. No flashing buttons. No emergency power.

No operational equipment at all.

"Full system failure," I muttered as my stomach clenched.

Without our engines, we were going down for sure. But this wasn't the kind of landing I wanted to make.

CHAPTER TEN

kyler centaurus

Here's the thing about engine failure in space:
As long as you're well outside a planet's atmospheric pull, the lack of gravity will keep you from free-falling. So you just drift. Which is all fine and good . . . unless you gathered a bunch of momentum before your engines failed, and now you're drifting *toward a planet*. Then, without a barrier to stop you, it's just a matter of time before gravity takes hold, and your ship becomes a literal ball of fire as you streak through the sky and plummet to your death.

And guess what? Because I had set the autopilot on a course for New Dakota, the engines had already propelled us in that direction, so we were about to get up close and personal with it.

Good times.

"I'm going to send a Mayday," Fig said, standing from her seat.

"With what?" I asked, gesturing at the lifeless transmission station, barely visible in the dim glow of sunlight that trickled through the windshield. "No power, remember?"

"I have a handheld comm in my room," she told me, then she muttered something about low battery life as she walked away. That didn't sound promising, so I brainstormed a way to change the ship's path before we gave New Dakota its next crater.

Physics, I thought to myself. *Remember the laws of motion.*

That was the answer. But how?

I thought about my first day on the ship, when I had used a fire extinguisher like a broomstick to propel me through the air. I could force open an exterior hatch and spray the extinguisher nozzle away from New Dakota, but that wouldn't do much good. The *Whirlwind* was too heavy, and she was drifting too fast to be reversed by the force of one dinky pressurized canister. So either I needed something with a lot more force than a fire extinguisher, or . . .

Or a fixed object to push off of, I realized.

Okay, so maybe *fixed* was the wrong word. Nothing in space was tied down. But if there was a heavy enough object within Cabe's roping distance, we could collide with it on purpose and change our path—like a living game of pool, with the force of one object transferring to another. At the right angle, we could skew ourselves away from New Dakota and then float along safe and snug until someone rescued us.

Now I needed a figurative cue ball to set my plan in motion.

I ran to the observatory and peered out the window, scanning the void for anything large enough to bump us along a new trajectory. Believe it or not, there was a surprising amount of junk in space—a side effect of people being, you know, complete slobs—and most of the clutter tended to gather around planetary settlements like this one. Garbage pods, broken-down shuttles, engine pieces, caskets (yes, that's every bit as creepy as it sounds), hazardous-waste capsules, building materials from old satellite stations. As long as the garbage was hefty, I could make use of it.

I squinted and made out a shadowy cone-shaped object floating in the distance, roughly the length of a football field away from me. I couldn't tell what the object was, but it seemed to be the same size as the *Whirlwind*, maybe even bigger. Cabe had more than enough line inside him to lasso the thing and tug it in our direction.

"Winner, winner, chicken dinner," I whispered.

Fig had snuck up from behind, making me flinch when she pressed her nose against the observatory window. "Chicken dinner? Did a food ship come to tow us away? 'Cause I could get down on some chicken and mashed potatoes right now."

So could I. The only thing that kept my stomach from growling was the threat of a fiery death on New Dakota. "No," I told her, "but I have an idea that might save us." I searched her face for a sign of emotion, a hint to tell me if she'd had any luck with her handheld comm. But all she did was fog up the glass and trace her name in it. Finally, I asked, "Did anyone respond to your Mayday?"

She scrubbed the side of her fist over the glass, erasing her doodles. "No. My battery died after I put out the distress call."

"Then why are you acting so chill?"

She turned to face me and leaned against the window. "Because I have an idea, too."

Something in her confident tone set me on edge. Ideas were all I had to offer. I liked being the problem-solver; it was my thing.

"Okaaaay," I said warily.

Her eyebrows formed a V. "What is *okaaaay* supposed to mean? You don't want to hear my idea?"

I held up a palm. "No offense, it's just . . . I consider myself more of an idea person."

"What does that make me?"

I shrugged. "Good with lasers?"

She glared at me. "Has anyone ever told you you're a smug know-it-all?"

I pressed my lips together. I wasn't about to admit that my brothers called me that on the regular.

"I'll take that as a yes," she said, reading my face. "You know what? You're a real piece of work, kid."

"Kid?" I repeated as my head cocked sideways. All of a sudden I didn't care that we were drifting toward a planet. "We're the same age, you know."

"Chronologically, maybe." She lifted one shoulder in an annoyingly superior way. "But there are different kinds of ages."

"What, like developmental?" I asked with a snort. "If you're trying to say I'm younger than you when it comes to smarts, then I've got a closet full of science trophies that say you're wrong."

"Street smarts, then."

"Those aren't as important as book smarts."

"Really?" She stood tall, gripping her hips. "Who saved your ship from pirates?"

"The same girl who wrecked it," I reminded her. "So thanks for the help . . . *kid.*"

She made a noise of aggravation and flipped her hair, looking like every human girl I'd ever known. "I'm done wasting my time with you," she called over her shoulder as she stomped out of the observatory. "If you need me—which I'm sure you will—I'll be suiting up and saving your bacon. Again."

"Wait, suiting up?" I said. "As in going outside the ship?"

"Yes, that's where the asteroids are."

"Asteroids? What do those have to do with anything?" I jogged after her, following down the stairs into the loading bay. "We have to talk about this. We don't have a plan."

"Sure we do." She crossed the loading bay and pointed at the blaster strapped to the floor. "I'm going to take that beautiful piece of tech outside and do what I do best."

"What, blast rocks?" I asked, unable to stop my voice from rising. "How's that supposed to help?"

"It'll get us noticed."

"That's crazy! Is blowing stuff up all you know how to do? There *are* other ways to solve problems, you know."

"As in?"

"As in science. It fixes everything."

"Not in my experience."

"What experience?" I asked as I ran around to block her

path. "When was the last time you were floating two klicks away from a planet's gravitational field?"

She frowned. The obvious answer was *never.*

"There's no room for error out there," I told her, thumbing at the airlock door. "I'd rather not die in a fire today, if you don't mind. We might only get one chance to save ourselves. Let's not waste it."

I explained the science behind my idea, and why it was sound. When I was done, she pursed her lips in thought for a few seconds, both arms folded across her chest, before she finally broke through her own stubbornness and agreed with me.

"All right, we'll try it your way," she said. "But you'd better not be wrong about this."

"Trust me," I told her. "Science is never wrong."

Twenty minutes and three arguments later, we were inside the airlock chamber, decked out in our thermal suits and oxygen helmets. Cabe stood between us, nervously whirring his cable reel despite the extra time I had taken to explain to him what we were about to do.

"No improvising," I reminded him. "Stick to the plan, okay?"

"Affirmative, Goosey."

Fig rolled her eyes and mumbled something I couldn't quite hear. I didn't ask her to repeat herself, mostly because I was tired of bickering with her, but also because every thump of my heart brought us a little closer to New Dakota's atmosphere. If we didn't change our path soon, we would crash. My palms were already sweating inside their insulated gloves. The last thing I needed was another wisecrack from Fig to undercut my confidence.

You can do this, I told myself. *Science fixes everything.*

"Get ready," I said, gripping the outer door latch.

In response, Cabe slid a long section of rope through a metal loop called a carabiner that was attached to the waist of my space suit. He tethered the cable to a hook on his chest, and then Fig clipped her carabiner to the same line. That way neither of us would float too far from safety. Now Cabe had both of his reels free, one to secure himself to the ship, and the other to retrieve the cone-shape mystery object in the distance.

With a deep breath, I slid the airlock latch upward and flinched as the chamber filled with the hissing sound of escaping oxygen. The room had to equalize pressure with the outside before the door could open, otherwise we would shoot into space like the contents of a shaken can of soda. Once the pressure was stable, the door opened with a *click*, and my boots drifted up from the floor as the vast chill of space unfolded before me.

I had never taken a space walk before, and even though my breaths came in gasps, a flutter of excitement tickled my chest. I was floating, drifting weightlessly in a sea of emptiness, with nothing holding on to me except a thin cable around my waist. It was like diving into a pool that had no bottom. The thrill topped any roller coaster or zip line I'd ever ridden on Earth.

But it was colder than I had expected, a bone-deep freeze that sliced through the layers of my thermal suit. In seconds, my sweaty hands were beginning to tremble, and I knew it wouldn't take long for the rest of my limbs to follow.

We needed to hurry.

"Okay, buddy," I told Cabe. "Time to go fishing."

"You got this, Cabe," Fig added encouragingly. "Just remember how clever you are. You know, for a robot."

Cabe fixed himself to the airlock and then aimed his remaining spool at the target, shooting out at it with maximum force. His cable sailed flawlessly through the darkness, but the motion caused the *Whirlwind* to rotate a quarter of a turn toward New Dakota. The sight of the planet looming there, all red and green and brown . . . and way too close for comfort . . . raised a lump in my throat that all the spit in my glands wouldn't wash down.

If Fig shared my fear, she didn't let it show. Her eyes gleamed wide and alert with readiness for her part of the job, probably because it involved a laser. I had agreed to let her bolt her laser cannon to the hull of the ship so she could help blast the cone-shape object into the right position when Cabe roped it in. The angle had to be precise when we collided with our "cue ball." According to Fig, *precision* was her middle name.

We would see about that.

Anyway, she got right to work, pinning the cannon between her knees and using her hands to scale the network of ladder rungs along the hull until she reached the top. And after that, I lost sight of her.

I stood on the middle-most rung and turned my attention to Cabe, who was still attached to the airlock chamber and unspooling metal rope as hard as he could. Whatever the cone-shape hunk of metal was, it must have been farther away from the *Whirlwind* than I had thought. I pulled a handheld density meter from my zipper pouch and used it to scan the object, discovering that its mass was heavier than I'd estimated, too. By more than half a ton. That wasn't a problem—it was actually a good thing—but I would have to account for the changes when I crunched the numbers. I tapped my helmet's MAGNIFY button and watched the end of Cabe's rope make contact with the cone. The industry-grade magnet I'd fastened to the tip of his cable latched on with a loud *click* that echoed like thunder in my ears.

"Target acquired, Goosey," Cabe said.

"Good," I told him. "Remember, no improvising. Just hold tight while I figure out what to do next."

"Affirmative."

I glanced at the object. Now for the hard part: reeling it in at just the right speed *and* calculating the precise point where it should strike the ship before I told Cabe to release the tether. I knew the right equation to use. It was simple physics, really. But I wasn't kidding when I had told Fig there was no room for error. The math had to be flawless.

Lucky for us, I mathed harder than a hurricane.

I licked my lips and studied the cone-shape object, calculating its mass in comparison to the ship's. The formula played out in my mind, and after a few minutes I saw exactly where, and with what force, the object needed to strike us. Just to be safe, I double-checked my math, but I knew I was right. In that moment, the hair on my forearms stood on end—not from fear, but from a sense of purpose. Almost like destiny. It felt as if every physics class I had ever taken had led me to this moment.

"Fig," I said through my helmet comm. "You ready?"

"Almost," she replied. "One more bolt to go, but I can't reach it." She tugged the cable securing both of us to the ship, sending a vibration to me along the metal. "My tether's too tight."

"Unhook your carabiner," I told her. "But just for a few seconds, then hook yourself back on. We don't want you floating away."

"Roger that." She went quiet for a moment. Then I heard a metallic *thud*, and she reported, "All done. I'm ready when you are."

I switched my comm link over to Cabe. "Okay, buddy, time to reel it in. I want you to start slow, on your lowest power setting, until the thing is twenty yards from the ship. Then crank into high gear and let it ram us. Got it?"

Cabe beeped nervously, but he obeyed. His internal motor whirred, causing the ship to lurch slightly as his line to the object tightened. I watched the metal cone approaching us and eventually realized it was the tip of an old space rocket, the kind early astronauts had traveled in when they'd first explored Mars. What I didn't know was how the capsule had ended up in New Dakota's orbit. Though faded by time, its name was still visible in block lettering: the *Orion*.

"I've got that ugly thing in my sights," Fig said. "Tell me where to blast it."

I nodded. "See the little dot above the letter *i*?"

"Yeah."

"Can you hit it?"

She sniffed a laugh. "Is a duck's butt watertight?"

I took that as a yes. "Then do it on my mark, but at fifty percent power."

"You're sure about this?"

"Positive," I told her. If I knew anything, it was that math and science didn't lie. That was what made them more reliable than people.

The *Orion* reached the twenty-yard mark, and the ship lurched again as Cabe increased his towing power to full capacity.

"On my mark . . ." I said to Fig. "After you fire, brace for impact."

"Ready," she answered.

The *Orion*'s cone raced toward us. I waited for it to rotate another few inches to the left. Then the timing was perfect. The force from Fig's blaster would skew the capsule enough to strike us in the perfect spot, just below the loading bay. All we would have to do then was hold on to our butts and glide to safety.

I told Fig, "Now!"

She fired a beam of white-hot light that forced me to shield my eyes. I felt heat wash over the front of my thermal suit, and after that, everything happened in a rush.

For the record, I'd like to say my math was correct.

At least based on the data that was available to me.

What I hadn't counted on was the presence of air trapped inside the *Orion*'s capsule, or how piercing the capsule's metal shell would release that air with enough pressure to turn the cone into one of those black-and-white pinwheels that catches the wind and spins so fast it blurs into gray.

A whirligig: that was what I had created.

The air hissing from the capsule sent it rotating faster than Cabe could detach from it. Before I could blink, the cable was wrapped twice around the cone's midsection and drawing closer to the *Whirlwind*. The rope pulled taut, jerking the ship out from under my feet.

Next thing I knew, I was falling. Not falling in the usual way of gravity pulling me toward the ground, but rather *tumbling* with nothing to hold on to. My boots tipped over and over again above my head. I windmilled my arms to anchor myself to something solid, but the cable around my waist had gone slack, giving me no traction. I stopped breathing. My stomach roiled, and I tasted vomit at the back of my throat. Then I opened my eyes and saw swirls of red and green flash alternately with black space as I soared toward New Dakota, and I truly lost it.

Let's just say there's no shame in leaking in your shorts at a time like that.

From somewhere over my shoulder, the clatter of metal told me the *Orion* and the *Whirlwind* had collided. Air continued to fizz and hiss like a demented snake. I was too dizzy to sense in which direction the impact had sent us, but the glimpses I caught of distant landmass seemed to be getting bigger with each of my flips. I pictured my body as a fireball streaking across the New Dakota sky, and the mental image shocked me into taking a breath.

"Cabe," I cried. "You have permission to improvise!"

His reply came as static that I couldn't understand. I called out for Fig, peering for her through my helmet, but all I could see was the constant flip-flopping of land and space.

If I could only steady myself . . .

My wish came true a little too suddenly as the cable around my waist brought me to a halt. I doubled over with an *oof* before pinging backward. I glanced over my shoulder while I sailed toward the tangled-up ruin that was my ship. The mass was still spinning, though slower now that the air from the *Orion* had begun to run out. I spotted Cabe right where I'd left him, fastened to the airlock chamber while he reeled me in.

But wait. Fig had been holding on to my cable, too.

"Where's Fig?" I asked, glancing all around and finding nothing. The *Whirlwind* made another rotation, showing me her blaster mounted to the top of the ship, but she was no longer with it.

"Fig!" I shouted.

I didn't hear her voice, but a sensation of being watched prompted me to look west. That was when I found her: arms outstretched, eyes wide, mouth agape in a silent scream, sailing away from me with the kind of velocity that could only mean one thing. She hadn't refastened her carabiner. She had fallen off the ship, and now she was caught in New Dakota's atmosphere.

My heart stuttered. My gloved hands reached out to her, but deep down I knew there was nothing I could do. The closest person I had to a friend was about to die right in front of me.

And it was all my fault.

CHAPTER ELEVEN

figerella jammeslot

Heat.

That was all I could think about. Not the fact that I was free-falling. Not the sensation of gravity pulling my spine into my navel. Not the ground rising up to meet me from somewhere I couldn't see. The only thing that mattered was the burn. It pierced my thermal suit and screamed across my nerves, growing hotter with each second. My face felt swollen, like I had held my breath for too long. And maybe I had, because the oxygen in my tank was thicker than soup. Sweat dripped into my lashes, blurring my vision. I wanted to take off my helmet, to wipe my eyes and feel the wind cooling my hair, but I couldn't unclench my fingers long enough to work the latch.

So hot.

I knew I should do something—scream or flail my arms or say a prayer to whoever the patron saint of mutants was—but in the moments before my death, I had a weird realization about the power of suffering. It made me think of all the action movies I'd seen, the ones where the hero was tortured for information, but in the end, he gritted his teeth or muttered a cool one-liner or spat in the bad guy's face or something equally savage like that. I had always thought I was savage, too, but now I knew better. Pain took me down a notch. It showed me how weak I was. I would give anything to make it stop. I was going to die in a blaze of shame, not glory.

That wasn't how I'd pictured it.

My muscles jerked, and I blinked hard. I must've passed out for a second. I didn't stay awake for much longer after that. I kept drifting in and out of awareness in rapid spurts until I finally let my neck go slack, and my eyes rolled back in my head. I didn't care anymore. Let the universe take me to wherever my parents were. At least we'd be together again. I wouldn't have to strain to remember which tune my father whistled when he was in a good mood. Or the direction my mother had braided my hair: under or over. I had forgotten those details. The years without my parents had been a thief, eroding my image of their faces, the curves and lines that had made them distinct. Sometimes I pictured my father's face as more round than oval, and then I wondered if his jawline had been square. And what had been the exact shade of my mother's eyes? True blue, or more of a bluish gray?

Soon I would know. That was some small comfort.

I had just begun to dream of my mother's irises—pale blue with flecks of amber—when I flinched awake again. But this time something was different. Several things were different, actually. I felt the hard press of metal beneath my body. A reverse tugging in my stomach told me I was falling up instead of down. I squinted through the moisture fogging my helmet and noticed a shadow looming above me, wide enough to block out the sun. A burst of air blew over me. It felt so good that I groaned out loud. As the air continued flowing over my suit, my senses returned one at a time.

I heard the low roar of an engine, and I realized the shadow above me was a ship, a cruiser roughly the same size as the one my parents had owned. A set of cables rose from my position into an open port in the ship, towing me quickly upward. That explained the backward falling—the ship's crew was bringing me on board. My focus sharpened, and I made out several pockmarks in the craft's underbelly. Something about the dents seemed familiar, but I couldn't figure out why.

Until the blood flow returned to my brain and I noticed the stenciled markings on the underside of the ship's hull. In neon-purple paint it spelled *Wanderlust.*

My hands turned cold in a way that had nothing to do with the breeze.

I knew this ship.

I don't mean I recognized it. I mean I *knew* it, the way my right hand knew my left. I knew the *Wanderlust* had a creaky third step leading to the main floor. I knew the galley smelled like onions, no matter what time of day it was. I knew the pockmarks on the underside of the hull had been caused by an asteroid demolition gone wrong. I knew the bookshelves in the common room were empty, because all of the books had been burned . . . *on purpose.* I knew the ship's robot was named Kirk, and that he needed to charge for at least two hours before he could punish me with a level-two electric shock. And most important, I knew the best way to escape any locked room on board was through the air ducts.

I knew this ship because I had been a "guest" here for a month after my parents had died. And by "guest" I mean indentured servant. When I'd ditched the *Wanderlust* crew, it hadn't been on friendly terms. I might have broken a jaw or two . . . maybe three, tops.

They had deserved it.

But still, they had to hate me. So why had they saved my life?

My body tensed as I entered the port and glanced at the rust flakes on the loading-bay walls. When I was part of the crew here, one of my jobs had been to sand down and paint over those rusty patches. I hadn't made it far before I'd run away. Maybe the captain had saved my life because he needed someone to finish the job in the loading bay, and a hundred more chores after that. Free labor, not much different than Quasar's prison farms. Or maybe he wanted a deeper level of revenge.

Peeking over my shoulder at the distant ground below, I had one final thought before the hatch closed.

I wonder if it's too late to jump. . . .

CHAPTER TWELVE

kyler centaurus

I'm not a touchy-feely kind of guy. Never have been. I think it's a side effect of growing up in a house full of dudes. If a situation called for physical contact—like Christmas or birthdays or whatever—my brothers and I traded manly pats on the shoulder. Or light punches. Those were even better. My mom was the only person in the family who wanted cuddles, so I threw her a bone every once in a while and rested my head on her shoulder when we were on the sofa watching a movie. But that was for her, not for me. Generally speaking, I didn't feel the need to hug people.

Except for Captain Holyoake.

After what he had done for Fig and me—saving our lives and towing our ship—I wanted to hold him like a stuffed bear. Heck, I would've planted a big, juicy, wet one right on his kisser if I didn't think he would punch me into next week for it.

The captain wasn't the affectionate type, either. I could tell by his rough, beefy hands, which hadn't stopped gripping his hips since he'd towed Fig into the cargo hold and docked the

Whirlwind to his spare port. Then there was his mouth, which had yet to crack anything resembling a smile. Combined with the fact that his biceps were bigger than my head, I decided to hug myself instead of him, crossing both arms over my rib cage and cupping my elbows as I gazed up at the captain.

He stood at least two heads taller than me, with a wide brow and an even wider jaw. His skin was covered in the reddish purple patches of all Wanderers, but the way his scars were arranged, forming downward slashes at the corners of his eyes and mouth, made him look even tougher than he already was. But most striking of all were his eyes, dark and piercing, and at the moment, laser fixed on Figerella.

I could tell the two of them knew each other from the way she glared back at him with her chin defiantly lifted. I almost wondered if he was her father or some other relative, because the charged silence between them reminded me of the times I had stared down my parents, waiting for a punishment to be given.

Fig broke eye contact and swung both legs over the side of the excavator the captain had just used to pluck her out of the sky like a toy in a claw machine. But she didn't seem to know where to go from there, so she just sat in place and sulked.

"Thanks again," I told the captain, because clearly Fig wasn't going to show him any gratitude. He ignored me. I used my eyes to send Fig a silent *what's-your-problem?* glare, but she ignored me, too.

Their silent showdown continued until the captain finally asked her, "You have nothing to say to me?" His gritty, pack-a-day voice made Fig flinch, but she tried to play it off by rubbing her upper arms like she was cold. "Nothing at all, Figerella Moonbeam?"

"Moonbeam?" I repeated. Despite the tension in the room, I couldn't help snorting. I guess cheating death had made me giddy. I raised my eyebrows at her and chuckled. "Your middle name is Moonbeam?"

"Shut up," she and the captain said at the same time.

I lifted an apologetic hand and made a zipper motion across my lips.

"After everything we've done for you?" he went on. Then his mouth pulled into the same frown my mom had always used on me when she wanted to inflict maximum guilt. At that point I really began to think he was her dad. Until he added, "What would your father say?"

All right, so the captain wasn't her father. But *whoa*, did that question make Fig angry. Like full-on, nuclear, hot-under-the-collar furious. She balled her fists while her face turned the color of strawberries in June.

"Don't talk about my father," she ground out between her teeth.

The captain opened his mouth, but he didn't have a chance to respond before the clatter of boots sounded from the stairs, and a pair of teenage boys came jogging into the loading bay. They stopped short at the sight of Fig. Judging by the pinch of their brows, they weren't happy to see her. A woman roughly the captain's age followed the boys, but in the slow, uneven steps of someone in pain. She wore a cool smile that didn't reach her eyes, so I supposed she wasn't thrilled with the company, either. Two more teenagers came skipping down the steps behind her, this time girls, followed by a little boy who butt-slid down the handrail. All of the kids' facial markings resembled the captain's, so I assumed this was his family. I leaned aside and peeked through the upper doorway to see if anyone else was coming, but that appeared to be it.

Seven people in all, just like my family—a big crew for such a small ship. I wondered how they got along without killing each other. Or maybe they didn't. One of the older boys rubbed his jaw and stared murder at Fig.

"Figerella," the motherly woman greeted with a nod. "Welcome home."

Fig's reaction caught me by surprise. If I had blinked, I would've missed it. But I didn't blink, and when Mrs. Holyoake said *home*, I saw Fig's shoulders tense. Like she'd been slapped. A cold feeling settled in my chest. Despite what the captain had done for us, something wasn't right here. I felt inside my pocket for Cabe's remote-control fob to make sure I still had it. Cabe was my only defense, though not a very good one. Right now he was powered down and charging on the *Whirlwind*.

The teenager who'd been rubbing his jaw pointed at Fig and said, "Don't think I've forgotten what I owe you." His mom silenced him with a lifted finger, but when she wasn't looking, he mouthed, *I'll tag you back.*

Either that or *I'll take your bag.* I'm not good at lip-reading.

That same boy noticed me, and his jaw dropped. "A human," he said. "What's Fig doing with him?"

One of his sisters wrinkled her nose. "He's Earth-born. I can tell. He reeks of that nasty planet."

"Hey," I objected. Then I discreetly sniffed my armpits, which SO didn't stink, by the way.

"Enough," the captain snapped at his kids. "You know better than that. We don't sink to *their* level."

Clearly he meant me. I began to understand how Fig felt when she spent time around humans.

"You there, boy," the captain said to me. He snapped his fingers as if trying to remember something. "Your name is Skylar, right?"

"Um, it's Kyler, actually." I shrugged, not wanting to poke the bear. "But no worries. Close enough."

"Tell me the news from Earth, Skylar," he went on. "Last I heard, our Council of Wanderers wanted to meet with your United Nations to negotiate the right for our people to come and go as we please. Has that happened yet?"

"Not yet," I told him. "But soon. I think the meeting is supposed to take place in a couple of days."

I didn't mention that the only reason I knew this information was because of all the doom-and-gloom news coverage surrounding the meeting. A lot of major networks kept interviewing "experts" who claimed the Wanderer population would use too much of Earth's resources and lead to the downfall of mankind. (Way to overreact.) Others warned that if Wanderers were allowed on Earth, they might marry humans and create a new generation of mutant babies. Which sounded pretty cool to me, but the point was, the news was doing a bang-up job of getting humans all frothy about Wanderers for a bunch of bogus reasons.

"I hope it works out," I added. "I never thought it was fair, the way Wanderers were cut off from Earth all those years ago. It would be cool if you came back."

Right away, I knew I'd said the wrong thing. The captain clenched his teeth, similar to the way my father did when he was mad, but harder, and with an unsettling muscle twitch in his jaw. From somewhere in the background, a couple of the crew members groaned.

"Do you, Skylar?" the captain asked. "Do you think it would be cool if we returned to the original planet?"

That seemed like a trick question, so I stayed quiet.

"Do you think it would be cool," he continued, "for us to return to a world that rejected us simply because we had the courage to leave? A world that spent the last five hundred years treating us like cockroaches because we developed abilities that they lack? A world that allows us to be enslaved for corporate greed? Do you think that would be *cool*?"

"Uh . . ." I cringed. "Maybe? I mean, not the enslavement part, but the going home part. If that's what some Wanderers want?"

He scoffed at me. "My people don't know what they want."

Fig spoke up, but in a small voice that cracked on the first note. "Yes, we do. We want the freedom to—"

"Let me rephrase," the captain interrupted loud enough to make everyone in the room flinch. "My people don't know what's good for them. They don't understand that we've outgrown humanity, that we're better than our ancestors were—stronger, fitter. Our bodies are made to live in space now. It's the universe that nourishes us, not Earth. The universe is our destiny, our goddess. Returning to the original planet would drag us backward, no different than if humans returned to the trees to live as primates."

His family nodded in agreement. One of them said, "Amen."

"It sickens me, the way my people hoard relics from Earth," the captain spat, his upper lip curling. "Clinging to their ancient books and their pictures of oceans and landscapes, thinking of these things as an anchor to their past. Those relics are nothing but anvils around their necks."

"Excuse me." I raised my hand, classroom-style. "What's an anvil?"

The captain huffed in frustration, but he seemed more irritated with himself than with me. "Of course you don't know what an anvil is. It's an outdated reference, proof that not even *I* can escape our ties to ancient Earth."

I was about to point out that he hadn't answered my question when he added, "That's why I burned every single Earth-made object that my ancestors brought on board this ship. All of them—films, clothing, photographs, music files, games. Oh, and books, of course."

Books?

I gasped so hard I nearly collapsed my own lungs. Horrified, I wrenched my gaze to Fig, who didn't look nearly surprised enough for my own comfort.

The Holyoakes burned books?

I couldn't think of many things worse than that. For the first time, I wondered if it really was possible that Wanderers had stolen the Fasti star. Because you know who else burned books? Dictators and tyrants—the kind of people who were okay with wiping out anyone who stood in their way. But I took a breath and reminded myself not to jump to conclusions. The captain was one man. He didn't speak for all Wanderers. He hated Earth, but he'd saved my life. That wasn't something he would have done if he loathed humans. If that were the case, he would've left me to die, either that or flushed me out the waste port. And he hadn't floated me . . .

Yet.

He turned to Fig with outstretched hands. "I made a promise to your father that I would watch over you, that I would keep you on the right path if anything happened to him. And I mean to do that, Figerella. Your parents left you in my care when they died. You're my responsibility, and I won't let you waste your life on humans."

My mouth dropped open. I hadn't known Fig's parents were dead. Now that I thought about it, I'd never asked her about them. My heart sank. If Fig and I were friends, then I wasn't a very good one.

"My parents were nothing like you," she argued.

"Only because I hadn't shown them the way yet," the captain said. "They would have come around. They were reasonable people. They would've accepted the truth and followed me into the next phase of our destiny."

"That proves you didn't know them at all," she said. "And they didn't know you."

The captain lifted one broad shoulder. "Then perhaps the universe took control and did what needed to be done in order to save you. Now your path is clear."

Whoa.

Had this guy seriously implied that it was a good thing Fig's parents were dead? If I didn't already think the captain was a few sandwiches short of a picnic, that clinched it.

He slashed a hand through the air. "No more arguing. That's what the enemy wants us to do—to fight with one another. They want to weaken and divide us with the same bickering they've sown on Earth. But as I've said in the past, we won't sink to their level." He snapped his fingers and called, "Kirk! Activate!"

Whoever Kirk was, the mention of his name made Fig's eyes fly wide.

That couldn't be good.

"I'm not going to lock you in your cabin," the captain told Fig. "Because we both know how well that worked last time. But I've disabled my shuttle, so you can forget about stealing it again." He thumbed at me. "And as for Skylar's ship, it needs a new core processor. Without one, his engines won't produce enough power to run a night-light."

"And don't even think about taking ours," one of the older boys called. He pointed at a closed door on the other side of the loading bay. "The engine room door is double bolted."

The captain nodded. "Basically, there's nowhere for you to go, Figerella. I hope you've matured enough during our time apart to be respectful of our hospitality."

Fig muttered something under her breath. It sounded like, "Hospitality, my butt."

A clicking noise drew my attention to the rear corner of the loading bay, where a metal robot made its way toward us using six crablike legs that tapered to points at the ends. And

I mean *sharp* points, as in "the better to impale you with, my dear."

This must be Kirk.

He croaked in a deep drone, "Activated and ready for your command."

Kirk looked like something out of a nightmare, with a set of pincers for hands and a cracked plastic head that must have been recycled from an old mannequin. As if that weren't freaky enough, whoever built him had given him glowing red eyes and the warbled voice of a demon.

I mean, come on. That was laying it on a bit thick.

Kirk stopped in front of the captain and snapped both pincers twice before bending at the legs in some sort of weird bow. I backed away toward Fig, putting a few feet of distance between myself and the robot. He was bigger than I'd originally thought. Even with his body lowered, the top of Kirk's head reached the captain's shoulders.

Captain Holyoake extended a hand toward Fig and me. In response, the robot swiveled its plastic face in our direction, giving me an epic case of the willies. "Kirk, do you remember Figerella?"

Kirk snapped his pincers again, which I took as a yes. Beside me, Fig went stiffer than a plank, which told me she remembered him, too.

"The universe has returned her to us," the captain said. "And this time she's going to stay. I command you to escort her wherever she goes, and make sure she follows the rules of the ship. You know what the rules are."

"As you command," Kirk droned in his devil voice.

"And this," the captain said, nodding at me, "is our guest, Skylar. He is to remain with Figerella in her cabin until we decide what to do with him. Is that understood?"

"As you command," Kirk repeated.

"Escort them to their cabin now."

Kirk turned to face us, his needle legs tapping the steely floor. "Figerella and Skylar, proceed to the stairwell."

I shivered. Hearing even my wrong name coming out of that monster's mouth felt like someone had shoved an icicle in my ear. "Wait, can we talk about this?" I asked the captain. "What did you mean when you said 'until we decide what to—'"

Before I could finish, Kirk reached out with one of his pincers and zapped the words out of my mouth. I yelped in pain, stumbling backward and landing on my butt, which caused the Holyoake clan to erupt in laughter.

Well, except for the captain and his wife. They didn't crack a smile.

"I should have warned you," the captain said. "Kirk has permission to discipline our guests. I suggest you follow his orders the first time. He doesn't like repeating himself."

I stood up and made for the stairs, rubbing my sore bottom. I would figure out what to do when I reached Fig's cabin. But when I climbed halfway to the top and turned around, I noticed Fig hadn't joined me. She was at the foot of the stairs, where one of the older boys had stopped her to whisper something in her ear. I tensed at first, afraid that he'd threatened her. But whatever he had said made Fig stop and grin sweetly at him.

Except Fig didn't grin sweetly at anyone.

She patted his jaw and then joined me on the stairs. When I raised a questioning eyebrow at her, she shook her head as if to say *Don't worry about it.* I gave the boy one last glance before fear of another electric shock outweighed my curiosity, and I continued up the stairs.

CHAPTER THIRTEEN

figerella jammeslot

"Cross us again, and we'll take you to the Council."

That was what Taki had told me.

And even though I'd pretended not to care, a cold finger traced my spine as I walked up the steps. The Holyoakes had told me horror stories about the Council and their kind of "justice." Sometimes a Wanderer got out of control—starting fights, or stealing, or acting recklessly in a way that put the whole ship at risk—but nobody wanted to get the Galaxy Guard involved. So the ship's captain could bind the offender and bring them to trial. When a case came up, the Council listened to both sides of the story and voted on whether to punish the crew member. I guess the sentences they handed down were better than a lifetime of slavery at one of Quasar Niatrix's prison farms, but in my opinion, the Council had a disturbing way of matching the punishment to the crime.

For example, one time I overheard Taki on a video call to his friends, and they were talking about a woman who'd had her fists electronically hobbled as a punishment for violence. But the hobbles made it impossible for her to defend herself, so when a drunk miner had targeted her at an outpost, she hadn't been able to fight back, and she'd ended up in the hospital with brain damage. Then there was a rumor about a man who'd stolen from his crew and had to wear I AM A THIEF in holographic ink on his forehead. Another man who had spied on his captain for proof of illegal blasting, hoping to collect a reward from the Galaxy Guard, had been found guilty and blinded with eye drops so he couldn't spy again.

See what I mean? Disturbing.

I wasn't afraid of many things, but the Council was one of them. They scared me the way the dark scared most kids. I couldn't help wondering how they would punish me for what I'd done the last time I was on board the *Wanderlust*, when I'd stolen the captain's shuttle and run away.

I shivered and shut down the thought.

It wouldn't do me any good to worry about things beyond my control. Instead I focused on the scent of onions that clung to the air as I passed the galley. Nonna, the captain's wife, believed onions had healing powers, so she put them in everything: chili, biscuits, oatmeal, even cookies. That was why the ship smelled so bad. As for the supposed health benefits of onions, I didn't buy it . . . unless burping was good for your health. In which case I was probably immortal from the month I'd spent on board the ship.

Kyler's stomach rumbled loud enough for me to hear. He rubbed his stomach and said, "Something smells good."

"Then you must love onions," I said. "Either that or you're extra-hungry."

"Or both," he told me.

We passed three closed doors and entered the last cabin at the end of the hall, a closet-size room with two folding bunks attached to the wall. I caught myself tensing my shoulders when I saw the bunk where I used to sleep. It still looked the same: a scratchy wool blanket tossed on top of a bare mattress that was covered in splotchy stains of unknown origin. There was no pillow, never had been.

"Home sweet home," I muttered. "I never thought I'd miss sleeping on the floor of a travel depot."

Kirk stood in the hallway, blocking our exit. Not that there was anywhere to go. As the captain had pointed out, I was stuck here. But I figured I might as well make the most of it, so I asked, "Can you bring us some food?"

Kirk clicked his pincers, something he did when he was processing input. "I was commanded to escort you to your cabin, Figerella."

"And you obeyed that command," I pointed out. "Your other command is to make sure I follow the ship rules. One of those rules is to eat a healthy diet."

There was clicking. Then silence, followed by more clicking.

"Besides," Kyler said, "the captain didn't say we *couldn't* have any food."

More clicking. "That is true, Skylar."

"Um, it's actually Ky—"

"I will retrieve your food," Kirk told us. "You will remain in your cabin."

Kyler held up both hands in surrender. "I won't move."

"Thank you for your cooperation, Skylar," Kirk said. Then he backed down the hallway, watching us with those burning eyes until he turned the corner and crab-walked out of sight.

Kyler made a face. "Is it just me, or is it a total mind freak when he uses that I'm-gonna-eat-your-soul voice to say thank you?" He shivered. "Whoever programmed him is nuts. How do you know these people, anyway?"

"Never mind that," I told Ky. "We don't have much time before Kirk comes back. I need to know what kind of shock he gave you."

"An electric one."

"Well, duh. But was it big or small?" When that didn't seem to make sense, I explained, "Kirk has two power settings for discipline. One of them is low. He can shock you all day long with that one. But the other one is high. It hurts like *whoa*, but he can't shock you that hard again unless he plugs in for a couple of hours. And by that time, he usually glitches and forgets to punish you."

"Ah," Ky said. "You want to know which setting he used on me before you decide how to behave."

"Basically," I admitted. "So how badly did it hurt?"

"I don't know. Bad enough to knock me on my butt."

"Okay, but on a pain rating scale, did it feel more like *Ouch, that's gonna leave a bruise in the morning* or was it more like *OMG my whole body is full of bees!*?"

"The first one, I guess."

"Darn. We have to be on our best behavior."

A slow grin crept across Kyler's mouth. "Or do we?"

"What do you mean?"

"Where's Kirk's charging station?"

"In the loading bay."

"Okay," Kyler said. "And after he punishes someone with a superhard OMG-my-body-is-filled-with-bees! kind of shock, he has to power up for two hours before he can deliver another one, right?"

I nodded.

"What would happen if he shocked you superhard and you didn't back down? Like, what if he punished you and then you broke an even bigger rule than the first one?"

"I don't know," I said. I'd felt that level-two shock, and my only instinct had been to back down. "Maybe he would go back to his charging station. Maybe not. It's hard to say, because he can be glitchy."

"That's good," Kyler said. "So if we want to ditch him and get out of here, all we have to do is *mis*behave. If I can provoke him into delivering a supershock and then you unleash your signature red-hot sass, he'll want to go to his charging station to power up."

"But what's the point?" I asked. "How are we getting out of here with no ship and no shuttle? You heard the captain. He's got everything on lockdown tighter than a clam with lockjaw."

Kyler glanced down the hallway, where Kirk had just rounded the corner carrying a tray of food between his pincers. "I haven't worked out all the details yet," Ky whispered. "Just follow my lead."

"Follow your lead?" I shot him a dirty look. We both knew what had happened the last time I'd done that. The phrase *out of the frying pan and into the fire* came to mind.

He shrugged. "Or you can stay here forever. Your call."

When he put it like that, there wasn't much of a choice. But I kept thinking, wondering if it was a better idea to play nice and earn the crew's trust, and then slip away at a travel depot or some such. That could take a long time, though.

While I was quiet, Kyler's eyes turned soft. "Hey," he whispered, scratching the back of his neck and dropping his gaze to the floor. "I'm, uh, sorry about your parents. I didn't know they were . . . um . . . gone."

Gone. That was the wrong word. A person can be gone and then come back.

"If you, uh, want to talk about it . . ." Ky added.

Hard pass. Talking about my parents was the last thing I wanted to do. I changed the subject to our escape plan. Well, *his* escape plan.

"We'll do it your way," I said. "Again."

Two hours and four bowls of chili later, nothing had changed in our cabin except for the smell of gas. The beans and onions had kicked in, so Kyler and I were burping a lot, and our tiny room stank like fart stew.

Ky pounded his chest, releasing another belch. "Holy onions."

I didn't answer him. It annoyed me that I still didn't know what he was planning. Night had fallen—or rather bedtime, because there's no day or night in space—and the Holyoakes were asleep in their cabins. I knew from the chorus of snores. We had been sitting in silence for so long that Kirk had gone into low-power mode outside our doorway, his eyes dim and his motor still.

"Psst," Ky whispered to me. He thumbed toward the Holyoakes' cabins. "Are they heavy sleepers?"

I nodded. Anyone who snored as loud as the Holyoakes would have to go into a virtual coma to sleep through all the noise.

"Good," Ky said, much louder. "Tell me about the ship rules."

At the sound of his voice, Kirk awakened with a hum.

That seemed like an odd question, but then Ky winked at me, and I understood. It was time to follow his lead. "The usual kind of rules," I told him. "No open flames, no running on the stairs, no horseplay, no tampering with—"

"I'm more interested in the *un*usual stuff," Ky interrupted. "Does the captain have any rules that are less about safety and more about his . . . uh, personal issues?"

Without meaning to, I glanced at the outline of a storage drawer on the underside of Kirk's belly. That was where Kirk had put my necklace after he'd stolen it from me. It had been my first experience with a level-two shock. Kirk had demanded I give up my "Earthly relic," and I had refused. So he'd shocked me, ripped the chain off my neck, and stowed it in his drawer. I couldn't help wondering if it was still in there. Probably the captain had burned it.

"Yeah," I told Kyler. "There are no artifacts from Earth allowed on the ship. The captain's pretty militant about that one."

"Huh. You don't say." Kyler pulled something from his pants pocket. Small and silvery, it appeared to be a key fob. "An Earth-made artifact like this?"

Now he had Kirk's full attention. Pincers snapped as Kirk stood to full height and ordered, "Surrender your contraband, Skylar."

"Oh, I don't think so." Kyler stood from the lower bunk and held up his object for show. "This is too valuable. It's an artifact replicator. It multiplies anything that was made on Earth. In five minutes, I could fill this ship from floor to ceiling with relics. In fact, I think I will!"

"This is your final warning, Skylar."

I felt a wave of fear for Ky, who teasingly dangled the fob in front of Kirk before yanking it away and stuffing it back in his pocket. "You can't have it. And for frick's sake, my name is Kyler, not Sk—"

A current of white-blue electricity shot out from Kirk's left pincer and connected with Kyler's torso. For a moment, Ky flopped on his feet like a fish out of water, then he collapsed onto the bunk mattress with a moan. Sympathy pains broke out along my spine. I knew how badly that shock hurt, and I looked at Kyler with respect.

He had taken one for the team. Now it was my turn.

Before Kirk could retrieve the fob, I said, "I have one, too," and dug in my pocket for my Bubble Pop game. I made sure

Kirk saw it before I stuffed it down my shirt. "The only way you'll get it from me is if you shock it off my body."

He lurched back and forth as if he couldn't decide what to do. Finally, he made a couple of grabs at me, which I easily dodged. That seemed to do the trick. After clicking his pincers twice, Kirk whirled around and skittered down the hall. Soon I heard the clinking of his legs as he descended the stairs into the loading bay, where I hoped he would settle onto his charging station for a couple of hours.

I shook Ky's shoulders. "Okay, he's gone. Now what?"

"Now I barf," he said.

And he did—a lot—the poor kid.

Ky groaned and wiped his mouth. "Chili doesn't taste so good when it's coming back up."

It didn't smell so good, either, but I chose not to mention it. We had more important things to worry about. "Please tell me you have a plan."

"I have a plan," he said.

"And . . ."

"And I'll tell you in the engine room." He panted. "Too tired to talk right now. Or move."

"Put your arm around my neck," I told him. "I'll help you."

I gripped his waist and half dragged him to the lower level.

As I predicted, Kirk was in the corner hovered above his charger, his red eyes sightless and pulsing. We passed him as quietly as we could. Kyler seemed to regain some of his strength by then, because his clumsy footsteps had improved to a stagger, but he still needed to sit down and rest when we reached the engine room door.

Kyler slumped against the wall and raised a weak finger toward the keypad. "Might as well try it, just in case they lied about locking it."

I pressed a palm to the keypad. Nothing happened.

"It's all right," Kyler said. "I can tell you how to override the lock. But first I should probably ask if you know what a core processor looks like. Because I have no idea."

"I do," I said. "I learned from watching your engine on the *Whirlwind*."

"Okay, good. Let's steal one." He nodded at the keypad. "The first step is to pry that panel off the wall. But do it gently. You don't want to rip the wires on the other side."

I grabbed a flathead screwdriver from a nearby toolbox and worked it around the edges of the keypad. It only took a few minutes until I pried it loose and pulled it about six inches from the wall. That was as far as it would reach. A tangle of colorful wires held it in place from the back.

"Now find the red and blue wires," Ky told me. "You're going to unplug them from the keypad and touch the ends together."

I did as he said. The instant the metal tips of the red and blue wires met, a *hiss* sounded, and the engine room door slid open. I grinned. "I can't believe it. That was too easy."

"Tell me about it," Ky said, not sounding pleased. "I learned that trick from my twin brothers. They have no respect for privacy."

I found the light switch and focused on the engine room, which, luckily for me, had the same layout as the *Whirlwind*. Because I knew exactly where to look, I found the core processor easily. But pulling it out was another matter. Rect-angular and the size of a shoebox, the processor was built like an antique battery cell, with tiny metal plates that matched receptors in the wall. There were no wires to disconnect, but the cell was *really* wedged in there. It took three tries and all my strength to wriggle it loose. Finally, it broke free.

At once, all motion stopped as the engine went dead. The lights went out, too. I had to feel my way out of the small room and into the loading bay.

Kyler was standing up and prepared with a flashlight, which he shone at the boxy tech in my hands. "That's it? I thought it would be bigger."

"It's small but mighty," I told him. I cast a glance toward the corner to check on Kirk, but I didn't see his red eyes glow-ing. The power outage must have interrupted his charging cycle. It gave me an idea. "Hey, do you think you can carry the processor to the *Whirlwind*? There's something I want to do before we leave."

Kyler tested his limbs. "I think so."

"I'll be right behind you," I promised, and handed him the core processor. "You don't need to suit up. There's an airlock chamber that connects the loading bay to the *Whirlwind*. Just wait for me inside and be ready to motor when I get there."

"What're you going to do?" Ky asked.

I held out my hand for his flashlight. "I'm gonna take back something that belongs to me."

"I don't like the sound of that," he said, but he gave me the flashlight and shuffled to the airlock chamber.

After making sure Kyler was strong enough to open the airlock door, I turned around and aimed the flashlight at Kirk's charging station, where he was crouched motionless. A distant creaking sound prompted me to turn an ear toward the upper level. When a few beats passed and I didn't hear the sound again, I continued to the corner.

I crept close to Kirk, close enough to wave a hand in front of the motion sensor on his chest. He remained still. I rested one hand on his shell and felt more warmth than I expected. That told me he'd absorbed a lot of power during his short charge. The crew must have upgraded his battery. But that didn't concern me. He seemed to have gone into sleep mode.

Careful not to stir him, I skimmed my palm along his midsection, feeling for the spot that would release his storage drawer. I recalled it had a spring latch, the kind you press to open. I found a small, round dip in his metal shell, and I paused. Then, holding my breath, I pushed the spot as gently as I could. The latch released with a faint *click*, and his storage drawer slid out ever so slightly, just enough for me to work a finger inside it. Now I could pull the drawer all the way free.

I still hadn't exhaled. I didn't know what scared me more: that I might wake up Kirk, or that my necklace might not be inside him. I paused to take a long, deep breath and told myself the drawer was probably empty. I shouldn't get my hopes up. But that didn't stop my pulse from racing when I pulled the drawer open.

My eyes searched at once—scanning past bolts, gadgets, small toys, antique watches, and a bunch of other junk—for my necklace. My spirits dipped. I didn't see it. But then a glimmer of red caught my eye from beneath a tangle of wires, and the next thing I knew, I was digging wildly for it. I recognized my pendant by touch, from all the times I had rubbed the ruby between my thumb and index finger. I untangled the silver chain while my heart soared. The chain's clasp was broken, but that was all right.

I'd gotten a piece of myself back.

But my eagerness must have made me clumsy. Because no sooner had I shut Kirk's storage drawer than his eyes glowed red hot, and he fired a bolt of electricity at me that knocked the wind from my lungs. My body flew backward, and I lost hold of my necklace. I landed hard and inhaled just in time to release a scream when he shocked me again. The second jolt wasn't as powerful, but it still hurt like the devil. At that point, he must have run out of juice, because he threateningly held one pointed leg above me and commanded, "Stay down, Figerella."

Then I heard the clamor of boots upstairs.

"Fig!" Ky shouted, his head poking out of the airlock chamber.

"Go!" I told him. "The crew is coming. Take the processor and run!"

To my surprise, Ky disappeared inside the airlock chamber. I hadn't expected him to leave me so quickly, and I felt a surge of dread. I wanted Ky to save himself, but deep down, I had also wanted him to save *me*. I was terrified to face the Holyoakes alone. They would turn me in to the Council for sure.

Fear clogged my throat as I looked up the stairs and saw the first pair of boots run into view. I'd just clamped my lips together to trap a sob when a distant voice echoed, "MORTAL DANGER! WEIRDO IS IN MORTAL DANGER!"

I whipped my head around in time to watch Cabe wheel like a maniac out of the airlock chamber and into the loading bay, his ropy arms waving in panic. He didn't miss a beat, and he didn't give any warnings. Instantly, he pivoted toward Kirk and fired a length of cable so fast it struck Kirk like a bullet. His crablike body skidded across the floor and landed upside down, his legs skittering uselessly in the air. Cabe secured Kirk to the floor with another section of rope and then turned his face toward the stairs, where the captain and his family stood, watching in horror.

Cabe yelled at them, "YOU WILL NOT PASS!"

The majesty in his voice gave me chills. He reminded me of Gandalf from the Lord of the Rings books. But instead of a magical staff, Cabe used his metal ropes to block the steps, trapping the Holyoakes at the top.

"Crew member Weirdo," Cabe said to me. "Are you free from mortal danger?"

I couldn't talk right away, so I stood up and I hugged him. Part of me knew it was dumb, but I didn't care that Cabe was made of metal and wires and that he couldn't sense my arms around his barrel chest. The hug was more for me than for him. He made me feel something I hadn't felt in years—safe.

I picked up my necklace and tucked it in my pocket. No one would ever take it from me again. To make sure the

Holyoakes knew it, I faced them full-on and flicked one thumb off my front teeth—the Wanderer version of the middle finger.

"I'm okay now," I said to Cabe. "Thanks to you."

He chirped happily, and my heart melted.

"You're pretty awesome," I said as we hurried into the airlock chamber to join Kyler. "You know that?"

"For a robot?" Cabe asked.

"No," I told him. "You're just plain awesome."

CHAPTER FOURTEEN

figerella jammeslot

I waved to the Holyoakes when I left them behind.
I didn't know if they could see me from inside their darkened ship, but I knew they couldn't follow me—at least not until they bought another core processor—and that put a smile on my face.

I nestled into the pilot's seat and set a new course to Earth, taking a longer but less traveled route to avoid the Galaxy Guard's no-fly zone. I could have set the autopilot, but I didn't want to. Kyler was taking a nap in his parents' cabin, and I was enjoying the feel of the *Whirlwind* under my command. Besides, I needed to brainstorm my next move, and something about the act of flying always helped me think.

I should probably call Corpse and Cadaver. We hadn't talked since the Fasti Sun Festival, a couple of days ago. Even though they'd told me to go to Earth and wait for more instructions, I wanted more information on what I was supposed to do. I figured they were the ones who'd stolen the Fasti star, but I didn't understand when or where I should blast it.

And a nagging part of me kept asking *why?* Why blow up a star?

Something about this job didn't add up.

And because getting the truth from pirates was about as likely as getting blood from a turnip, I decided to try the microphone hack Kyler had taught me and listen in on Corpse and Cadaver after our call ended. With any luck, they would be feeling extra-chatty today. I set the autopilot and moved to the next seat, in front of the transmission station. After prying loose the cover on the control panel, I linked the yellow and purple wires and hoped for the best.

I tapped the transmission screen and unlocked the main directory. But I had just begun to input Corpse and Cadaver's number when I stopped and deleted it. There was someone else I wanted to contact first.

Centaurus residence, Earth, I typed in the search bar. The results populated, and I scrolled through a page of images until I recognized Kyler's mom from the recording she'd left him, and I knew I had found the right family. I selected her transmission number and typed a message on the touch screen.

Dear Mom and Dad,

Hi. It's me, Kyler.

First of all, I'm safe and sound, and I'm not alone anymore. I found a nice person to help take care of me, so you don't need to worry. I'm sorry I've been such a selfish jerk and that I ignored your calls. I'm on my way back to Earth now, so I plan to be home in a few days. I shouldn't have made you stress. That was really awful of me, and I hope you ground me for a long time. Like, for years. Because I deserve it. Also from now on, I'm going to stop being an annoying know-it-all who thinks I'm the only person with good ideas and a working brain.

Love, your idiot son,

Kyler

I tapped the TRANSMIT button and deleted the call history before I had a chance to think too hard about why I had sent the message in the first place. I had never met Kyler's parents. They didn't even know I existed. But his mother's image had stuck in my mind, haunting me like a ghost, all red-eyed and frazzled and reminding me of lavender face cream. I had to get rid of her somehow.

Maybe now I could focus on my real job.

I typed Corpse and Cadaver's number into the comm screen and checked over my shoulder to make sure I was still alone. For good measure, I lowered the volume setting and leaned in close to the screen. The call beeped ten times before Cadaver answered, and when his image finally appeared, I lurched back at the sight of his holographic skull mask.

"Ugh," I said. I would never get used to that.

He snapped his fingers and made the skull illusion disappear. It was a lot easier looking at his pretty face than at a mask of bones. "Sorry, kid. I didn't recognize your call number. How come you're not using the comm link I gave you?"

"The battery died. I haven't had a chance to charge it yet."

"You almost to Earth?"

"Not exactly," I said. "There's been a small delay. I'm back on course now." I glanced behind him to get a feel for his surroundings. The dim artificial lighting told me he was on a ship. No surprise there. The real clue came when I spotted a logo painted on the wall in the background. It was a bold letter *F* with a Saturn-like ring around it, the logo for the Fasti Corporation. Cadaver was on board the hijacked star barge. "Well, that answers my first question. You're the ones who stole the sun."

His proud smile confirmed it. "Easy as knifing a puppy."

I wrinkled my nose in disgust at his words. There was something seriously wrong with this guy. I guess I needed a reminder that his personality didn't match his looks, because his angel face kept throwing me off.

"We have a man on the inside," he added before seeming to catch himself. "Oops. Probably shouldn't have mentioned that."

"It's okay," I assured him. "My lips are sealed. I want to hear more about what happens next. When do I blow up the star? And how? You said something about dark matter, but you didn't tell me what I'm supposed to do with it. I've never detonated a star before. I have to know exactly where to hit it and with how much power, otherwise it won't work."

"Don't worry about the dark matter," he said. "It's already

loaded into the sun's core. I'll send you a set of coordinates for dead center—and I do mean *dead center*. If you miss the mark by the tiniest bit, you won't hit the package and the sun won't explode. But if your aim is as good as you say, all you have to do is fire your laser at the coordinates, and you're done." He mimicked an explosion with his hands. "That star will blow its chunks like a watermelon in a pressure chamber." He shrugged. "Either that or implode and create a black hole."

"Wait, *what?*" I said. Black holes were deadly. And impossible to escape. Could I really open one? Because if so, Corpse and Cadaver would have to find someone else to finish the job. Sure, I was broke, but what good was money if I didn't live to spend it?

A new voice said, "No, not while the star is shrunken," and Corpse's red head appeared behind Cadaver's shoulder.

"Either way," Cadaver told me, "you'd better fire the shot and make tracks."

Corpse cut her eyes at him. "Don't scare the kid. You have no idea what you're talking about."

"Are you sure it's safe?" I asked.

She raised her right hand as if swearing an oath. "Sure as the sunrise."

That was an ironic thing to say, but I didn't mention it. "All right," I said. "You told me to go to Earth, but that doesn't make sense. I can't demolish the star if it's too close to an inhabited planet. Are you sure it's not a better idea to meet you—"

"Just be there in two days, and be ready," Corpse interrupted. "Have your comm turned on. We'll tell you what to do."

"How will I get paid when I'm done?" I asked. "I'm all out of—"

Before I could finish my sentence, Corpse reached out and tapped her screen, turning off the video feed.

I blew out a sigh. She had better not be trying to stiff me.

I cocked an ear toward the comm station, hoping the hack had worked. When I heard the soft rustle of clothes from the other end, I grinned. The trick had done its job. Now I needed Corpse and Cadaver to spill their guts.

"Kids are so annoying," Corpse said in her raspy voice. "I should've hired that old mutant with the twitchy eye."

"But the boss wanted the best," Cadaver said. "And that's what we got him."

Corpse grunted.

There was a pause. Then Cadaver asked, "Think she'll make it out in time after she fires the shot?"

"Who cares?" Corpse said. "If she doesn't, it's not like anyone will miss her. She's a mutant . . . *and* an orphan. She's so far off the radar that she's practically dead, anyway."

Cadaver snorted. "Plus, if she dies, we can keep her share."

"Please," Corpse sneered. "As if I was going to pay her. I already spent her share. If she's dumb enough to come around looking for money, we'll off her."

My jaw dropped. They *were* trying to stiff me!

"What about the mutant Council?" Cadaver asked. "Those ghosties don't mess around. I don't want to end up on their burn list."

"You won't," Corpse told him. "The boss said not to worry about the Council."

"Why?"

"Because soon they'll have bigger problems to deal with than one random girl."

"Problems like what?"

"Oh, come on." Corpse made a noise of frustration. "Seriously? You can't figure it out?"

"Maybe if you give me a hint . . ."

"Ugh," she said. "I think I absorbed all of the brain cells when we were in the womb together."

A voice behind me whispered, "Whose womb are we talking about?"

I jumped in my seat and whipped around to find Kyler standing in the doorway. I froze, wondering how much he had overheard. If he found out I was working with the Fasti kidnappers (or starnappers), he would rat me out in a hot second. Luckily his expression seemed more curious than angry, so he must have just walked in. I released a breath and rested a hand over my heart. That was a close call.

"I don't know," I whispered. "I decided to do some investigating into what happened on Fasti, so I looked up the transmission code for the stolen star barge and called it using the hacking trick you taught me."

Ky's eyebrows shot up. He seemed impressed. "That's the Fasti barge?" he asked, pointing at the comm station.

"Yeah, but they haven't said anything useful yet."

"Wait a minute," Ky said, wrinkling his forehead in thought. "I recognize those voices. Aren't those the pirates who tried to steal my ship?"

I faked an *aha* face. "You might be right."

From the barge's transmission station, a beep announced an incoming call. Corpse answered, and a man spoke in a harsh tone: "Where's my star? I wanted it here a week before the vote."

"Sorry, boss," Corpse said. "It's going to take another day or two. We're going as fast as we can. A star's not easy cargo."

The man huffed an angry breath. "Make changes, not excuses. Have the star here tomorrow, or you're not getting the rest of your money."

Corpse grumbled to herself. "I guess I could lighten the barge by dumping some equipment."

"Whatever it takes," the man said. "And park the sun a few klicks closer to Earth than my scientist told you to. I want the voters to feel the heat."

"But won't that fry the planet?" Corpse asked.

"Not if your sharpshooter is as good as you promised." The man paused in a way that made the silence feel like a threat. "Which had better be the case. I want people scared, not torched."

"Our shooter is the best," Corpse told him. "I guarantee it."

"Then get it done," he ordered. "Or else."

Another beep sounded, and the man disconnected.

"What a jerk," Corpse muttered. "It's a good thing he's rich, or I would've killed him a long time ago."

"Guess we should figure out how to make the barge faster."

"Come on," Corpse told her brother. "We've got to lighten the load. Let's start by dumping anything we don't need— furniture, storage containers. . . ." Her voice trailed off as both of them walked away from the transmission station.

On my end, I uncrossed the yellow and purple wires while I took a moment to figure out what was going on. My stomach dipped as I realized Mystery Man had hired Corpse and Cadaver to steal the Fasti star and use it to scare the people of Earth. And my role was to blow up the star . . . and if it was too close to Earth, possibly destroy the planet.

I shivered, suddenly cold. No way was that going to happen. I darted a glance at Ky, double hoping he would never find out I had been involved with these monsters. But he wasn't looking at me. He was staring at the comm screen, his skin as pale as milk.

"I know who that was," he murmured. "The guy in charge. I recognize his voice because I've heard it a hundred times on my dad's data tablet."

"Who is he?" I asked.

Kyler gulped. "Quasar Niatrix."

"*The* Quasar Niatrix?" I asked, though I didn't know why I was surprised. Quasar was the same money-hungry jerk who had rigged the prison system against my people, so risking an entire planet seemed right up his alley.

"What did the pirates say before I got here?" Kyler asked. "I know you told me it was nothing useful, but try to remember any detail you can. It might be more helpful than you think."

"Uh . . . let me see . . ." I dropped my gaze, pretending to think it over while I searched for a detail to share that wouldn't bust me. "I remember them saying they had help stealing the star, someone on the inside."

"Where? Like in the government? Or the Galaxy Guard?"

"They didn't say."

"Anything else?" he asked.

"Hmm . . ." I thought of another detail. "They mentioned dark matter."

Kyler's eyebrows shot into his forehead. "What about it?"

"Not much. Just that it's been loaded into the sun, to help it explode or something."

"Wait a minute." Ky paused. "That's actually a huge clue. It would take someone really skilled, like an expert in the field, to put dark matter in a man-made star. So that means the person Quasar had on the inside must be—"

"Someone from the Fasti lab," I finished. It made sense. "Maybe the lady who invented it all, Doctor Norbert. She knows stars better than anyone."

"Doctor *Nesbit*," Ky corrected. "And no, she would never do that."

"How do you know?"

"Because she's my mentor," he said. "Well, kind of. She called me once. I have her number in my comm."

"That doesn't mean you know her," I pointed out. "Plus, it kind of makes sense that she was the one, because she's the best. Quasar doesn't seem like the kind of guy who would want the second best."

Ky shook his head. "Trust me, it had to be one of her assistants, someone who studied her research and had access to the lab. But either way, it's obvious Wanderers didn't steal the star. Quasar is framing them."

"Not surprising," I said. "People always throw us under the bus."

Ky thumbed at the comm speaker. "It sounds like Quasar

wants to scare voters into thinking Wanderers are going to launch the star into Earth, and that he's the only one who can save the day. You heard him. He has a sharpshooter standing by. He said he wants people scared, not torched. So his plan must be to swing the vote and take control of Earth."

"But he also wants to bring the star closer than his scientist told him to," I pointed out. "If it's too near Earth, there won't be a planet left for him to control."

Kyler chewed his bottom lip. "I need to call home and warn my family. And you should send a transmission to your Council."

I froze.

"They should know what's going on," he added. "The meeting with the United Nations is tomorrow. They're going to decide if Wanderers should be allowed to live on Earth. It's not going to go well if they think you're a bunch of terrorists."

There weren't enough credits in the galaxy to convince me to call the Council. I wanted to stay so far off their radar that I was an actual ghost. But I couldn't admit that to Kyler, so I scrambled for an excuse.

"But what proof do we have for the UN?" I asked him. "They're not going to believe the word of one boy and a mutant girl over Quasar Niatrix. Besides, if Quasar is willing to frame my people for the star theft and terrorism, then he won't hesitate to use his media connections to smear us even more."

Ky frowned. "He's already doing that. My dad said it's a smoke screen, that Quasar is stirring up lies about Wanderers in order to scare voters into letting him run the planet."

"See?" I said, pointing back and forth between us. "Your

people haven't exactly rolled out the welcome mat for mutants. We're not allowed to live on Earth. That's why we've been flying around the galaxy for hundreds of years looking for a way to scrape together a living. And humans hate us for that, too. They say we're taking away their jobs. We can't win with you guys. So what do you think will happen if the Council goes public and announces it's Quasar Niatrix behind the star theft? Humans will think the Council is delusional."

"All right, point taken," he admitted. "My dad knows a lot about politics. Maybe when I call home, he'll have an idea to get the truth out there."

"Better do it before you lose your nerve," I told him. He'd been avoiding his parents for too long already.

He exhaled a long breath that puffed his cheeks. Then he tapped the transmission screen and entered a contact number. He hesitated for one more moment until he tapped SEND.

But nothing happened.

"Connection error, static interference," he read on the screen. "That's weird."

"What's weird?" I asked.

"Static interference usually happens when a ship has its shields up. Something about the tech won't let the signal through." Ky furrowed his brow. "But we don't have a shield, and neither does Earth."

"Maybe it was a fluke," I said. "Try again."

He did, five more times, and got the same error message.

Kyler went pale. He wiped a sheen of sweat from his upper lip. "Something's wrong. We have to call the Galaxy Guard."

"What?" I demanded. "Are you nuts? Half the Guard is in Quasar's pocket."

"But the other half isn't," he argued. When I glared at him, he added, "Look, there's a miniature sun headed for Earth. We can't sit on that information. We have to tell someone."

"They won't listen."

"Maybe they will."

"But you can't trust . . ."

I trailed off because Kyler made the decision without me. He entered the Guard's number and sat back in his seat while the transmission connected.

A bald man with a bushy brown mustache appeared onscreen. He wore a polite grin that dropped as soon as he looked at Kyler and realized he was talking to a tween. It was a good thing my face wasn't visible from the pilot's seat, otherwise the guy probably would've disconnected without a second thought.

"This line is for emergencies only, kid," the man warned.

"That's why I'm calling," Kyler said. "It's about the Fasti star."

"We're handling it. Our ships are already trailing the barge."

"But there's more." In a rush, Ky told the man everything we'd learned about the star theft. "I know it sounds wild, but Quasar Niatrix really is—"

The line disconnected, leaving behind one last image of the man rolling his eyes and releasing a sigh that puffed his mustache.

"Told you," I announced. "You can't trust the system."

Ky cut his eyes at me. "Thanks. That's real helpful."

"So what do we do now?"

He scratched his temple in thought. Then he came up with an idea that was even dumber than calling the Guard. "We'll catch up to the star barge and send a transmission to the Guard ships chasing it."

"Seriously?" I asked. "I mean . . . *seriously?*"

"This time it'll work," he said. "This time I'll make them listen."

CHAPTER FIFTEEN

kyler centaurus

Have you ever been caught off guard in gym class and taken a soccer ball to the gut? It's the actual worst, enough to turn you off sports forever. The force of the blow expels the air from your body, and once your lungs go flat, it's wicked hard to inflate them again. So you open your mouth and try to coax air down your throat, but nothing happens. Your eyes bulge and start to water. Your face turns red. You feel like you're suffocating, because in a way you are.

If you know that sensation, then you understand how I felt after learning a star was headed for my home planet. There was nothing physically wrong with me. My lungs were working just fine, but each time I pictured my family sitting around the dinner table, having no idea they might become crispier than twice-fried bacon bits, my chest went tight and my brain spun inside my skull. It was all I could do to set the autopilot for a new course. Luckily, we were close to the barge, no more than a few hours away.

Hours that passed in awkward silence.

I could tell that Fig thought my idea was dumb, in part from the disbelieving looks she kept throwing at me, and also because the only time she spoke to me was to say, "This is a dumb idea." So it was probably a good thing that we approached the barge quicker than we had expected.

I leaned forward and squinted at the navigation screen, taking in the chaos we were about to enter. We weren't close enough to the barge to see anything except the blinding light from the miniature sun, but the screen showed dozens of flashing dots (Guard ships) flying in circles around a craft so enormous it reminded me of an elephant with flies buzzing around it.

"Which one is in charge?" I wondered aloud. "There are so many ships."

"The one that looks most evil, I guess," Fig muttered.

Since that was no help, I decided to send a transmission to the nearest Guard cruiser. "Computer," I said, "connect me with the ship at the following coordinates." Then I called out the cruiser's position and waited for someone to answer.

A young guy responded, friendlier than the last man, but with a similar bushy brown mustache that covered his upper teeth when he smiled. What was the deal with Guards and their mustaches? Was it part of the uniform or something?

"What can I do for you, son?" he asked me.

I slid a smug glance at Fig. Not all Guards were jerks. "I have information on the Fasti star," I told the man. Then I shared everything I knew with him. The whole time I talked, he really listened—not a single eye roll or weary sigh. When I was done, he nodded in a way that said he believed me. I can't tell you how good it felt to be taken seriously for once.

"I need you to come on board so I can take an official state-ment," he said. "Tell your pilot to approach our hangar slowly, and then wait for permission to dock. I'll be inside waiting for you."

I nodded, and the transmission ended.

"No way," Fig said, her hands fisting the wheel. "I'm not flying us inside a Guard ship. Have you forgotten there's an illegal blaster on board?"

"It's hidden in the storage bay," I reminded her. "But they can't search the ship without a legal reason, and they don't have one."

"You think they can't make up a reason?" She laughed bit-terly. "You really *are* a chump."

"Hey," I objected. There was no need for name-calling. "I'm trying to do the right thing here. In case you've forgotten, Earth is in danger. The fate of an entire planet is more impor-tant than your illegal laser cann—"

A blast shook the *Whirlwind*, knocking the words out of my mouth. I glanced up just in time to see another shock wave rippling toward us from the Guard cruiser. The wave collided with our ship so fiercely it rattled the bolts in the triple-reinforced hull.

"What the—" My mouth dropped open. "They're firing on us!"

"Of course they are," Fig said, veering left to avoid the next blast. "You just spilled your guts to one of Quasar's paid men."

"How could I know?"

She gritted her teeth and zigzagged away from the cannon

fire. "Because half of them are in Quasar's pocket! I told you that!"

"So what do we do now?"

"My cloaking device," she said, waving a hand toward the console. "It's around here somewhere. It might have one use left in it."

I tore through every nook and drawer until I spotted something that looked like a tube of lipstick. "Got it!"

But then I had to find the cord—because, you know, outdated tech. And it wasn't easy fishing through the junk drawer while the ship spun and jerked all over the place. By some miracle, I found the cord and jammed it into the matching port on the console.

I held my breath, watching the tiny tube. "Is it working?"

"Only one way to find out," Fig said.

She circled around to the other side of the Guard cruiser and shut down the engines. We floated in their line of vision. When they didn't fire on us, we had our answer.

I exhaled in relief, but I knew it wouldn't last long. Fig's cloaking device didn't have much juice left in it. Which meant at any moment, we could reappear and be blown to bits by Mr. Mustache. Oh, and as a bonus, now it was up to Fig and me to stop the miniature sun from reaching Earth.

No pressure.

Fig piloted the ship to an asteroid floating nearby, barely large enough to hide us. After we were concealed by the rock, she rounded on me and demanded, "Are you happy now? Your idiocy almost got us killed! We should've tried shutting down the barge on our own!"

"I was trying to help," I argued. "The Galaxy Guard is supposed to"—I flashed both palms—"wait for it . . . *guard* the galaxy. So calling them was the logical thing to do. Now I know better. But I had to try."

"No you didn't," she snapped. "You could've thought outside the lines. Or listened to someone else for a change."

"Are you saying I can't think for myself?"

"Yes! You trust all the wrong people! You're the dumbest smart person I've ever met!"

Her accusation stunned me into a beat of silence. Besides the Galaxy Guard, who were *all the wrong people*?

"Like that scientist," Fig went on. "The one who invented the Fasti stars. You think that just because you talked to her, she's an honest person. But she's practically a stranger. You don't know anything about her."

I shook my head because that wasn't true. "I know that Doctor Nesbit started the field of celestology. She cares so much about finding new homes for people that she dedicated her whole career to it. That's why I trust her."

"That's not a good enough reason."

"Says who?"

"Says me."

"Well, I think you have trust issues."

Fig threw up her hands in frustration. "You're one to talk! You put your faith in strangers, but you don't trust your own family. That's messed up."

"What?" I asked. Who did this girl think she was? "You have no idea what I deal with at home."

"Your parents seem like good people."

"They are, but that doesn't mean things are okay. They look the other way and let my brothers terrorize me."

"Oh, please," she said in disgust. "You're part of a family, an actual flesh-and-blood family, with a mom and a dad and brothers, and probably a floofy little dog, too. And until today, you couldn't be bothered to tell them you were safe!"

She was right about the last part, but I couldn't admit it. So I mumbled, "I don't have a dog."

"Well, I don't have parents," Fig spat. "I used to, but one day they were here, and the next day they were gone. Just like that." She snapped her fingers. "I didn't get a warning. And you know what? It's not fair, because I always loved them. I didn't take my family for granted like you do. They've been gone for two years, and I miss them every single day. I would do anything to have the same thing you ran away from."

My cheeks went up in flames.

"So don't judge me, Kyler friggin' Centaurus," she said. "I might have trust issues, but you suck at being a son and a brother, and that's a thousand times worse!"

Her words stung. Even though I knew she had lashed out at me in anger, I couldn't deny there was a kernel of truth in what she'd said.

But how big a kernel?

Was she right? Was I a bad son and brother?

My first instinct was to say no, but when I considered the evidence, it didn't look good. Now that I thought about it, I'd done a lot of things to push my family away. I had fought with my brothers, even though it made my mom sad. I'd spent more time with my books than my parents. I had told myself that I didn't belong in a home with a bunch of jocks and protesters because I was different from them. *Better* than them. I might've run away by accident, but I'd wanted to leave my parents and my brothers behind. That was why I'd set the course for Fasti in the first place.

My shoulders sank.

Fig was right. I sucked at being part of a family. It chilled me to think I might lose them. Would the universe do that to me? Take away my family to teach me a lesson?

"You're a jerk," Fig said. "After we save Earth, I'm done with you."

Fig and I didn't speak for the next hour.

But her words kept echoing in my ears—not just what she had said about me, but how she'd lost her mom and dad. She had never talked about her parents before, not even on the Holyoakes' ship when I'd tried to get her to open up about them. I couldn't imagine losing my parents. They weren't perfect, but at least they were mine. I had so many questions for Fig. I wondered what her life had looked like before the accident, because no matter how hard I tried, I couldn't picture her as a normal kid with normal kid problems. I mean, think about it: Fig sitting in the galley of her parents' ship, whining about having to eat broccoli?

Yeah, no.

Fig was so tough I figured she'd been born that way. But maybe I was wrong. Had she been like me once, a sheltered kid who'd had to toughen up after she had lost everything? What had that been like for her? How had she survived all by herself?

So many questions, but I couldn't bring myself to ask them. I didn't feel like I had the right to invade her privacy, and besides, the icy silence between us told me she didn't want to talk to me, anyway. So while we floated behind the asteroid, I focused on bigger problems than the ones inside my head.

Like how to steal a sun from pirates.

Because that was what we had to do. And despite the fact that I'd stolen a spaceship in my sleep, I had no useful skills. Not compared with the professionals. Anyone crafty enough to hijack a star barge was no one to take lightly. Then there was the fact that the Galaxy Guard itself was trailing the barge, half of which were secretly working for Quasar.

I blew out a breath and glanced at Fig, who sat beside me in the copilot's seat, quietly reading a data tablet. I could see from the text heading she was researching the Fasti star barge.

"I'm calling a truce," I said. "Let's hit the defrost button long enough to wreck these pirates, then you can go back to freezing me out."

"Fine," she agreed, not looking at me.

"Tell me what we're up against."

"Basically the barge is a fortress inside a force field," she said, pointing at the barge's image on the navigation screen. "The hull is reinforced with a crap ton of layers to protect it from the star's radiation, and then the whole thing is surrounded by a force field to protect passing ships and planets from the same radiation. There's one sealed tube that allows shuttles to come and go inside the force field, but it's controlled from the barge's pilothouse, so the pirates would have to let us in."

"That's why the Galaxy Guard—the good ones, I mean, the ones who are actually trying to do their jobs—can't get inside."

"Yep," she told me. "The barge and the star are in a bubble that no one can pop, not unless they want to be incinerated. That's why Corpse and Cadaver can sail right down the center of the galaxy with their middle fingers out the window."

I lowered an eyebrow in confusion. "Corpse and Cadaver? Who are they?"

"The pirates who stole the barge."

"How do you know their names?" I asked.

Fig parted her lips, her eyes going wide. It was a look I knew well, the face of a kid who'd done something wrong and had just busted herself.

"I heard it on the Guard scanner," she said.

I didn't buy it. Something was up. "What aren't you telling me?"

She snapped her gaze to mine and instantly made me regret that I'd asked. "There's a lot I'm not telling you, Kyler," she spat. "Like how much I hate your face right now. Do you really want me to vent my spleen, or should I stick to what's important? Because I was kind of under the impression that we don't have a lot of time to mess around."

My gut still told me she was hiding something, but I didn't have time to figure out what it was. "Whatever," I said to get us back on track. "Let's think about our options. If we can't pop the force field bubble, then we'll have to stop the barge another way."

"Like how?" she asked. "A roadblock won't work. The

pirates will mow down anything we put in their path." She pointed at the enormity of the barge in comparison to the Guard ships flying behind it. "Look at the size of that thing. It's like a glacier sliding through snowflakes."

A glacier sliding through snowflakes...

Her words gave me an idea. "Even glaciers can be worn down by the elements."

She shot me a skeptical glance. "Are you suggesting we melt the sun?"

"No, but maybe we can shrink it somehow," I said. "Think about it. If the Fasti scientists can keep a star in a miniature form until they deliver it, there might be a way to make it even smaller. Or unmake it altogether."

"Unmake it?"

"Yeah." I took a moment to consider the possibility. It didn't seem too far-fetched. "The star is man-made, right? So if people can build a star, it stands to reason that people can take it apart, too."

Fig didn't answer. She stared out the windshield, either dazed, tired, or deep in thought, I couldn't tell which. We approached the star barge as close as we dared without entering the Guards' line of sight, but it was still near enough that the brightness forced us to engage the *Whirlwind*'s sun filter. Even after the windshield dimmed, Fig kept gazing out into space until she asked in a soft voice, "What about black holes? Don't they form when a star dies?"

"Sometimes," I told her. Maybe that was why she was acting weird, because she was worried about opening a black hole.

If so, I couldn't blame her. That was scary stuff. "But that's the case with natural stars," I pointed out. "I don't know about the man-made kind. The rules are probably different for the Fasti star because it was formed in a lab."

"*Probably* different," she emphasized. "And this one has dark matter in it."

"That does complicate things. No other stars were made that way."

"The recipe for man-made stars is top secret," she said. "So you can't know for sure how they're made, just like you can't know for sure whether we'll create a black hole if we try to 'unmake' one. You can't guess based on limited information. We both know how well that worked out last time."

"So I'll call Doctor Nesbit and find out."

"I don't trust her to tell us the truth." Fig went quiet again, gnawing on her lower lip for a moment. "What if we could take control of the barge and fly it away from Earth?"

"We'd have to get inside it first."

"What if I could do that?" she asked. "Get us inside?"

I huffed a laugh. "How? With Floo powder and portkeys? Or did Hogwarts teach you to Apparate?"

"Be serious." Fig refocused me with a light smack upside the head. "Never mind *how* I get us inside the barge. What if I could do it?"

"That would change everything," I told her, rubbing my scalp. "Our battle plan would go from shrinking the star to hijacking the barge, a completely different mode of attack. Less science, more sabotage."

She slanted me a glance so full of mischief it made my lips twitch in a smile. She looked like the old Fig. I hadn't realized how much I hated fighting with her until then.

"That's right up our alley," she said.

"*If* you can get us in," I reminded her.

She sprang from her seat, calling, "Leave that to me," over her shoulder. Then she raced out of the pilothouse before I could ask her any more questions.

CHAPTER SIXTEEN

figerella jammeslot

It was a good thing I'd remembered to charge my comm link when I restored power to the *Whirlwind*, because the innocent buttonlike device in my hand was also my golden ticket inside Corpse and Cadaver's stolen star barge.

Assuming I spun the right lie.

So it was also a good thing I could lie like a rug.

I pinned the comm link to my shirt collar and sent a call request to Cadaver, the dumber of the two pirates. As soon as he answered, I used my most panicked voice to tell him, "I'm right behind you in the *Whirlwind*. Quick, you have to bring me on board!"

"Whosey whatsit?" was his reply.

I rolled my eyes and spoke slower for him. "I was flying to Earth, just like you told me to do. But then I got busted for breaking curfew, and the Galaxy Guard saw my blaster. They tried to pop me for illegal weapons possession, so I made a run for it. They're on my tail right now, hailing me. If I don't surrender, they'll use a shock-wave bomb to hobble my engine."

When I paused to take a breath, I could hear Cadaver scratching himself wordlessly, as though he still didn't understand.

"If they catch me, they'll send me to a prison farm," I told him. "You know what'll happen after that. I'll never come out again . . . unless I give up information in exchange for my freedom. Information like the names of the people who hired me to blow up the sun you're towing."

On the other end of the comm, Cadaver went as silent as a tomb.

"Mainly Quasar Niatrix," I added. "I know he's the mastermind behind this whole steal-the-sun-and-use-it-to-scare-Earth thing."

"Didn't anyone ever tell you snitches get stitches, ghostie?"

"Then don't make me be a snitch," I said. "Let me on board the barge. If I get arrested, you'll have no one to fire the big demo shot. You said yourself the aim has to be dead accurate to hit the dark matter at the sun's core. You're fooling yourself if you think anyone in the galaxy has better aim than me."

Cadaver grumbled to himself while I held my breath, willing him to give in. Then with a grunt, he replied, "All right. Fly your ship to the bottom of the barge. There's a circle of lights to show you where the chute is. Position your ship inside that circle, and I'll let you through the force field."

I silently pumped my arm in victory. "Thank you!"

"Don't thank me yet, kid. If you can make it here *alone*, I'll let you in. But if any Guard ships try to follow you in, I'll clamp that chute down so fast it'll squash you like a bug."

I shuddered at the mental image he had painted. "I'll ditch

the Guard," I assured him. "Just be ready to beam me up when I get there. I'll see you in ten."

I ran back to the pilothouse and took the wheel, ignoring Kyler's questions as I searched for the quickest path through the maze of Guard ships to the barge. If I was lucky, maybe I could sneak past the lot of them before they had a chance to fire.

Too bad luck was never on my side.

I had barely entered the fringes of the Guard fleet when the same cruiser that had fired on us before sent another shock-wave blast at our hull. It was skill, not luck, that saved us as I tipped the *Whirlwind* out of the way. Two more shots followed. I dodged them both before an idea came to mind. Veering off my path, I flew deeper into the fleet and slowed down to make myself an easy target. The next blast came, just as I knew it would. But I was ready for it. I zipped away, just in time for the shock wave to hit the Guard ship behind me. That created enough havoc for me to fly right into position beneath the barge, undisturbed.

Kyler started to say something, but the *Whirlwind* lurched, making us both gasp. The barge's wireless piloting system had taken over our controls. I let go of the wheel as a circle of flashing lights appeared high above us on the starboard side of the barge. Out of nowhere, a translucent chute appeared, sucking us inside it and closing quickly behind us to create a bubble.

"Whoa," Ky murmured. He leaned toward the windshield and gawked at the shimmery tunnel surrounding our ship.

I admired the view with him. The star's force field was made of energy that rippled and moved like a living waterfall. Silvery and electric, it pushed us up the tube at speeds fast enough to send my stomach dipping into my lap. I'd read that the force field wasn't technically solid but made of zillions of molecules linked together to form a shield stronger than titanium. I didn't have to be a science geek like Kyler to find that cool.

"Did you look up the floor plan?" I asked, mostly to keep him from prying into how I had managed to get us inside the force field. "And what about the pilothouse controls? We need to know how to set the barge's navigation course to return to Fasti. Either that or disable the engines until someone can come fetch the star and take it to the system where it belongs."

"Yes and yes," he mumbled absently. He shook his head as if to clear it, coming out of his trance. "The barge is huge, like the size of two football fields, but most of it is made up of engines and radiation scrubbers, so we won't have as much ground to cover as you think."

I nodded. "That makes sense."

"There are only three main levels we need to worry about," he continued. "There's the hangar, where we'll dock the *Whirlwind*. Then up one level is the crew's living quarters. That whole floor is empty because the crew never had a chance to come on board, but there's a cafeteria, a few common areas, and a rec room." He wagged his eyebrows. "There's even a bowling alley and a movie theater up there."

"Nice," I said. "I'm in the wrong line of work."

"No joke. Anyway, the level we're interested in is at the top." Kyler craned his neck and pointed at the barge's domed roof. "That's where the towing controls and the pilothouse are, and probably where the pirates will be, too . . . if they're smart."

"That's a big *if*," I said, but a shiver passed over me. I had no idea what to expect from Corpse and Cadaver. I had basically blackmailed Cadaver into bringing me on the barge, so he wasn't bound to be happy about it. Beyond that, I didn't know if he would meet me in the hangar, or whether he had told Corpse I was coming on board at all. I hoped to steer clear of them, at least until I was alone. The last thing I needed was for one of them to start talking in front of Kyler and blow my cover.

"Got all the supplies?" I asked Ky. "The Mega Über Lube?"

"Check."

"The rope?"

"Check."

"The EZ-Doze and the homemade blow darts?"

"Check and check," he said. "Just to recap: I'll use the air ducts to crawl to the pilothouse ceiling. Once I see the pirates through the ceiling vent, I'll load the blow darts with enough sleep medicine to drop a mule, then I'll open fire from above. You'll be waiting outside the door to bust in and take control of the barge. Then we'll fly it away from Earth and save the day."

"Divide and conquer," I agreed, anxiously bouncing my leg. I couldn't wait to get on with our plan. The sooner we split up, the less likely Kyler would find out my secret. "Let's not waste a second. The moment we touch down in the hangar, you head for the nearest air duct, and I'll take the elevator upstairs. We don't want to lose the element of surprise."

He shifted me a sideways glance. "Yeah, I know. I literally just said that. It was my idea, remember?"

"Oh, sorry." I flashed a what-was-I-thinking? grin. "Just nervous, I guess."

"Yeah, nervous," he repeated, looking at me like I was a math problem to solve.

A math problem—that was fitting, considering my lies were starting to feel like arithmetic. Each time I told a lie, I not only had to remember the exact details of what I'd said, but also who I had told it to. So as the deception added up, the false details multiplied while my brainpower divided into fractions. Honestly, it was exhausting. Between remembering the lies I had already told and juggling new ones, bending the truth was becoming a full-time job. I envied people who had the luxury of being honest, who could say what they meant and who meant what they said.

I couldn't think of a good excuse to set Kyler's mind at ease, so I stayed quiet until the *Whirlwind* rose to the top of the force-field tube, and the barge's massive hangar door inched open. That fascinated him enough to turn his attention to the dash. Our ship drifted forward through the open hangar onto a wide landing pad made of steel. The ship touched down and landed with a *boom* while the hangar door closed behind us. We didn't have to turn off our engines because the barge's wireless system did that for us.

I have to say, it was kind of creepy.

I looked for Corpse and Cadaver through the windshield and released a breath of relief when I didn't see them. The only sign of life on the landing pad was one small shuttle parked nearby, a sporty model with an emblem of a planet-juggling octopus painted on the side. I recognized the symbol as belonging to Quasar Niatrix's corporation.

Kyler had noticed it, too. "The pirates are flying under Quasar's logo," he said. "They're basically advertising the fact that they're working for him. Maybe they're not the sharpest knives in the drawer and this will be easy."

"The shuttle is probably stolen, just like the barge," I pointed out. "Don't assume anything will be easy, even if the pirates are idiots. Smart people can be reasoned with. It's the dumb ones you have to watch out for. Some of the most dangerous people in the galaxy are complete morons."

"Good point," Kyler said. He shrugged, and we finished scanning the hangar.

All around us, metal floors stretched to curved walls. I was surprised by how small the enclosure was. I had thought the landing pad would be bigger, based on the enormity of the barge. But then I remembered the hull was crazy thick to protect the crew from radiation, and I imagined the barge as one of those wooden nesting dolls—deceptively big on the outside with a small core. I couldn't decide if that was a good thing or not. A small interior meant less ground to cover to get to the pilothouse, but it also meant fewer places to hide if the pirates turned the tables on us. Without thinking, I reached down and patted my leg for the laser I kept tucked in my boot—the one Kyler thought I had lost in the galley explosion. I relaxed when I felt it there, strapped against my lower calf. It always calmed me to know I could blow things up if I needed to.

Ky stood up and slung his rucksack of supplies over one shoulder. "Ready?"

"Born ready," I told him.

We jogged down the stairs to the *Whirlwind*'s loading bay and lowered the boarding ramp, passing Cabe along the way. We had debated bringing him along with us on our mission, but he was too much of a wild card. We couldn't have him going mental and fusing us to the walls with rope or something like that. So Ky had shut him down and wheeled him into the corner to charge. But when Ky wasn't looking, I paused to kiss Cabe's metal cheek before I left the ship. Quirky or not, I considered him part of our crew.

Kyler and I made it to the base of the ramp and braced ourselves for what we might find on the other side. A quick glance around the hangar showed it was still empty. I ignored the weight of suspicion tugging at my stomach and told myself we were lucky. Corpse and Cadaver clearly didn't view me as a threat, otherwise they would have met me in the hangar with their guns drawn. Lots of people underestimated me. That was something I could use to my advantage.

I pointed at one of the air-vent screens on the opposite wall. "You go first," I told Kyler. "I'll stand watch and refasten the screen behind you."

He nodded, and five minutes later I was watching him crawl up the air duct. When he was out of sight, I pulled my comm link out of my pocket and prepared to send another call to Cadaver. But before I had the chance, it beeped with an incoming message.

I tacked the device to my shirt and answered.

"It's me," Cadaver said. He sounded like he was in a good mood, and that made me suspicious. "I saw you shake those Guard ships. That was some halfway decent flying, ghostie."

"Thanks," I told him. "I manage."

"Are you alone?"

"As promised."

"Where's the kid that was traveling with you? The Centaurus brat?"

I recited the lie I had prepared for this exact question. "I ditched him. It's less complicated with him gone. He was starting to ask too many questions."

Cadaver grunted. "Too bad you didn't bring him with you. His parents might have paid to get him back." I heard the rustling of a shrug. "Oh, well. A kid's ransom is chump change compared to Quasar's payroll. Which reminds me, we've got the rest of your money if you want to come and get it."

I brightened for a split second . . . until I remembered overhearing Corpse say that she'd already spent my share of the credits and had no intention of paying me.

Cadaver was setting a trap.

"Sweet," I said, faking pep while my mind raced with ways to outsmart him. Luckily, he was as dumb as a bag of hammers. "Where are you? In the pilothouse?"

"Nah, the autopilot is doing all the flying. We're in the cafeteria." He let out a hearty belch. "It's dinnertime—burgers, spaghetti, tamales, fried chicken, mashed potatoes with gravy so thick you could swim in it—we've got a real spread going on up here. You should join us. I'll bet you're hungry."

My traitorous stomach growled. I pressed a hand over it. I

didn't care if there was a chocolate river flowing through that cafeteria. I wasn't setting foot in it. "Hungry enough to eat my boots," I said. "Save me a drumstick. I'll be there five minutes ago!"

As soon as the call ended, I ran to the elevator and tapped the screen for the third floor, where the pilothouse was waiting for me, nice and empty. My heartbeat raced as a sense of urgency took control. I had to hurry. Corpse and Cadaver were expecting me in the cafeteria on the second floor. If I took longer than a few minutes to get there, they would know something was wrong and come looking for me.

I tapped my booted toe and waited for the elevator doors to open. When a minute passed and nothing happened, I pressed UP again. After two more tries, I quit waiting for the elevator to respond, and I made for the stairwell.

I threw open the metal door and stopped short.

I wasn't alone.

"Hey there, ghostie," Cadaver said from inside a glass helmet that covered his entire head. "Want to hear some wisdom?"

"Wisdom? From you?" I asked. "Isn't that an oxymoron?"

But despite my sass, I could barely force the insult past the lump in my throat. My whole body was frozen in fear. It took a moment to shake my muscles loose and step back. I didn't make it far, though, because Corpse lurched out from her hiding place in the corner of the stairwell and snagged my arm in her anaconda grip. She wore a glass helmet, too. She didn't say anything as she tightened her hold on my arm. Instead, she let the wicked curve of her grin do all the talking.

"Never trust a pirate," Cadaver said.

Way to state the obvious. That was about the level of wisdom I'd expected from him. I swallowed hard and said, "Next you'll tell me water is wet."

Corpse squeezed my arm, making me hiss in pain. She pulled a small canister from her pocket. I had just enough time to bring the can into focus before she sprayed something cool and misty in the air near my face. It was then that I understood why she and Cadaver were wearing helmets. I held my breath to keep from inhaling the poisonous gas while I struggled to break free from Corpse's iron fist, but it was no use. All she had to do was stand there and wait me out.

Which she did.

My lungs screamed as the moments passed. My body strained for air. It wasn't long before nothing else mattered except for breathing, not even the knowledge that my next breath might kill me. I tried to fight my body, but I lost the battle. My chest expanded and filled my lungs to bursting. It felt exquisite for a fraction of a second, until a bitter taste crossed my tongue, and my brain felt like it was turning to goo and leaking out of my ears.

My eyes rolled back in my head as everything turned dark. The floor slid out from under my feet, and the entire galaxy seemed to dissolve and fold inward like a black hole with me at the center.

CHAPTER SEVENTEEN

kyler centaurus

Want to hear something gross?

I hope so, because I'm about to drop some major truth bombs on you about your largest organ, the skin, otherwise known as the epidermis. Your skin will make up about twenty square feet of your surface area by the time you're fully grown, and you probably have no idea, but it sheds a lot of cells. And I mean *a lot* of cells, like somewhere in the neighborhood of one and a half pounds per year. Kind of mind-blowing when you consider the fact that a cell weighs next to nothing.

We shed so much skin that our cells make up a decent percentage of the dust in our homes. You know that layer of dullness on your furniture? Might as well think of it as a skin graveyard. And those tiny dust motes floating gracefully in the air like miniature snow crystals? Hate to break it to you, but you're breathing your family's DNA. Now here's where it gets freaky. There are these microscopic bugs called dust mites that love nothing more than to chow down on our dead skin flakes.

Not only do dust mites nosh on your bodily leftovers, but

they hang out and get frisky with each other, which leads to laying eggs and hatching another generation of literal flesh-eating monsters. Oh, and did I mention that they poop? (Everything poops; that's the first law of biology.) Mites drop tons of microscopic deuces, and you're breathing in those fudge nuggets even as we speak. And dust mites are everywhere—on your skin, in your socks, under your pillow. . . .

In your ventilation system.

Especially in your *ship's* ventilation system, because the air in deep space is dry and cold, so your oxygen has to be heated and humidified before it's safe for you to breathe it. And you'll never guess what kinds of places dust mites love to make their homes. That's right, in *warm and humid* places.

Places like the air duct I was crawling through.

My hands and knees kept skidding on the metal floor below me, which was especially fun considering the vent was on a steady incline toward the upper levels. I squinted through my night-vision glasses, barely able to see twelve inches in front of my face. The goggles were older-model hand-me-downs from Duke. There was a brighter headlamp in my backpack, but I didn't want any light leaking from the exterior vents and giving away my position.

Even in the dark, I could tell from the greasy feel on my palms that more than humidity had created this residue. Little bits of grit and clumps of hair told me the intake vents had sucked in decades of "souvenirs" from past crew members—not just skin cells, but oil and mucus and heaven only knows what other cooties—and not one of the geniuses from Fasti had thought to clean the ductwork in all that time. Apparently, creating man-made stars was no big deal, but basic hygiene? *Noooo*, that was reaching too far.

"Disgusting," I hissed, pausing to shake the slime off my palms. "When I make it out of here and save Earth, I'm going to bathe in disinfectant."

I crawled a little farther and tried not to think about what I was wading through. I had just begun to trick myself into believing I was on an algae-covered waterslide when I noticed the *smell*, and all my illusions came crashing down. I alternated between breathing through my mouth, which made me gag because I was basically inhaling crew cooties, and breathing through my nose, which made me gag from the stink. Either way I couldn't win.

After another twenty minutes—or maybe an hour, it was impossible to tell—the slope of the ductwork evened out, informing me I had reached the barge's second level. I took a moment to orient myself before recalling the site map, then I turned left and began crawling up a new incline to the third floor. I barely made it a few more yards when I heard something strange coming from ahead of me, and I paused to cock an ear toward the sound. A noise clicked nearby, like fingernails tapping on metal. I increased the power on my night-vision glasses and peered around for the source of the clicking.

What I saw made the bottom drop out of my stomach.

Remember how I said dust mites are microscopic? I should have been more specific. The dust mites on *Earth* are microscopic. But dust mites in space? They're the size of my fully splayed hand . . . a fact I didn't realize until that very moment.

I froze, staring in horrified fascination at the semi-translucent arachnids happily munching on clumps of dust and grime with their sharp pincers. Crouched there, trapped in the dark, I had to remind myself that dust mites didn't consume living flesh. (At least not the ones on Earth. I hoped the space variety hadn't mutated too far from the original specimens.) There were three mites within view: one female and two males, judging by the slight difference in the size of their abdomens. They each swiveled a head toward me in eerie slow motion, blinking almost lazily, as if they'd noticed me and couldn't decide whether I was worth the effort of investigating any further. I must not have seemed impressive to them, because they turned their buggy eyes back to the dust clumps and resumed munching.

I studied them, taking in the bend of their eight legs, the coarse hairs protruding from their backs, the graceful lines of their exoskeletons. Their hard shells explained the clicking sounds I had heard. It made me think back to all my trips on the *Whirlwind*, and the occasional weird noises the ship had produced in the night—the ones my parents had dismissed as the products of my overactive imagination. I bet we had giant dust mites in our ventilation system. There's an old saying that everything is bigger in Texas. That might have been true five hundred years ago, but not anymore. Now everything is bigger in space, thanks to the advanced levels of radiation.

As quietly as I could, I unzipped my backpack and pulled out my headlamp, a stretchy elastic band with supercharged

lighting along the front. I wanted a closer look at the gargantuan mites. I strapped the device to my forehead and tapped
the power panel to illuminate the bulbs. The area in front of
me lit up so brightly I had to shield my eyes, and then something happened I couldn't have predicted.

The dust mites lost their friggin' minds.

They screamed. I didn't think bugs were capable of
screaming, but there was no other way to describe the ear-
splitting screech that emanated from their jaws. Their pointed
legs clicked in a frantic dance against the metal floor, sending
up a clatter I could feel more than hear . . . you know, because
of the wailing. I was so captivated by the organs pumping
inside their translucent exoskeletons that I ignored the chaos
for a beat. But then they seemed to get angry, because their
pincers snapped out at the air in front of them. It wasn't until
they advanced on me that I noticed their eyes were squeezed
tightly shut, and I figured out what was wrong.

The headlamp. They hated it. Like deep-dwelling ocean
creatures on Earth, the dust mites must have spent so much
time existing in the dark that they'd lost their pigment and their
ability to tolerate bright lights. As I scrambled back from their
snapping pincers, I tapped the power panel on my headband.
The light began to fade but not quickly enough to satisfy the
arachnids.

I pulled off my backpack and held the tear-proof fabric in
front of me as a shield. Then an idea came to mind. I yanked
open the top of my bag and positioned it in front of the charging mites. All three of them scampered inside, and I zipped
the bag shut as the last beams of light extinguished from my

headlamp. Encased in darkness once again, the mites stopped their screaming and scampering.

I blew out a long breath. "Settle down, big guys," I whispered, switching on my night-vision glasses. I grabbed a "tasty" chunk of dust and opened my backpack just wide enough to drop it inside, then refastened it and gently hooked both arms though the straps. "You guys don't mind if I take you back to my lab, do you?"

The bugs didn't answer. Not that I expected them to.

"No dissections or anything like that," I promised. "Just scientific observation. I'm not a monster."

At that point, I realized I was having a one-sided conversation with a trio of mutated space mites when what I needed to be doing was crawling to the pilothouse and taking out the pirates so I could save Earth.

Priorities, I said to myself. *Focus, Kyler.*

I resumed my slippery climb to the third floor, passing more clusters of mutated dust mites as I crawled along. Much like the trio in my backpack, the other bugs weren't interested in me. Most of them didn't even bother to move out of my way, forcing me to arch over at an awkward angle to avoid squashing them beneath my hands and knees. I half expected to come across a massive egg stash or maybe a queen, but I observed that the space mites gathered in clusters of three or four, as opposed to colonies. Behaviorally, that made them more like mammals than insects, but I didn't dwell on that point for very long. As soon as the air duct leveled out, announcing my arrival to the third floor, I heard the low rumble of adult voices and focused my attention on the pirates.

I couldn't hear what Corpse and Cadaver were saying, but from the location of their voices, I could tell they were in the pilothouse . . . right where I needed them to be.

Perfect.

I lowered myself onto my belly for maximum stealth and shimmied toward the sound of the pirates' voices until I was directly on top of them. The homemade blow darts were already loaded in my bag, but I still needed to reach the air vent a few feet in front of me. I inched forward and paused when the pirate woman spoke clearly enough for me to hear.

"What should we do with *her*?"

Based on the way Corpse had said *her* like a swear, I could only assume she meant Fig. Did that mean the pirates had captured her? To hear them better, I used the side of my fist to scrub clean a section of ductwork before pressing my ear to the metal.

"Leave her right where she is," the man, Cadaver, said. Then he clarified, "Alive."

I swallowed a lump. Yeah, they'd definitely taken Fig.

"She's a liability," Corpse argued. "She proved that when she threatened to rat us out to the Guard." A set of knuckles cracked. "I should've hired the other ghost. Everyone knows kids can't keep their mouths shut."

I wrinkled my forehead. Corpse had hired Fig? To do what?

"It's too late now," Cadaver said. "She's the one we hired. And that's why we have to keep her alive—to finish the job and blow this star to kingdom come."

My heart stopped. Fig was the sharpshooter Quasar had mentioned.

"Yeah," Corpse agreed. "Then we off her."

"And keep the ship she conned off the Centaurus kid. That's a double win."

Corpse snorted a laugh. "A triple win when you consider we already spent her share of the payout."

"Well . . . *you* spent it," he muttered, until Corpse silenced him with a smack. Then they both went silent.

Lying there with my ear pressed to the greasy metal, surrounded by filth and mutated bugs, I realized my mouth was hanging wide open, and I snapped it shut. I couldn't believe what I was hearing, and yet it explained so much. Fig had been working with the pirates, and by default, Quasar Niatrix, the whole time. Now everything made sense: how Fig had "rescued" me from Corpse and Cadaver, how she'd known their names, how she had stumbled upon their transmission to Quasar Niatrix, how she'd gotten us on board the barge.

Oh, and apparently she planned to con me out of my ship, too.

My heart throbbed like an infected tooth. At the same time, my face heated with embarrassment. I couldn't decide which was worse: that Fig had lied to me since the moment we'd met, or that I had fallen for her scam so easily. Because I had. She'd played me like a game of cards, and I'd handed her the whole deck without thinking twice about it.

She was right. I was the dumbest smart person in the galaxy.

The warmth in my cheeks turned to anger. It was bad enough that Fig had tricked me, but she'd gone too far when she had used my ship to carry out her dirty work. No way would I let her get away with it. More than ever, I was going to bring this barge to a halt, and then I would hand over all three scumbags on this boat to the Guard—the redhead, her partner, and the Wanderer who pretended to be my friend.

But the question was how to make that happen. For all I knew, Fig could have told the pirates I was on the barge. I might not have the element of surprise anymore. That changed everything.

I glanced in front of me, where slats of light from the pilothouse ceiling filtered through the intake vent. The vent would give me a perfect overhead view, but I would have to be silent. One peep out of me, and the pirates would not only know my position, they would have me trapped like a hamster in a cage. All they would have to do is aim a laser pistol in my general direction, and it would be game over for me. Which could mean game over for my whole family and the rest of Earth, too.

So, yeah. Stealth was the main objective. Time to go full ninja.

I slithered ahead, barely making enough noise to rival the sound of my breathing as I approached the vent slits. In my backpack, I felt delicate pin-tipped legs tapping against my spine, and I paused, remembering how the dust mites had screeched at my headlamp. Without knowing whether my sack's canvas was lightproof, I couldn't risk getting any closer to the intake vent. I slid one arm free of the bag strap, and then the other. Once I had set the backpack to the side, I closed the distance to the vent until I lay squarely on top of it.

The slats were wide enough to show me nearly the entire pilothouse. I peered at the front end of the room, where buttons flashed and navigation and engineering screens displayed the barge's position and system status. Squinting, I brought the controls into focus until I identified the emergency shutdown panel, a sequence of two buttons and a key that had to be pressed and turned at the same time. I knew from my research that once the key was removed, the barge couldn't be started again without a new access code from Fasti headquarters, which the officials would never give to pirates who had just stolen a sun. The shutdown panel was situated to the right of the pilot's chair . . . so close yet so far away. My fingers twitched to set the sequence in motion, but I squeezed both hands into fists.

Stealth, I reminded myself. *Patience and stealth.*

I tore my eyes away from the controls and scanned the rear of the room. I spotted Corpse at once. I would recognize her muscles anywhere. She stood with her clownish red head tipped close in conversation with Cadaver. They were whispering too low for me to understand what they were saying, but I had a pretty good idea they were discussing Fig. I say that because Fig was positioned between them, tied to a chair with both hands behind her back.

For the briefest of moments, my chest ached with panic for her. Then I remembered how she'd double-crossed me, and I put my sympathy on lockdown.

I didn't know what the pirates had done to Fig, but I could tell she was just waking up, because her eyelids drooped, and her neck was bent back like a wet noodle under the weight of her head. A rag was stuffed in her mouth to keep her quiet.

The bluish hue of her lips told me she had been deprived of oxygen, but now that she was conscious, she pulled in several deep breaths, and the color returned to her skin.

I didn't move or make a sound, and I certainly didn't want to attract her attention, but she must have sensed me watching her, because all of a sudden her gaze latched on to mine. Her eyes widened. She blinked. Then she shook her head in a small movement as if trying to send me a silent message without the pirates noticing. I shook my head back at her, glaring to send a message of my own:

Eat snot, traitor.

I'm guessing my message got lost in translation. She shook her head even harder.

"What?" Cadaver asked her. "You got to pee or something?"

Fig's eyes brightened as if an idea had come to her. She nodded vigorously.

"Well, too bad," he taunted with a laugh. "You're gonna have to hold it."

"Mmphhmphmm," she muttered through the gag. "Mmphhmphmm!"

Cadaver heaved a sigh and pulled the rag out of her mouth. "What?"

Fig glanced at me and said, "Eyrethay earingway odybay armoryay."

My brain took a moment to catch on. By the time I realized she was speaking pig Latin, I'd forgotten half of what she'd said. The only words I recalled were *odybay armoryay.*

Body armor.

"Aimway orfay ethay ecknay," she told me.

Aim for the neck.

The pirates were wearing a protective layer under their clothes. Now I understood what to do. It would be a challenge to aim for their necks, but luckily I'd brought plenty of blow darts. I backed away a few inches to reach my bag.

I shouldn't have done that.

Remember how I was lying on top of an intake vent? Well, unknown to me, the only thing holding that vent to the ceiling was a basic latch . . . a latch that dislodged as soon as I slid my body backward. Before I knew what was happening, the steel panel gave way and clattered to the floor, leaving my upper body dangling from the ceiling like an idiot chandelier.

Blood rushed to my head while I swung my arms for something to hold on to, but it was no use. My legs slid against the air duct, unable to get enough traction for me to swing myself back up and crawl away. The only thing I managed to do was hook one foot around my backpack strap, so when Corpse marched over and plucked me out of the ceiling, she got my bag of supplies as a bonus.

"Two hostages for the price of one," she said, baring her gums in a grin as she yanked back my head and identified me. "Kyler Centaurus."

It might seem silly, but all I could say was "Hey, you got my name right. No one ever gets my name right."

"You know what helps me remember a person's name?" she asked in a tone that made it clear she wasn't looking for an answer. To drive the point home, she held her knuckles in front of my nose. "When that person bounces me on the floor a bunch of times and then dumps me out the garbage chute. Now shut your ugly face hole before I plug it up with my fist."

I didn't want her fist in my "face hole," so I took her advice and shut up.

Cadaver kicked the chair that Fig was tied to. "You said you ditched him."

"Never trust a pirate," she told him. "Or a mutant who's—"

Cadaver stuffed the rag back in her mouth. "What now?" he asked his partner.

"Send a transmission to the kid's house," Corpse said, shaking me to demonstrate which kid she meant. "Tell them to send half a million credits to our account if they want to see him with all his fingers and toes attached. They have twenty-four hours. For each hour the money is late, I'll start sending him home in pieces."

I felt the blood drain from my face. I reminded her, "In twenty-four hours, you'll be terrorizing Earth with the star you're towing. If the banks close for bogus holidays like Columbus Day, I'm pretty sure they'll shut down for the end of the world, too."

"Good point." Corpse nodded thoughtfully and told Cadaver, "Better make it six hours."

Well, that backfired.

My family didn't have half a million credits, especially considering that our most valuable asset—the *Whirlwind*—was docked two floors below me in the barge hangar. I glanced around the pilothouse, brainstorming ideas to turn the tables before the pirates started liberating my niblets to mail back home to Mom and Dad. There was nothing to use as a weapon, and I hadn't brought my remote control fob to activate Cabe. I might be able to make a run for the door, but where would I go? Where would I hide? What was the point in playing cat-and-mouse if I couldn't lay any traps? All of my supplies were in my backpack.

My backpack.

Inspiration struck. I looked for my bag and found it resting on the floor where it had landed.

"All right, you can call my parents," I said. I bit my bottom lip and flicked my gaze to the backpack. "But whatever you do, please don't tell them what's in my bag. They'll kill me for taking it."

One of Corpse's red eyebrows arched with interest. "Why?"

"Yeah," added Cadaver, scratching his jaw. "What's in the bag?"

"Something I stole when I ran away from home," I told them. For effect, I made my chin wobble. "A family treasure. They'll hate me if they find out—or worse, they won't pay the ransom."

Corpse snorted a laugh and rolled her eyes as if to say *Kids are so stupid.*

With a shove, she sent me stumbling into the copilot's chair. My eyes darted to the emergency shutdown panel, just out of reach. If I tried to begin the sequence now, Corpse would only grab me before I could finish it. I needed to wait for the right moment.

While Corpse and Cadaver stalked toward my backpack

with greed curling their fingers, I shot a glance at Fig and mouthed, *Get ready.* Even though she was the enemy, I didn't want her freaking out and ruining my plans. Then I turned away from her to watch the pirates. After that, several things happened in a rush.

1. Corpse and Cadaver knelt over my backpack and unzipped it.
2. They peered inside.
3. Light entered the bag.
4. An unholy screech tore through the air.
5. Two giant dust mites leaped up and latched on to the pirates' faces.
6. Corpse and Cadaver screamed as they scrambled across the floor, clawing at their faces in an effort to pry the arachnids loose from their ugly mugs.
7. Most important, I saw my chance, and I took it.

I bolted up from the copilot's seat and ran to the emergency shutdown panel. Using one hand, I pressed both buttons while I used my other hand to turn the key. The barge responded at once. The whirring of the engines ceased, and the floor no longer vibrated. But one of the pirates landed on top of me—I'm guessing Cadaver, because of the awful smell that slammed my nostrils. His weight forced my body onto the controls, mashing a bunch of other buttons. I managed to wriggle out from beneath him. Then, to make sure he couldn't restart the engine, I removed the key and ran to the opposite wall, where I pitched the key out the waste chute.

An alarm buzzed in three loud blasts that forced me to

cover my ears. I didn't know what I'd done to trigger it. Corpse and Cadaver shared a look of panic and bolted out the door without a backward glance. Something about that didn't feel right, so I glanced at Fig and found her shouting muffled nonsense through her gag and bouncing in her seat hard enough to make it jump back and forth.

I jogged over to her and pulled the gag from her mouth. She told me in a rush, "You can't mess with the control panel after an emergency shutdown!"

My stomach took a dip. Not only because I had the sense that something bad was about to follow, but because the barge lurched upward hard enough to send my guts careening toward the floor. I stumbled and righted myself against the wall.

I was almost afraid to ask. "Why? What'll happen?"

Fig didn't have to answer me. The overhead speakers did the job for her. An automated voice crooned in a tone far too smooth and chipper for the message it was about to deliver, "Self-destruct sequence initiated. Detonation will commence in sixty seconds."

CHAPTER EIGHTEEN

kyler centaurus

I have a theory that the laws of physics are flexible, at least when it comes to the passage of time. I'm no Einstein, but allow me to explain my reasoning. Have you ever noticed that sixty seconds feel like an eternity when you're doing something painful, like holding your breath underwater, or listening to your brother talk about his game-winning touchdown, or watching your parents suck face at the kitchen table after they had too much wine with dinner?

(Blech! Pass the brain bleach.)

My point is during moments of boredom or torture, it's almost as though time slows down. Like the universe is an evil monster that wants to prolong your suffering. On the flip side, if you do something you enjoy or if you're racing against the clock, it's over in a flash. Now imagine a critical task that has to be done quickly ... like, oh, say, running for your life from an impending explosion ... and you'll see that a minute goes down faster than a bowling ball on a waterslide.

I was thinking about that while I sprinted to my ship, wondering where the sixty seconds had gone.

"Detonation in twenty seconds," the computer chirped.

It probably goes without saying that I had untied Fig. Right off the bat, that cost us more than a few precious beats. Then there was the trip from the pilothouse on the third floor to the hangar on the bottom level, which included a long, bendy hallway and two flights of stairs. Even at top speed, it had still taken us thirty seconds to reach the *Whirlwind* where it was docked at the far end of the landing pad.

"Detonation in fifteen seconds," droned the computerized voice as Fig and I raced up the *Whirlwind*'s ramp. From my periphery, I could see Corpse and Cadaver strapping into their shuttle, and I knew they wouldn't give us the courtesy of letting us make it inside our own ship before they opened the hangar door and blew us into space. If Fig and I didn't hurry, we would end up as human Popsicles.

"Fourteen . . ."

Fig must have been worried about the same thing, because she pulled a laser out of her boot and fired it at the shuttle. I recognized it as the same weapon she had used to blow up my galley—the one I'd insisted she hand over to me.

"Hey!" I shouted. "You said that was lost in space."

"Are you seriously complaining right now?" she yelled back, taking another shot at Corpse and Cadaver's shuttle. The pirates were forced to shield their heads, giving us a few moments to make it inside our ship.

"Point taken," I panted.

I punched the button to seal the *Whirlwind*'s door shut behind me.

"Twelve . . ."

Pumping my legs, I took the stairs two at a time, yelling, "Computer, ignite the main engine and prepare for emergency takeoff!"

"Affirmative," she replied. "Preparing for rapid launch."

"Eleven . . ."

The engine hummed to life. That was a good start, but we still needed to make it out of the hangar, travel through the force-field chute, and fly far enough away from the barge to avoid the blast. Or rather the *objects* that the blast would shoot at us like bullets from a loaded gun. Because when it came to explosions, the rules were different in space. It wasn't the heat and flames I was worried about. The lack of oxygen outside would choke a fire before it could spread. But at great speeds, heavy shrapnel—hunks of metal hull and framework from the barge—could slice my ship in half like a knife through warm cheddar.

"Ten . . ."

"Faster," Fig yelled, passing me. She skidded sideways across the floor and landed upright in the pilot's seat. As much as I wanted to revoke her crew status, she was the better pilot, so I sat in the other chair. She strapped into the seat harness and told me, "Buckle up. This'll get bumpy enough to scramble your eggs."

"Nine . . ."

I strapped into my seat.

"Eight . . ."

Fig grabbed the wheel and lifted off, bringing the ship around to face the main hatch. Corpse and Cadaver must have already signaled the hangar door to open, because the air had depressurized, and the massive hatch was halfway ajar. The two of them wasted no time zipping out of the hatch in their small shuttle.

"They already dropped the force field," Fig said, pointing.

"Good," I said. "That's one less obstacle in our way."

We approached the exit, but the *Whirlwind* was a full-size sedan, not a shuttle, and way too big to fit through the gap. So we lost two more seconds waiting for the door to open fully before Fig could punch the thrusters.

With six seconds to go, we rocketed out of the hangar so fast my body was practically welded to the seat. The force of acceleration must've made Fig tug harder on the wheel, which in turn drove the thrusters harder. The engines roared and whined, propelling us at speeds high enough to time-travel. (That's an exaggeration. But we were going RFF: Really Friggin' Fast.) And before I knew what had happened, we'd shot past the entire Galaxy Guard convoy.

Which reminded me . . .

"We should warn them," I said. As quickly as I could, I entered the Galaxy Guard call code on my transmission screen. "Maybe they'll have enough time to—"

I was interrupted by a thundering *boom*, followed by another and another. On and on it went, until the distance between our ship and the barge grew wide enough to dull the noise to distant thuds. I chewed the inside of my cheek and tried not to think about the Galaxy Guards on those ships. Whatever Quasar had paid them, it wasn't worth dying for. Quasar wouldn't care about the loss. People were disposable to him. He would just hire more minions and go about his day. But the guards weren't replaceable to their families back home.

Home.

My heart leaped with fresh panic. I'd been so focused on escaping from the barge that I'd forgotten about the star it had been towing. I glanced out the windshield, looking for the man-made sun and seeing only debris.

"Where's the star?" I asked.

Fig pulled up the navigation screen. I saw the *Whirlwind* represented as a tiny flashing dot, and a few klicks away, a larger circle was sailing toward Earth. I didn't want to believe my eyes, so I closed and reopened them twice. But the truth didn't change. In their rush to drop the shield and escape, Corpse and Cadaver must've freed the star from its tether.

As terror sank in, it became clear that not only had I failed to save my family, I'd doomed them. Because without a barge to anchor the miniature star, it was going to gravitate toward a mass larger than itself, namely a planet of more than six billion people.

The star was on a collision course with my home planet.

With no way to slow it down or stop it.

The only hope was to evacuate Earth during the time we had left, to save as many lives as possible . . . and pray that my family could escape, because I had taken away their only ship when I'd stolen the *Whirlwind*.

I released a shaky sigh and wiped my cold, clammy palms on my pants. The last time I'd tried to call home, the connection had failed. "I have to try again," I heard myself say in an empty voice. "I have to warn my parents."

CHAPTER NINETEEN

figerella jammeslot

Have you ever been to a big holiday dinner where there wasn't enough room at the table, so some of the guests, usually kids, got stuck eating in a reject place like the living room, where the grown-ups could ignore them? Well, for me, being around humans was kind of like being one of those extra kids. There was never a seat for me at the table. Usually that didn't bother me. I had always taken pride in my weirdness because it made me special. Most days I didn't give a rat's furry backside about fitting in, or being included.

But today wasn't one of those days.

Today I would've given my right arm to be a part of something bigger than myself, a part of a unit. After three attempts, Kyler had finally reached his family. And I'd never felt more like a mutant than I did right then, standing next to Cabe in the hallway, one finger pressed to my lips in a message for him to be quiet so I could listen to the conversation. I was literally on the outside looking in.

And I won't lie. It sucked.

On tiptoes, I leaned through the pilothouse doorway and snuck a peek at the transmission screen, where a blond woman was smiling at Kyler with one slender hand resting over her heart. Tears shimmered in her eyes, but they seemed like the happy kind of tears. She had a soft, round face that most people would probably consider more kind than pretty, but to me, that made her more beautiful than a hundred fashion models. I wanted to keep gazing at her. It's probably going to sound stupid, but Kyler's mom had the sort of face that made me think of warm things like fuzzy blankets and chicken noodle soup and curling up on the sofa with a good book on a dark day.

Yeah, that definitely sounded stupid.

Still, I couldn't look away from her. I held my breath and focused on the conversation, as if I could live Kyler's life if I tried hard enough.

"Mom, I need you to listen to me," Kyler said. "You're all in—"

"Kyler Gregory Centaurus," she interrupted. "I'm going to kill you!" In the very next breath, she broke down in fresh tears and added, "Thank goodness you're all right, baby. I love you so much!"

"Me too, Mom," he said. "But listen—"

"You're grounded for eternity," Mrs. Centaurus snapped, immediately followed by "I promise we'll take you on more trips, honey, wherever you want to go. Museums too. We're sorry we didn't pay attention to you. We didn't know you felt so trapped at home."

She kept doing that, contradicting herself. Next there was

"You're so brave and smart, surviving out there all alone," and then "What were you thinking, doing something so selfish and idiotic as flying away in our ship? I'm surprised you can walk and chew gum at the same time!" After that, she threatened to murder him again, restart his heart, and then hug him for a thousand years. Kyler tried to talk the whole time, but it was as though she couldn't hear him over the noise of her emotions.

It made me smile . . . and it made my chest burn with jealousy. My mother used to love me like that, fierce enough to lose her mind.

"I didn't know what to think when I got your message," Mrs. Centaurus said. "The writing didn't sound anything like you. I almost thought someone was holding you for ransom, but they didn't ask for any money."

"What message?" Kyler asked, but then his dad poked his head into the frame. Mr. Centaurus was also fair-haired and dark-eyed. His image was followed onto the screen by four boys who looked like various size clones of him. Relief washed over the dad's face, relaxing his jaw and easing down his shoulders. Meanwhile, four grins sprang to the boys' mouths.

"Hey, it's Ky," said two boys simultaneously. They looked like twins.

"He's not dead," added the oldest boy, judging by his gargantuan size. "Who would've guessed?"

A shorter boy extended a hand to his big brother, palm up. "Score! You owe me ten bucks, loser."

His demand for payment went ignored. "Dude," the large

boy said to Kyler. "Running away to another planet? Seriously uncool. There's nothing you won't do to get out of playing laser hockey."

"Yeah, there's no *I* in *team*," one of the twins said.

"But there's a *u* in *Ky's grounded*," the other twin added with a snicker.

The shortest boy elbowed the largest. "Hey, for real. Pay up, bro. Ten bucks."

The larger boy made a fist. "How about I give you a knuckle sandwich instead? I'll even supersize it for free."

At that, the younger boy shifted his hips toward the older brother and farted loud enough to break glass. Which resulted in a sucker punch to the upper arm that knocked the younger boy into the twins, who bonked their heads together and glared at the other two. From there it descended into a brawl that moved offscreen.

I grimaced. I never thought Kyler would be the normal kid in his family.

"Um, guys," Kyler said, folding his arms and cocking his head to the side as if this sort of thing happened all the time. "Mom? Dad? I have to tell you something. Could you try to focus on me for longer than ten seconds?"

His parents were only half listening, distracted by the *thud*s and *thwack*s that were taking place out of view. I could tell from their wrinkled foreheads that they weren't sure whether to intervene or let the boys fight it out and establish dominance like a litter of wolf pups.

"Hey," Ky said, waving a hand to get their attention.

"Long-lost son over here. . . . Remember me? I didn't call just to say hello. There's an emergency I have to tell you about."

The word *emergency* got his mother's attention. It also got Cabe's attention. Cabe's inner reel hummed with panic, and I had to whisper, "It's all right. We're not in mortal danger." He calmed down just as Mrs. Centaurus whipped her gaze to the screen.

"An emergency? What's wrong? Are you—"

"I'm fine," Kyler told her. "You're the ones in danger. Remember that stolen star from Fasti?"

She and her husband nodded.

"It's headed for Earth," Kyler said. "And fast. It should be there by morning. You guys have to find a ship and get off the world as fast as you can."

His mom tipped her head in confusion. "Last I heard, the Galaxy Guard had the barge surrounded and was bringing it to a stop."

"It was announced a few minutes ago," Mr. Centaurus said. "I'm sure if we were in danger, we would know. It would be all over the news."

"But who spins the news?" Ky asked. "Who pays off the people who report the stories? Who controls the airwaves and the worldwide network?"

Mr. Centaurus peered at Kyler as though he didn't understand the question. "You mean Quasar Niatrix?" For a moment, I thought I saw his eye twitch.

"Exactly," Ky said.

"Since when do you believe me about Quasar manipulating the media?"

Kyler flapped a hand. "Doesn't matter. I get it now. What matters is that Quasar is the one who stole the star, not a crew of Wanderers. I think he had help from someone on Fasti, and he hired two pirates to steal the star barge. Now the star is headed for Earth, and it can't be stopped."

"That doesn't add up," Kyler's dad said. "Listen, you know I hate Quasar, but I can't believe he would destroy Earth. That's his customer base. There'd be no one to buy property on his colony planets. He'd be shooting himself in the foot." Mr. Centaurus delivered a stern look. "Where did you get your information, Kyler? You know you can't believe everything you read. I told you how important it is to check your sources before—"

"I'm the source," Ky interrupted. "I know it's true because I lived it."

He told his family a brief version of everything that had happened . . . except for meeting me and finding out I had been working for the pirates. I didn't know why Kyler was protecting me, or even if that was what he meant to do, but it caught me by surprise.

"No way," the large boy said to Ky after the story was done. "Did pirates really try to kill you? Because that's completely bogus."

"Yeah," one of the twins said. "Pirates can't kill our brother."

"Only *we* can kill our brother," the other twin finished.

"It's our God-given right," the first twin agreed.

Kyler's mom and dad shared a hesitant glance that said they weren't sure what to believe. I couldn't blame them. Even to my ears, the story sounded too wild to be true, and I had been there for most of it.

"But why?" asked Ky's dad. "What's Quasar's motive in all this?"

"To control Earth," Kyler said. "He wanted to convince everyone that Wanderers were trying to destroy the planet. His plan was to tow the star close enough to Earth to make voters panic, then save the day and look like the hero. But it backfired. Now the star is loose, and there's no stopping it."

His parents went quiet. They still didn't seem convinced.

"Aw, come on." Kyler threw his hands in the air. "If you never listen to me again, just trust me this one time. You need to evacuate. Find a ship and go visit Nana. What do you have to lose?"

During the exchange, I saw Cabe working himself into a lather again, his inner reel buzzing and his bendy legs creaking as he tried holding back his worries. I pressed a calming hand to his chest, but it was no use. He lurched into the pilothouse waving his cable arms around wildly and crying, "Mortal danger! The Centaurus family is in mortal danger!"

Kyler spun around. "Whoa, whoa. Stand down, Cabe. That's an order."

Cabe let his arms go slack and reeled them inside his body until they were only long enough to clasp together at the ends.

Kyler thumbed at him. "I activated him; he's been a big help. You can believe Cabe. You are in . . ." Ky hid his lower face behind one hand and mouthed the words *mortal danger* so Cabe wouldn't hear him and lose his marbles again.

"Uh-huh," said Mr. Centaurus flatly. "I'd like to point out that Cabe also thought my beard trimmer was an instrument of death. Remember when he snatched it out of my hand and chucked it out the airlock?"

Kyler heaved a sigh. He wasn't getting through to anyone. I could finally see that he wasn't the only person to blame for the problems in his family. His parents didn't seem to have much faith in him.

I gripped the edge of the doorway, hesitating to come forward. I knew Kyler didn't want me around, not after what I'd done. Besides, I felt like I didn't deserve to talk to his family. I was part of the reason they might die, along with billions of other innocent people. But in the end, I swallowed my fear and my shame, and I walked into the room. The least I could do was make Ky's mom and dad believe him.

"He's telling the truth," I said. "My name is Figerella Jammeslot, and I was hired by two pirates to blow up the Fasti star."

"Whoa," the youngest boy breathed. "A mutant!"

Ky's mom elbowed the boy, and he corrected, "A Wanderer, I mean."

She made an apologetic face and nodded for me to go on.

"The star is filled with dark matter," I told them. "The pirates said that if I hit it at dead center, it would explode. Or implode. They weren't quite sure which way it would go." I bit my lip and peeked at Kyler, who stood rigidly beside me, refusing to meet my eyes. I wanted so badly for him to know I wasn't a monster. "I had no idea what they were really planning. If I had, I never would've taken the job. Please believe me."

He folded his arms.

"I needed the money," I told him. "But after I found out what Quasar Niatrix was up to, I tried to stop him. I still want to stop him." I shifted in place. "I'm not a bad person."

Kyler's dad pointed back and forth between us. "How did you two end up on the *Whirlwind* together?"

"Long story," Ky said. "But do you believe me now?"

His father scratched his head in thought. "Let's say a star really *is* coming—"

A series of beeps interrupted him, and a voice in the background of the Centaurus house said, "This is an emergency alert from the Earth Link Broadcast Network. This is not a test. I repeat, this is *not* a test. The following message will be translated into all known languages."

Kyler pointed behind his parents. "Move the camera so I can see."

His mother adjusted the lens, bringing the family telescreen into view. The screen flashed with the face of a handsome man with tanned skin and waves of glossy brown hair that touched his shoulders. His blue eyes were solemn, his mouth unsmiling as he sat behind a mahogany table with both hands folded atop it. A flag representing Earth stood behind him.

Quasar Niatrix.

"My fellow citizens," Quasar said in the velvety voice of a Hollywood actor. "The Earth Link Network has provided me with this airtime because our planet is in danger, and the government can't help us. And why can't they help us? Because they're too busy helping the enemy. While the United Nations was negotiating with Wanderers for the right to take away our land and our jobs, a group of mutants destroyed the Fasti star barge, killing hundreds of Galaxy Guards in the process. And that's not the worst of it. Before the explosion, the mutants launched the stolen star at Earth, and it's traveling toward us at an alarming speed. The estimated time of impact is in ten hours."

An image appeared onscreen of the miniature Fasti star, surrounded by a rippling force field and dragging its broken tether behind it like an enormous comet tail.

"I made a decision to step up," Quasar said. "Where the government failed to protect you, I will use my resources at Niatrix Industries to save our precious planet."

"See?" Kyler shouted. "He wants to be the hero."

"I have a sharpshooter standing by," Quasar said, "to destroy the star before it reaches Earth. This should prove to you, the citizens of our great world, that no threat is a match for the power of Niatrix Industries. A vote for Niatrix is a vote for survival."

"He's lying," I said. "The sharpshooter he's talking about is me, and I'm nowhere near Earth."

"Quick," Kyler told his parents. "Don't wait for him to finish. Evacuate now!"

"For your protection," Quasar added with one hand pressed to his chest, "I'm placing a force field around Earth to shield you from radiation."

"Oh no," I murmured. So much for evacuating. A force field would block ships from entering or leaving the atmosphere. Everyone on Earth would be trapped on the ground.

"As for me, I will serve as our last line of defense," Quasar said. He indicated his lavish surroundings, and for the first time, I noticed the artificial lighting that hinted he was in space. "Here, in my remote headquarters."

In other words, he had ensured his own safety by escaping. If the star was somehow destroyed, Quasar could take credit for it. And if he failed to save the day, he could blast off to one of his oasis planets and leave the rest of mankind to die.

"Try not to panic," he went on. "I won't let you down."

The transmission flickered, drawing my focus back to Kyler's family. They were huddled together with their lips parted in disbelief. I felt the same way, even knowing Quasar's plan in advance. It was so evil it almost seemed like an elaborate prank.

Ky's mom was the first to speak. "So what do we do—" Her words cut off as the screen flickered again. A moment of static followed, and then there was nothing.

"No!" Kyler shouted. He tried two more times to reconnect and failed.

"It must be the force field," I said. "It's messing with the signal, like the first time you tried calling home. Quasar must have been testing the shield that day."

Ky turned to me with panic etched on his face. "We have to do something."

I agreed that we couldn't give up. It didn't matter that we had no plan, no allies, and no heavy equipment. We had to go down fighting. The worst kind of failure was not trying at all.

"What if we blow up the star?" I asked. "I have my laser. There's dark matter in the sun's core. If I hit it dead center, it'll blow." The aim would be tricky, because the sun was in motion. But my experience blasting asteroids had taught me to hit a moving target. "I know I can do it."

Kyler shook his head. "It's too risky. Earth could get fried like a chicken."

"Then let's brainstorm while I fly," I said. "We're wasting time."

Ky held out an arm, stopping me before I could reach the wheel. "You mean while *I* fly. I downgraded your crew privileges."

"But I'm the better pilot. I can get us—"

"Not happening," he snapped.

I backed down and took the copilot's seat while Kyler set a course for Earth at maximum speed. Right away, the *Whirlwind* rotated thirty degrees and rocketed away fast enough to press my spine into the seat.

"Just saying," I muttered. "It might be a good idea to give me flight privileges. I mean, what if you're hurt? You could hit your head or get sick. Or what if we're headed for an asteroid?"

"The autopilot would steer around it."

"Still," I argued, "it would be smart if we—"

"There is no *still*," he interrupted. "There is no *we*. And in case you need me to spell it out for you, there is no deal. I'm not taking you to Earth, assuming we can save it. After what you've done, you'll be lucky if I don't turn you in."

"I tried to make things right," I said. "And I *did* rescue you from pirates."

"Pirates you were working for!"

Cabe's chest whirred. "Goosey, you are displaying higher than normal levels of aggression toward a fellow crew member. Stand down."

I gave Cabe a nod of thanks for having my back. He was a better friend than most humans. Kyler waved him off. "It's all right. We're just having a . . . heated debate . . . about Fig's crew privileges."

"Fig?" Cabe asked. "I have no record of—"

"Weirdo," Ky interrupted. "I meant *Weirdo's* crew privileges."

Cabe beeped in understanding. "Please keep your verbal communication below eighty decibels. My programming states that I must—"

"Break up our fights," Kyler said, his eyeballs practically doing backflips. "I know."

I lowered my voice to a loud hiss. "What does it matter if I was working for the pirates? I still saved your bacon. That should prove I'm not a bad person."

Ky shot daggers at me with his eyes. "Well, here's a new deal for you: If you can come up with a way to save my planet and my family, maybe, just *maybe* I'll dump you at the nearest transport station even though you were part of the worst terrorist attack in human history." He thrust a hand at me. "What do you say? Should we shake on it?"

I smacked his hand away, then made an innocent gesture when Cabe *bwoop*ed at me in warning. "I told you I had no idea what was going on when Corpse and Cadaver hired me. All they said was—"

"To blow up a star," Kyler finished. "Right. Because that sounds like a totally innocent job. I mean, what could possibly go wrong with blasting apart a giant ball of radiation? What reason would someone have to blow up a star except for kicks and giggles?"

"I didn't think about it like that," I said. "I needed the money."

"Oh, come off it," he told me. "It was about more than the money, and you know it. I'll bet you couldn't wait to blast that star to bits just because it was big and beautiful and there for you to demolish. Let's be real, Fig. You get a high from blowing things up."

I bit my lip. I couldn't deny the sun had put an itch in my trigger finger.

"I'll tell you something else." He looked at me again, and there was a new emotion in his eyes, something raw and tender. I had hurt him. "You were right when you said I put my trust in the wrong people. I trusted *you*. I thought we were friends. I tried to be nice to you, and I ended up with a knife in my back."

I took a sudden interest in my boots.

"I can't believe I actually thought . . ." Ky shook his head. "You know what? It doesn't matter. I wouldn't want you for a friend, anyway. You did me a favor by turning out to be a liar and a thief."

My eyes started to prickle. I blinked them dry and spat, "Then I guess you should thank me."

I could tell he was gearing up to have the last word. And

he would've had it, too, if it hadn't been for the laser blast that shook our ship. We lurched forward in our seats while an alarm blared and an automated voice droned, "Level-one surface damage to the rear hull. Consult your authorized Pro Lux dealer to schedule a repair."

"Mortal danger," Cabe cried. "We must defend the ship!"

"Cool your reels," I said. "We're not in mortal danger."

I glanced at the navigation screen to see what kind of craft had fired on us. Level-one surface damage wasn't a big deal. It basically meant there was a cosmetic burn mark in the paint. But still, it was a strange (and really rude) way to get our attention.

"The Galaxy Guard?" I wondered out loud, squinting at the beacon trailing us.

That didn't make sense, though. The ship attacking us was too small.

Another blast shook the *Whirlwind*, jerking me in my safety harness.

Cabe was practically vibrating with worry now. I felt bad for him, so I reached behind his neck to power him down until we figured out what was going on.

"Okay, seriously," Kyler snapped. "Who is doing that?"

I glared at the flashing icon. "Someone who's going to get my boot up their tailpipe if they don't knock it off. I have a T-class laser, and I'm not afraid to use it."

"Whoever it is, they're flying a sedan-class model like mine, but they weaponized it," Ky said. "Why would a ship have a laser cannon mounted on the outside?"

To me, the answer was clear. "To blast asteroids."

"So they're Wanderers?" he asked.

"That's my bet."

"The Holyoakes?"

"No chance," I said. "Even if they replaced their core processor, there's no way they could catch up to us this fast."

The *Whirlwind*'s computer alerted us to more "level-one surface damage" to the hull. Then the feminine voice said something that sent ice churning through my veins. "Incoming transmission from the High Council of Galactic Wanderers. Do you accept?"

Now I knew who was chasing us—and why.

"The Wanderer Council?" Kyler said. He thumbed over his shoulder. "That's your government shooting at us?"

My mouth was too dry to respond. A sensation of dread came over me, so strong it was like the bottom had fallen out of my body.

Cross us again, and we'll take you to the Council.

The Holyoakes hadn't been bluffing.

"They want to take me away," I mumbled, more to myself than to Ky. He hated me too much to care right now. "They want to put me on trial."

"Who? The Council?"

I nodded. "They have their own court. It keeps the Galaxy Guard out of our business."

"What do they want to try you for?"

"Theft," I said. "I stole the Holyoakes' shuttle, the first time I escaped. Then I stole their core processor with you."

Kyler reached for the ACCEPT button on the transmission screen, but right before his fingertip connected, he paused. "Does the Council give out punishments?"

A shiver rolled over me. "Yeah."

"What will they do?" he asked. "Like . . . send you to kid jail?"

I shook my head. My people didn't do kid jail. "Way worse."

"Like what?"

I lifted a shoulder. "No telling. They like to get creative with their punishments."

"Oh," he said, his finger still poised above the button.

I sagged against my harness, suddenly tired. I wasn't sleepy tired, more like exhausted, deep down in my spirit. I didn't have the energy to fight anymore. I just wanted the struggle to be over. Besides, there was nothing the Council could do to me that would make me feel worse than I already did.

"Just stop the ship," I told Ky. "I'm the one they want. Do what they say, and they'll quit firing on us. You shouldn't have to suffer because of me."

"Do you really mean that?" he asked.

I dipped my chin. "Of course. Go ahead and let them have me."

Kyler pressed his lips together and seemed to think about it for a few beats. Then instead of tapping ACCEPT, he hit DENY. "Nope," he said. "Sorry, but you're not getting off the hook that easily."

I blinked at him.

"We made a new deal, remember?" he told me. "I'm not turning you over to anyone until you help me come up with a plan to save Earth. So if you want to rot away in some torture chamber, first you'll have to undo the mess you made. Then we'll talk about the Council. In the meantime, they can wait their turn."

My mouth opened and closed, but no words came out.

"Hey, look at that, I left you speechless," Ky said. "That's a nice bonus." He tightened his hold on the wheel and told the ship, "Computer, increase speed to full velocity and begin evasive maneuvers. We're under attack."

CHAPTER TWENTY

kyler centaurus

Fig was fidgeting with her hands, darting constant glances at the navigation screen to keep tabs on the Council ship, which, for now, was ten klicks behind us and well out of firing range. But who knew how long we could outrun them. "Next we'll probably lose our main—"

"Shhh!" I lifted a finger to stop her from jinxing us. "Don't tempt fate."

"What are we going to do?"

That was the real question. And I didn't know the answer. In the last few minutes, our problems had doubled. It was hard enough trying to stop a runaway star without the Wanderer Council attacking us from behind.

I blew out a sigh. "If the universe would stop yanking our chain, that would be great."

Fig snorted. "More like spanking our butts. Right now I feel like the kid in a story my mom used to tell me, about a boy who had to fight a giant using nothing but a pebble and a catapult."

"It wasn't a catapult," I said. I'd heard that story, too. "It was a slingshot—the old-fashioned kind that was basically a leather pouch attached to a string. Which is pretty impressive when you think about it. It's hard to hit a target with a primitive slingshot." I demonstrated by circling one hand over my head. "First you whirl the ammunition, a rock or whatever, around and around a bunch of times to build up momentum, then you have to let it fly at just the right moment. . . ."

I trailed off as an idea teased at the edges of my mind.

I imagined a slingshot attached to a long tether. But instead of leather, the string was made of a force-field cable, and instead of a rock, the slingshot pouch held a miniature star. Taking it a step further, I pictured myself grabbing the force-field cable and whipping it around my head a few times, building enough momentum to send the star flying into another solar system. Then I released the cable and watched the star sail into the distance.

It was a wild, ridiculous fantasy.

So wild that it brought a smile to my lips.

In theory, why couldn't I fling the man-made sun away from Earth? With the right equipment and enough force, it just might work.

"I have an idea," I said. "But brace yourself, because it's going to sound crazy. Like full on badoinky-doink nuts."

"Crazier than you stealing a spaceship in your sleep?" Fig asked. "Or scaring away two pirates with septic tank gas and candy-stuffed pasta noodles? Or me free-falling through a planet's atmosphere and almost catching on fire? Or us trying to steal a sun?"

I lifted a shoulder. "Okay, maybe it won't sound so crazy."

"Spill it," she said.

So I did.

After explaining my idea, I waited a minute for the details to soak in before I asked, "What do you think?"

She shifted her eyes toward me. "You care what I think?"

"Well, yeah," I said. That didn't mean I was okay with the lies she had told. Or that I was ready to forgive her, or even trust her. But I couldn't deny that Fig had a brilliant mind and a special set of skills that I didn't have. If I had listened to her sooner, maybe things would have turned out differently. "I want us to be on the same page this time. Whatever we do, it won't work if we're divided. That's what went wrong on the barge—we stopped being a team, and it weakened us."

"Well, here's what I think," she said. "It's not enough to shoot the star away from Earth. That'll cause a new set of problems for anything in its path. We have to shoot the star away from Earth and then destroy it."

"Blow it up?" I asked. "But what about the dark matter? We still don't know if it'll cause a black hole."

"Then let's find out." She pointed at the transmission station. "Ask your scientist lady, the one who invented the star."

"Doctor Nesbit? I thought you didn't trust her."

"I don't," Fig said. "But we're pretty crafty. I'll bet we can come up with a way to find out if she's honest."

"Okay, then I guess we have a plan," I said. "Is it just me, or does it sound kind of nuts?"

"Oh, nuttier than squirrel poop," Fig agreed. "But still, it's a solid idea."

"Really? You think we should run with it?"

"Like a kid with scissors."

"All right." I unfastened my safety belt and stood up from the pilot's seat, indicating that Fig should switch places with me. It was time to start acting like a team, and that meant trusting her to take the wheel. "I'm going to power up Cabe and restore you to level-three crew privileges."

Fig's eyebrows jumped. "Really?"

"Really," I told her. "Let's do this."

CHAPTER TWENTY-ONE

kyler centaurus

I pulled up Dr. Nesbit's private number in my comm and held my breath while I waited for the call to connect. As I sat there, nervously tapping a finger against my knee, part of me hoped she wouldn't answer. I know that sounds strange, but I couldn't stand the thought that she might have been involved with Quasar's scheme. If my personal hero was crooked, I would rather not know at all. The disappointment would crush me.

The call connected. Dr. Nesbit said, "Hello?"

I nodded at Fig, who had spent the last hour stitching together audio clips from speeches Quasar Niatrix had posted online. The end result wasn't perfect, but Fig had crafted a few sentences that should convince Dr. Nesbit Quasar was calling instead of me.

"Hello?" she repeated.

Fig played the first recording. I held my comm close so Quasar's voice blurted loud and clear into the receiver, "You had one job, and you failed. Now it's a disaster."

"*I* failed?" screeched Dr. Nesbit. "*I'm* the one who failed?" Then she lowered her voice to a hiss and called Quasar a name I'm not going to repeat. "How dare you blame this on me?"

The recording repeated, "You had one job."

"I *still* have one job," Dr. Nesbit snapped. "My *job*, you arrogant"—another word I won't repeat—"is to create stars, not weapons. I wanted nothing to do with your plan. I warned you from the start it was a terrible idea. But did you listen? No, of course not. You forced my hand, and I hate you for it."

An ache opened up behind my ribs. I glanced at Fig, who bit her lip and dropped her gaze. At least she didn't gloat, though she could have. She'd been right all along. Quasar Niatrix had wanted the best on his team, and that was Dr. Nesbit, the scientist I had spent half my life admiring. The person I had wanted to be when I grew up. Now I didn't know what was real. I felt like someone had reached into my head and torn out half my brain.

With numb fingers, I tapped my comm screen and switched the call to video. I couldn't see Dr. Nesbit at first, because she hadn't turned on her camera. But that was okay. I didn't want to see her face. That was how far she'd let me down.

"How could you?" I asked in my own voice.

There was a pause. "Who is this?"

"Turn on your video feed."

After another pause, Dr. Nesbit's image appeared on my screen. Right away I could tell she'd lost weight. Her cheekbones were too sharp, and her skin had lost its glow. She seemed miserable, which made me feel better. Maybe she would help undo the damage she'd done.

She arched her brows and breathed, "Kyler."

At least she remembered my name.

"What's this about?" she asked, looking behind me for clues. "What's going on?"

"Quasar's not here," I told her. "I used his voice to test you, to see if . . ." I had to pause to clear the thickness from my throat. "I know you helped him steal the star."

Dr. Nesbit froze, wide-eyed. "I . . . I . . . don't know what you're talking about."

"Please don't do that. Don't deny it. This is hard enough as it is."

Fig added from the pilot's seat, "Plus, we don't have time."

"That too," I said to Dr. Nesbit. "I'm chasing down your star, and I need to find out how to blow it up. I know you loaded the star with dark matter so it could be destroyed and make Quasar look like a hero. I know this because the sharp-shooter Quasar hired is sitting right next to me."

Fig leaned toward the comm and waved, then returned to piloting the ship.

"What I *don't* know," I went on, "is how to detonate the star without frying Earth. Or opening up a black hole. We're only a few klicks away from it, and I'm not sure what to do. We have one chance to save Earth. I need your help so we don't waste our only shot."

Dr. Nesbit licked her lips, saying nothing. Maybe she was afraid of admitting what she'd done because she was ashamed. Or maybe she didn't want to go to jail. Either way, I had to convince her to trust me before she would give me the information I needed.

"I'm not trying to get you in trouble," I said. "I just want to save my family. I think you want that, too. Because deep down, I believe that anyone who dedicates her life to celestology does it because she wants to help people, not hurt them. And I believe that if someone makes a bad choice, that doesn't make them a bad person . . . as long as they're willing to do the right thing in the end."

She fidgeted with her collar for a moment or two, until she gave me a slow nod. "All right. The most important factor in safely destroying the star is distance. Make sure it's no less than five klicks away from Earth before you fire at the core. That's going to be tricky, though, because it's traveling toward Earth."

"I have an idea about that," I said. "The star has a force field around it, including the tether from when it was being towed. What if I could attach the tether to my ship and then swing the star around a few times and slingshot it away from Earth? When it gets far enough away, we could blow it up. Would that work?"

"Yes and no," she told me. "I can send you the calculations for which speed and angle to use in aiming the star away from Earth, but a passenger ship has less power than a barge. Your engine can't generate enough force for a slingshot maneuver. You would need to circle the star around to change its path and then tow it in the direction you want it to go."

My stomach sank. "So I need a second ship?"

"Either that or you can set an autopilot course to tow the star, and eject yourselves."

I rubbed my temples and shared a worried glance with Fig.

If we abandoned ship, we would be on our own because of the no-fly zone. And no one on Earth could save us, because Quasar had everyone trapped on the ground. I guessed we could survive for a few hours in our thermal suits and oxygen helmets, but after that, we would be toast.

"How about radiation from the star?" I asked.

"The force field should protect you," Dr. Nesbit said. "It's a one-way shield, meaning things can get in, but not out. So your sharpshooter friend will be able to hit the sun with her laser, even with the shield intact."

I didn't like the way she said the shield *should* protect us, but I nodded.

"Do you want me to send the calculations?" asked Dr. Nesbit. "If so, I need to go back to my office and run the numbers."

"Yes," I murmured. "What about opening a—"

She disconnected before I could ask about black holes.

Fig and I sat in silence for a while.

I knew what we had to do, but I was too scared to say it out loud. When we'd agreed to do whatever it took to save Earth, it had never crossed my mind that we might not live to see the next day. I still wanted to take care of my family, and every other family on the ground—losing two lives to save six billion people was a worthy trade—but given the choice, I would rather not die in the cold void of space.

"I can't believe we're losing the ship," Fig said. "The *Whirlwind* is the closest thing to home I've felt in a long time." She slumped over in her seat. "By the way, I guess I should apologize for trying to steal her. Sorry about that."

As much as I loved the *Whirlwind*, she was just a collection of metal parts. "That's your biggest worry right now? Not potentially dying?"

"You don't get it," Fig told me. "I thought this ship was my ticket to a new life. No more sleeping in transport stations, no more begging for jobs, no more ending up at the mercy of people like the Holyoakes. Without a ship, I have nothing to live for anyway, so yeah, I guess you could say my biggest worry right now is losing it."

"But you never had it to begin with."

"In my mind I did," she said. "And it gave me hope, enough to keep going."

The sadness in her eyes plucked at my heart, and in the beat that followed, I put myself in her shoes. Her parents were dead. She had no friends, no family, no money, and no home. And to add another layer of garbage to her dumpster-fire of a life, her own people were hunting her down like she was some kind of intergalactic serial killer.

No wonder she felt hopeless.

"I'm sorry, too," I told her.

She peeked at me. "For what?"

"For being a bad friend. For not asking about your parents sooner." I paused, thinking of my brothers and their biggest complaint about me. "For not treating us like a team."

Fig's grin told me I was forgiven. "Better late than never, right?"

"Friends?" I asked, extending my hand for her to shake.

She gripped it. "Best friends."

"Wow, I finally have a best friend . . . just in time for us to die together," I joked.

Neither of us laughed.

In front of me, the transmission station beeped to announce a new recorded message. I glanced down, expecting to see a formula from Dr. Nesbit, but instead, my twin brothers' faces appeared on the screen. I pressed PLAY and leaned in closer to listen.

"Hey," Devin said. "Hope you can see this. Quasar's force field is blocking the main comms, but it takes more than that to defeat a Centaurus. We're using old tech to get a message through. Just wanted to say—"

"—get Figerella here, quick, and blast that star to pieces," Rylan finished.

"Yeah." Devin thumbed at his twin. "What he said."

Duke elbowed his way in front of the camera. "Dude, you can't give up. The game isn't over till the ref blows the whistle. You gotta go down fighting. Like the time I threw a twenty-yard pass with two seconds left in the—"

"Booooooooring," Bonner interrupted, poking his head into view. He pointed at me and said, "I have faith in you, bro. Hearing how you stood up to those pirates gave me the guts to tell Lori Ann McCallum that I love her."

Duke snorted. "And then she slammed the door in his face."

"But still, I told her." Bonner shrugged. "Anyway, you got this, Ky."

"Yeah," echoed the others.

A smile lifted the corners of my mouth. My brothers believed in me.

"Tell your Wanderer friend she's got this, too," Duke added.

He huffed a dry laugh. "Maybe she can blow up Quasar's yacht while she's at it."

"We gotta go," Bonner said. "But first, one more thing." He extended an index finger toward the camera. "Pull my finger, Ky."

I rolled my eyes hard enough to see my frontal lobe.

"I felt it!" Bonner yelled. "You pulled my finger with the power of your mind. Now I owe you one when you get home—a wet, juicy one. Prepare yourself, bro. It's coming, and it's gonna be epic!"

The screen went blank.

Fig glanced at me with wide eyes. "Did you hear that?"

"Yeah, he's always asking me to pull his finger." I made a face. Just thinking about it evoked the stench of sewage and rotten eggs and maybe something hot and steamy like boiled cabbage. "As if I haven't learned by now."

"No, not that," Fig said. "The part about Quasar's yacht."

I drew a gasp, because I understood what she was getting at. "Of course. I can't believe we almost missed it."

We were wrong before. Quasar didn't have *all* the ships trapped on the ground. There was one floating above the force field, and it was a whopper. Quasar's yacht would give us someplace to go after we ejected, and if a luxury cruiser didn't count as a ticket to a new life, I didn't know what did. Plus, we seemed to have ditched the Wanderer Council, but even if they caught up with us, we could always land Quasar's ship on Earth. The Council couldn't touch Fig there.

"We can steal his yacht, right?" I asked.

Fig tried to hide a grin, almost as if she was afraid to hope. In the end, her enthusiasm won out. The twinkle in her eyes told me so. "We broke into a pirate barge. Some billionaire's space cruiser is bound to be a piece of cake compared to that."

"All right, then. First we'll lasso the sun, then we'll blow it up and figure out a way to steal Quasar's yacht."

"An ordinary day," Fig joked. She nodded at the blank transmission screen. "By the way, what happens when you pull Bonner's finger?"

"You seriously don't know?"

"No, why would I?"

"Well, trust me, you don't want to find out," I said. "Be glad you don't have brothers. They're the worst."

"Doesn't seem that way," she said. "They cheered us on and helped us figure out what to do. That's something."

I opened my mouth to argue, but I closed it again. "All right. They were cool today. I'll give you that."

"So maybe brothers aren't the worst."

I snickered under my breath. "I'll tell you what. If we actually save Earth and make it to the ground alive, ask my brothers to show you what a NWARF is. Then you can decide for yourself whether they're the worst."

"What's a NW—"

"Nope," I said, cutting her off with a lifted hand. "It's best if you find out from the source." I teasingly added, "Now you have a *real* incentive to save the world."

CHAPTER TWENTY-TWO

figerella jammeslot

After two hours of pushing the *Whirlwind* to the max, we reached the miniature star, which looked more like a comet than a sun as it sailed toward Earth. Compared with a planet, the Fasti star was deceptively small. Even the moon, looming in the background, was ten times its size. Hard to believe such a tiny package could end mankind.

I dimmed the windshield and gazed at Earth, swirling with bright blue and green, and felt my heart swell until it nearly bumped my rib cage. I had never seen the original planet until now. I wasn't prepared for how vibrantly it stood out against the stars, so teeming with life that it glowed. All of the outer planets, even the designer colonies, were muted in color, made up of different shades of brown and offset by water that looked more gray than sapphire. I had thought some of them were pretty, but I didn't know true beauty until now. All of a sudden I got it—I understood why Earth was special.

There was no replacing the original.

"How close are we to the tether?" I asked Kyler. I didn't

like how quickly the star was sailing away from us. My insides felt like an antique watch, winding tighter and tighter with each moment. "If we don't latch on soon . . ."

"I know," Ky muttered, his eyes fixed on the screen in front of him. Dr. Nesbit had called to say she was almost finished with the formula to slingshot the star away from Earth, but first we had to connect to the star's tether. Kyler activated a camera at the bottom of the ship near the boarding hatch, and zoomed in on the image of a broken ring that had once connected the star to its barge. "We're right on top of the ring. Can you keep us here?"

"Yep," I said, gripping the wheel.

After that, Kyler used his remote-control fob to talk to Cabe, who was waiting in the airlock. "Okay, buddy. We're in position. Go ahead and work your magic."

"Magic is not a part of my programming, Goosey," Cabe replied.

I snorted. Leave it to Cabe to make me laugh at a time like this.

"I meant do your thing," Kyler said. "You know, repair the link and attach the star to the *Whirlwind*."

"Affirmative," Cabe answered. "That is within my capabilities."

Despite the tension building in my chest, I smiled while I watched the camera footage of Cabe using his metal ropes to build a new ring and fuse it to the ship. Cabe was a goofball, but we would never have survived without him. More than that, he accepted me for who I was and didn't try to change me, only protect me. He was the closest thing I had to a family.

I glanced at Kyler and wondered if Cabe meant the same to him. Before I knew it, the words popped out of my mouth. "Hey, you know how your family kept Cabe in a closet for two years?"

Kyler nodded, still watching the screen.

"Well, they probably wouldn't miss him if he was gone, right?" I asked. "If we live through this, do you think they might let me have him?"

When Ky looked up, his lips parted, and I knew Cabe meant as much to Kyler as he did to me. Maybe more.

"Never mind." I flapped a hand and distracted myself by gazing at the space yacht floating above Earth's atmosphere. I told myself a yacht was better than a quirky robot, but it felt like a lie. "It was just an idea. Anyway, I'm getting ahead of myself. We have more important things to worry about than who ends up with what."

Speaking of important things, the transmission screen beeped and displayed an incoming message from Fasti. I tried to read the text, but all I saw was a jumble of letters and numbers.

"It's from Doctor Nesbit," Kyler said. "She sent the formula."

I pointed at the screen. "That makes sense to you?"

"Sure. It's basic physics, with a little extra strategy thrown in."

"Huh. I just use instinct when I'm blasting." I suddenly felt useless. We didn't need my flying skills now that we were attached to the star. It was time to set the autopilot and eject. My next moment to shine wouldn't come until the star was far enough away to blast it to smithereens.

"Tell me what I can do," I said.

"You can go to the loading bay and get our things ready for when we eject," he suggested. "We'll need—"

"Suits and oxygen," I finished, standing up. "And a way to propel ourselves to the yacht after we're outside the ship. Plus, my blaster, of course." That would come in handy even after I destroyed the star. No way was Quasar going to open his doors for us. I would have to rip a hole in his airlock. "I'm on it."

"Work fast," Ky said. "We blow this Popsicle stand in T-minus five minutes."

CHAPTER TWENTY-THREE

kyler centaurus

"Cabe," I called through the comm link. "Is the star still latched on good and tight?"

"Affirmative, Goosey."

"Okay. Now that the star is fused to the ship, I want you to detach from the line and come inside. We're going to need both of your cables free to pull this off, buddy."

"Affirmative."

"How about Fig?" I asked. "I mean Weirdo. Is she ready to evacuate?"

"I'm ready," she shouted in the background.

While we spoke, I entered Dr. Nesbit's formula into the ship's autopilot program. I knew Fig was a good enough pilot to follow the instructions, but whipping the ship around would create a wicked amount of force, and I didn't want to risk either of us puking or passing out and mucking up the operation. So in other words, in order to save the human race, I had to eliminate human error.

Kind of ironic, I know.

"Here we go," I called through the ship's speaker system. "Hold on to something."

I punched the EXECUTE button and sat back in my seat. To picture what happened next, imagine holding a string attached to a ball. (Obviously, that ball represents the star, and the string is its force-field tether.) Now imagine you want to circle the string over your head and whip the ball around, but there's a major catch: You're doing all of this underwater. That was the challenge we faced: generating movement in space, where gravity was wonky.

The motion began as a slow pull to the right that revved the engines to maximum power but barely changed the ship's position. The engine lulled, almost as if catching a breath, and then it geared up for the next movement, which swung us around a little farther. I glanced out the windshield and noticed the miniature star beginning to change direction.

My heart fluttered. It was working.

The ship completed three more rotations, each faster than the last. When the next circle swung me around hard enough to press my ribs into the armrest, I took that as my cue to make an exit. After double-checking the autopilot commands, I braced myself against the wall and half walked, half stumbled into the hallway and down the stairs.

In the loading bay, Fig was struggling to keep the pile of equipment she had gathered from sliding across the floor—a space suit and helmet for me, a couple of rucksacks filled with who knows what, and her giant laser. Cabe stood nearby, but he wasn't helping Fig. Instead, he was examining his chest, which didn't seem right.

"What's the matter?" I asked him.

The reel inside his chest whirred. "My cable supply is critically low, Goosey."

"Critically low? That can happen?"

"Affirmative."

It had never occurred to me that Cabe might run out of metal rope. I had assumed he could make as much as he needed. It was a good thing he'd had enough cable to connect the ship to the star's force-field tether.

Fig pointed at Cabe while tossing me a thermal suit. "We'll have to be careful when we eject, only use as much cable as we need to get us to Quasar's yacht."

"Do you have that much?" I asked Cabe. "We're about a hundred yards away."

Cabe's innards whirred again. He chirped, "Affirmative. I have one hundred yards remaining."

That was good.

I managed to pull on my thermal suit while rolling across the floor, a feat for which I deserved a trophy, or at least a ribbon. After slinging a clunky rucksack across my chest, I fastened my oxygen helmet to my suit and switched on the mask comm.

"Testing," I called to Fig and Cabe.

"I read you loud and clear," Fig said from within her own helmet.

"Okay, so here's the basic plan." I handed Fig her laser cannon. "We'll eject from the airlock at the height of the next swing. Cabe will rope us together with one arm. Once the star is far enough away, you'll blast it. The force-field netting should capture all the radiation. When we're done saving the world, Cabe will use his other arm to reach out and attach to Quasar's yacht. After that, it'll be as easy as reeling us in and blasting our way inside one of the yacht's airlocks with the laser."

"And the *Whirlwind*?" Fig asked. She swept a sad gaze across the room. "Is there really no way to save her? Can't we track her down in a few weeks and cut the tether, then tow her back for repairs?"

I shook my head, feeling the same tug at my heart that Fig obviously did. I was going to miss the *Whirlwind*. I had programmed the ship to make the right number of swings and then tow the star away. After that, we would never see her again. Even if the hull survived, the engine would be shot.

I faced the heart of the ship and saluted. "I like to think of it as going out in a blaze of glory. The old girl will live on in our memories."

Fig released a long breath, right before the ship lurched and she had to bend her knees to keep from falling over. "We should go while we still can. I don't want to go out in a blaze of glory, too. At least not today."

I agreed. If we waited any longer, we could end up plastered against the wall like two kids in an old-fashioned carnival ride.

We grabbed as much as we could hold, and we made our way into the airlock. From there, I took a moment to calculate the right time to open the outside door so we ejected toward Quasar Niatrix's yacht instead of away from it.

"Prepare for evacuation," I told Cabe. In response, he threaded one of his cables around Fig and me, pulling us tightly against him. The chamber hissed as the air pressure changed. I grabbed onto the barrel of Fig's laser cannon, just in case her grip slipped. "In three . . . two . . . one . . . now!"

I levered open the door precisely as the *Whirlwind* made an arc toward the yacht. We flew out of the airlock in unison. The momentum sent us sailing in the right direction at a perfect speed and trajectory. I couldn't have asked for a more flawless evacuation.

Except for one thing.

We had barely traveled twenty yards when I heard a loud crack coming from the *Whirlwind*. The noise turned into a steely groan that sounded like metal twisting, but I was too far away to see the problem.

"Cabe," I said, hoping he was still synched with the ship's computer. "Can you check the damage report and tell me what's wrong?"

"Please stand by." He went silent for a moment. "Towing capacity for the rear hitch is compromised, Goosey."

"The towing hitch is breaking?" asked Fig.

"Affirmative, Weirdo."

My breath locked. The sun was too much for our ship to handle. And now that we had ejected, there was nothing I could do about it.

"The star isn't far enough away," I murmured. "It has to go at least another three klicks, or Earth's gravity will pull it back in, and the whole planet will die."

"Die?" Cabe repeated in a squeaky pitch. "My chief programmer, Moon of My Life, and her copilot, Darling, are on

Earth. Crew members Doodlebug, Cutie-Patootie, Squirt, and Stinky are on Earth. If the planet is threatened, then the Centaurus family is in MORTAL DANGER. I must defend the planet!"

I glanced at Cabe's whirring chest. He only had a hundred yards of cable on his reel, which wasn't enough for him to create a new tether, plus detach and rejoin us to storm Quasar's yacht. Cabe only had one job left in him. He would have to attach one of his arms to the star and the other one to the ship, basically stretching between them like a prisoner on a torture rack.

My body went cold. Cabe's line was strong enough to hold the connection, but he would be lost, along with Fig and me, because we would have no way to reach Quasar's yacht. We would just float there and die as soon as our oxygen ran out.

I looked to Fig. She nodded her approval. Then I glanced over my shoulder at Earth, and the decision made itself.

"Cabe," I said tightly. "You're right. This is not a drill. The Centaurus family is in mortal danger."

"Goosey, my programming—"

"Is to protect us, I know," I told him. "You can let go of me and Weirdo. Then I want you to attach your left cable to the ship and your right cable to the star's force-field tether. After that, you have to hold them together, no matter what it takes." I swallowed a lump the size of a peach pit. "Do you understand, buddy?"

He beeped in a somber tone that pierced my heart. "Affirmative, Goosey."

"I'm gonna miss you," I told him.

Fig sniffled from inside her helmet. "Me too."

Cabe tightened his grip on us and made a sad whirring sound.

I clapped a gloved hand on Cabe's shoulder. "Go ahead, buddy. Save our family."

The metal rope around my waist went slack. I gripped Fig's hand, and together we drifted in place while we watched Cabe unspool one of his lines toward the *Whirlwind* and attach it to the bent towing hitch. He reeled himself in until his legs touched the ship, then he kicked off at an angle that sent him soaring to the star's force-field tether. It was a perfectly executed movement, and in less than a blink, he was in between the ship and the star, holding them together.

In that moment, he was my hero.

The ship continued on its path, towing the star farther from Earth. I used my helmet's distance finder and kept watching until the star was far enough away to destroy it. Then I squeezed Fig's hand. Strangely, I wasn't afraid anymore. What we were about to do would change history, and that knowledge filled me with pride.

"Here's your big moment," I said. "Ready to blow up a star?"

Fig released a sad sigh. "This isn't how I pictured it."

"Well, we're going out with a bang, not a whimper," I pointed out.

That made her smile.

"For real." I nudged her with my elbow. "I'm pretty sure

blowing up a star is a once-in-a-lifetime opportunity, so you might as well enjoy it."

She turned to me with a lifted chin. "You know what? You're right."

"Say that again," I teased. "I didn't hear you."

"YOU'RE RIGHT."

"Ah," I said, smiling. "Music to my ears."

We worked together to crank up the laser to level 100 and then position it on top of Fig's shoulder. She nestled the cannon and took aim through the scope. I let myself float slightly behind her while hooking a finger beneath her belt so we wouldn't drift apart. All I could do now was be still and let her stabilize for the shot.

"It's all up to you," I said.

She snorted. "No pressure or anything."

"You got this."

She nodded. Her chest expanded as she drew a deep breath and held it. She went still, not moving a muscle, and peered through the cannon scope for several long seconds. In the distance, the star trailed behind the *Whirlwind*, so far away that I couldn't see Cabe or the ship anymore. Fig waited for another beat. Then she exhaled long and slow, and she squeezed the trigger.

What happened next was nearly indescribable.

The cannon fired a red laser beam wider than both my arms spread apart, and in an instant, it struck the star at dead center. The sun's core changed color from bright yellow to soft orange and then morphed into the pinkish purple of a twilight sky. Like cosmic fireworks, the hues glowed wild and electric, bursting outward and making the edges of the star tremble.

The glow was too bright for my eyes, but I held them open, refusing to blink, refusing to miss a single beat, because each microsecond brought a new change that was more breathtaking than the last. As the star continued to vibrate, something dark and sparkly formed in its center and began to swirl upward like a tornado of diamonds. Pinpricks of light flashed from all around the vortex, as if the universe was winking at us. And maybe it was, because I could swear that with each new flash, I glimpsed the distant starscape of another galaxy.

My insides hummed with so much awe that I almost couldn't take it anymore. Just when I felt like I might burst, the star swelled and shrank, swelled and shrank, again and again, faster and faster, until it was practically bouncing in place. Then in an instant, it collapsed in on itself and disappeared with a final wink of light.

Just like that, it was gone. As a bonus, it didn't open a black hole.

"Whoa" was all I could say.

"Oh yeah," Fig breathed. "*That* was worth dying for."

I nodded in agreement. But as the minutes ticked by and the rush wore off, dying started to seem a whole lot more real—and terrifying. I glanced all around us, looking for anything that might propel us to Quasar's ship, but there was only empty space between us and the yacht. All of a sudden, it occurred to me that Quasar had won. He had promised to bring in a sharpshooter to save Earth, and the people on the ground would think that was what he'd done. They must have noticed the star imploding. It was impossible to miss, even without a telescope, which plenty of people had in their backyards.

Quasar was going to take credit for all of this.

"No one will know the truth," I said, shaking my head at Quasar's yacht. "That's the worst part. He's going to get away with it."

"We'll see about that." Fig chuckled darkly and knocked on her laser cannon. "If we were really working for Quasar, would we do this to his ship?" She took aim and blasted a hole in the yacht's fuel tank. "I don't think so. Let him try to explain his way out of that one."

"At least he can't go anywhere."

I spoke too soon. The hangar door opened, and a glimmer of chrome appeared from inside. It was a shuttle, and a fast one, too, judging by the fact that it took off like a bullet before Fig could aim the laser cannon at it.

I sighed. "So much for him not going anywhere."

"Well, people will know that he ran away," Fig pointed out. "And left them trapped on the ground by a force field. That's enough for them to put together the truth."

I could see the force field ripples encircling the planet. "Too bad he didn't turn it off before he left."

"Yeah," Fig said. "That would've been nice."

For a long time, neither of us spoke. We just floated there, holding the laser cannon between us, looking down at Earth. I thought about what my family was doing at that moment, hoping they were proud of me. I didn't ask what was on Fig's mind, but I assumed she was thinking of her parents, too. Soon the air in my tank began to run out. I knew there wasn't much time left when I started yawning and feeling confused.

I figured I should say something. So I told Fig, "Look on the bright side. Soon we'll have no problems."

"No drama," she agreed. "No worries or . . ." She trailed off and glanced over her shoulder. I did the same and noticed a ship approaching us from behind. Even through my brain fog, I recognized it as the cruiser that had fired on us.

"So much for no worries," she muttered. "The Council is here."

CHAPTER TWENTY-FOUR

kyler centaurus

Here's a plot twist for you.

Quasar didn't get credit for saving the world.

"In breaking news," said a reporter on my living-room telescreen, "Doctor Sally Nesbit, famed inventor of the Fasti stars, called a press conference this morning to confess her role in the star theft that nearly destroyed Earth last night."

A video appeared of Dr. Nesbit standing behind a podium. Her eyes were fixed on a data tablet as she read a statement that described Quasar's entire plan and why she had been a part of it. "Years ago, I secretly experimented with dark matter," she admitted. "It was highly illegal and would have resulted in the loss of my lab if anyone had found out. Quasar Niatrix had proof of those experiments, and he threatened to expose me if I didn't help him. He blackmailed me, but that's no excuse for what I've done. I'm coming forward because I want to make amends. If that means going to jail, then that's a consequence I'm willing to face. The truth is more important than my freedom."

So in the end, Dr. Nesbit had done the right thing. That made me happy, and I'd like to think I was partly responsible for her coming clean. I still respected Dr. Nesbit's research, and I hoped we could work together someday.

"The unexpected heroes," the reporter went on, "are a Wanderer-human duo: Figerella Jammeslot and Myler Centaurus—"

I sighed. Of course the news got my name wrong.

"—both thirteen years old, who, with the help of an older-model Cable Aid robot, were able to divert the star away from Earth and destroy it. As for the galaxy's most wanted fugitive, Quasar Niatrix, no trace has been found of him, or of his hired pirates. Anyone with information on his whereabouts is encouraged to come forward."

From there, the reporter said Wanderer-human relations were on the mend for the first time in history, thanks to proof that Wanderers didn't steal the star. It also helped that the Council had rescued Fig and me in their ship, making them look like heroes . . . Never mind the fact that they'd chased down the *Whirlwind* earlier and fired on us.

The news didn't mention that.

The news also didn't mention that the Council had taken over Quasar's damaged yacht to use as their headquarters, and without a travel visa, Fig wasn't allowed on the ground. So she was trapped in space with the Council. Which was beyond bogus, not that our "rescuers" had listened to me. I'd been shoved headfirst by a very tall, very rude Wanderer into an Earthbound shuttle without having a chance to say good-bye to Fig.

I didn't know what the Council planned on doing with Fig, but I knew this: No one, and I mean *no one*, was going to punish my best friend, or even put her on trial.

I wouldn't allow it.

I cracked my knuckles and prepared for battle. It didn't matter that I had never held a gun, or studied kung fu, or thrown a single punch in my life. It didn't matter that the enemy had the advantage of mass numbers and laser cannons. Because what I possessed was a weapon that would make even the grittiest warrior hide under his bed covers:

I had four brothers, and they were the actual worst . . . and the actual best.

So prepare for defeat, Council!

It was game time.

CHAPTER TWENTY-FIVE

figerella jammeslot

A boot shook the edge of my bunk. I opened my mouth to yell at Kyler for waking me up, when a deep voice said, "Time to get out of bed," and I remembered I was a prisoner in the galaxy's most weirdly posh jail.

Shielding my eyes from the light streaming through the doorway, I blinked sleepily at the seven-foot-tall mutant who'd shown me to my room last night. I didn't know his name, but the guy walked around like he had a burr in his butt. He hadn't even let me say good-bye to my only friend before he'd shoved Kyler into a shuttle and sent him home.

Rude.

"What time is it?" I asked.

"Two in the afternoon," he said in the judgy tone of a morning person. "I wanted to wake you up at dawn, but I was outvoted. Anyway, come on. The Council has better things to do than wait around for one girl."

My mouth went dry. I wasn't ready for my trial to begin.

To stall, I touched my tangled hair and asked, "Shouldn't I freshen up first?"

He answered by jerking a thumb toward the hallway.

"Seriously?" I said. "Can't I have a comb?"

"No."

Instead, he gave me an escort to the conference room.

I put up a brave front while I followed the guy through a maze of yacht corridors and up two flights of steps. But my sass wore off, and I caught my footsteps slowing as I approached the conference center.

Through the open doorway, I could see Earth's flag mounted on the wall, the same place where Quasar Niatrix had filmed his final message to the planet yesterday. As I walked closer, I noticed the rest of the walls were lined with glittering mirrors that reflected a long teakwood table. Around the table stood more than a dozen cushioned leather chairs so deep I could sleep in them, all of them bathed in the rainbow glow of a crystal chandelier. Only two of the seats were filled, one by a young woman with blue hair piled atop her head in a bun, and the other by a man who, as my father used to say, was old enough to fart dust.

These were the mutants who would decide my fate. I'd thought there would be more of them. Fear brought me to a halt. The tall guy corrected that by nudging me into the room and shutting the doors behind us.

The blue-haired woman indicated a chair on my side of the table. "Figerella," she greeted me warmly. "Please have a seat."

Her smile threw me off, making me wonder what she was

up to. I was too nervous to sit down, so I stayed on my feet and gripped the back of a leather chair. "I'd rather stand," I told her. "If that's okay," I said to the giant behind me. I didn't want to give him a reason to start shoving me around again.

The guy grumbled under his breath, but he didn't object. He walked around to the other side of the table and took a seat next to the blue-haired woman.

"I'm Hazel," she said. She touched the elderly man's shoulder. "On my left is Billaby, and the tall gentleman to my right is Clarence."

Gentleman? I thought. *That's a stretch.*

"We make up a small part of the Council," she continued. "I apologize that the rest of the group couldn't be here. Great things are happening on Earth, so there are many meetings to attend. I'm sure you understand."

"Uh-huh." I understood that part. What I didn't get was why Hazel was being so nice to me. What game was she playing?

The old man, Billaby, spoke up. "Young lady, we want to begin by commending you for your bravery. You're a credit to us all. If it weren't for your heroic actions last night—"

"Just stop," I interrupted. All of this politeness was weirding me out. "You don't have to pretend to care. Can we just cut to the trial and get it over with?"

Billaby scrunched his nose. "The trial?"

"Yeah," I said before I lost my nerve. "Dragging it out will only make it worse. If you're going to convict me and hand down some twisted sentence, just do it already."

Billaby traded a confused look with Hazel, who shrugged.

She tilted her head at me. "Why do you think we asked to meet with you today, Figerella?"

Asked to meet with me? I couldn't help snorting at the way she phrased it. "You didn't *ask* anything. You chased me down like a dog until I had nowhere else to run. Then you held me prisoner on this yacht."

"What?" Hazel drew back. "We did no such thing."

"Then why am I here?"

"Because you don't have a travel visa," she said. "You can't visit Earth without one. In the meantime, where else are you going to sleep? In space?"

I bit the inside of my cheek. She had a point there. "But you fired at my ship," I reminded her.

At that, Hazel cut her eyes at Clarence. "I told you that was a bad idea."

He shrugged his massive shoulders. "I was trying to get their attention. They wouldn't answer our calls. What else was I supposed to do?"

Hazel gave me an apologetic grin. "He has poor social skills."

"Then don't put me in charge of the comms," he muttered.

I shook my head again. "So you weren't trying to catch me to put me on trial for stealing the Holyoakes' core processor?" I quickly added, "Not that I'm admitting I did that. Just saying it as an example."

"No," Hazel said. "When we saw the *Whirlwind* chasing the star, we assumed you were planning to divert it away from Earth, and we wanted to help." She gestured beyond the yacht, toward deep space. "After we picked up you and Myler—"

"Kyler," I corrected, not that she noticed.

"—we even tried to retrieve his family's ship. I'm afraid there was no saving it, but we brought back their android."

"Cabe?" I asked, almost afraid to hope. "He's still in one piece?"

"Several pieces," Clarence said. "But he should be repairable."

My chest filled with warmth. But at the same time, part of me warned that if something sounded too good to be true, it probably was. "Just to be clear," I said, "you don't put mutants on trial?"

Hazel spread her arms at the men sitting on either side of her. "We couldn't, even if we wanted to. There aren't enough of us. We're just a small committee that fights for better rights on Earth."

"And you don't punish mutants by hobbling their fists?" I asked. "Or blinding them with eye drops?"

Clarence drew back like he'd sucked a lemon. "That's horrible!"

"Heavens, girl," Billaby said, coughing on his own spit. "We're not monsters."

"Of course not," Hazel told me. "Whatever gave you that idea?"

I opened my mouth to answer but fell silent as the pieces clicked into place. The Holyoakes had lied to me. They'd used the Council as a bogeyman, filling my head with nightmares to keep me in line. And I had fallen for it. I'd spent the last two years hiding from the only people who actually wanted to help me.

"Never mind." My cheeks heated. "Must have gotten my stories mixed up."

"The reason you're here," Hazel said, "is to talk about the next step in your life."

"The next step?"

"Yes." She folded her hands on top of the table. "You've been surviving alone, which, believe me, is admirable, but it's not a healthy path for you, Figerella. We can't let that continue. You're a minor, and you need a legal guardian."

"Oh." I didn't know how I felt about that. Part of me didn't want to be alone anymore, but when I imagined living with people like the Holyoakes, being alone sounded way better.

"You have plenty of options," Hazel told me. "You're a popular girl on Earth, as you can imagine. Offers have poured in from boarding schools, corporations, and so on. But what I'm most excited to tell you"—she leaned forward to give me a pointed look—"is that you might have an uncle."

"A *what?*" I asked.

"I know this is a shock." Hazel flashed a palm. "His name is Lavar Jammeslot. He says he's your late father's brother. Lavar told us that he and your father were estranged for years, but he's been looking for you ever since your parents passed away."

"But my parents said they didn't have any brothers or sisters. How do you know he's telling the truth?"

"We can't run a DNA test until we have access to a lab," Hazel admitted. "But he showed us some of your father's personal articles, things a stranger wouldn't have. I know it's not proof, but I can't see a reason for him to lie about this. Of course we'll verify everything as soon as we can. He doesn't want to pressure you, but he wants very much to be your guardian. In fact, he came here to meet you."

By reflex, I checked over both of my shoulders.

"Not here in this room," Hazel said with a grin. "We gave him one of the suites on the third floor. I'll introduce you to him when you're ready."

"Wow." I scratched the back of my neck and tried to process what I'd learned. "An uncle. I can't believe—"

Suddenly, the doors burst open, and a voice called, "Stop!"

I spun around to find Kyler standing at the front of the conference room with his hands on his hips like some sort of superhero. Two of his brothers, Duke and Bonner, stood beside him on the right, and the twins, Rylan and Devin, flanked his left side. All of them folded their arms and puffed out their chests as if they'd come here to do battle . . . or challenge the Council to a dance-off.

"You," Clarence growled at Kyler.

Ky glared at him as if to say *We meet again.*

"I sent you home," Clarence said.

"You can't get rid of me that easily." Ky lifted his chin. "I've battled pirates, taken down a star barge, uncovered a conspiracy, and saved the world. I've got skills."

"All right," Hazel said, sounding just as confused as I was. "We can all agree that you have skills. But why are you here, Myler?"

"Kyler," he corrected. "And I'm here to present critical information that I guarantee will change the outcome of this trial."

Billaby threw up his wrinkled hands. "Why does everyone think we're running a court in here?"

Ky paused and looked to me for an explanation.

"There's no trial," I whispered. "Long story."

"Oh." Kyler gave the Council a sideways glance. "You're not trying to convict Fig for stealing the Holyoakes' shuttle?"

"Whoa, there." I lifted a finger. "Borrowing without permission. Not stealing."

Hazel pinched the bridge of her nose. "No. For the tenth time, we don't do that sort of thing."

"Then why—"

"We're here to discuss Miss Jammeslot's custody arrangements," she snapped. "If you'll give us some privacy."

Kyler formed a huddle with his brothers. They exchanged a few whispers, and then he asked the Council, "Actually, would you mind giving *us* some privacy? We want to talk to Fig about something important."

Hazel rolled her eyes before looking to me for approval.

"It's all right," I told her. "I'll make it quick."

The three council members filed out of the room, and to my surprise, Kyler's mom and dad walked inside. I didn't know why I was so shocked to see them—obviously someone had to have flown Kyler and his brothers to the yacht—but I hadn't expected this, and I found myself backing away toward the rear of the room.

With the extra space between us, I took a moment to study Ky's family.

His brothers looked slightly different than they had on-screen. Duke was even bigger in real life, a mountain of a boy with biceps big enough to crack walnuts, but with an easy posture that made him seem like a gentle giant instead of a bully.

Rylan and Devin watched me with a curious intensity that hinted Kyler wasn't the only genius in the family. As for Bonner, the youngest, there was a sparkle in his eyes that couldn't be captured on camera. . . . It told me he was trouble on two legs, but in a fun sort of way. I wanted to ask what would happen if I pulled his finger, but the timing felt wrong. Instead, I waved a shaky hand at the boys, and they waved back.

Mr. Centaurus stood at the head of the conference table with one arm wrapped around his wife. He unleashed a brilliant smile that drew out a pair of dimples in his cheeks. I liked him at once. Beside him, Mrs. Centaurus pressed a hand over her heart and peered at me with the same watery gaze she had given Kyler during their call. Her lips parted as if she wanted to say something, but she seemed too choked up to get the words out.

"Figerella," said Mr. Centaurus. He left his wife's side and strode to meet me where I was still frozen at the rear wall. "I'm Frank." He thumbed behind him. "And that's my wife, Ronalda, or Ronnie for short."

His hand was warm when he shook mine, and he brought with him the scents of peppermint gum and spicy cologne. I cleared my throat and told him, "Nice to meet you. You can call me Fig . . ." I shifted on my feet. "If you want to."

"Fig," he repeated with a grin. "I feel like I already know you from everything Kyler's told us about your adventures." He pressed another hand atop mine. "We're so grateful to you, Fig. I can't express how much." Squeezing my fingers, he added, "And I'm amazed by your skills with a laser. You probably don't know this, but I started a charity to clear asteroid fields from underprivileged worlds. I could use a sharpshooter like you on our team. In fact, I have a question to ask you. . . ."

"Yo, Dad," Bonner called, waving him over. "There's a call for you in the pilothouse. I think it's that lawyer guy on Earth."

Frank held up an index finger for me. "Hold that thought, Fig. I'll be right back."

As he left the room, Mrs. Centaurus closed the distance between us in slow, easy steps, as if she knew how nervous I was. When she reached me, she leaned down until we were eye level, so close that I could smell her lavender face cream. The scent caught me off guard, because it was different on her skin—warmer and sweeter, as though she brought out something special in the perfume. Until that moment, I'd forgotten it was like that with my mother—not the same scent, but a unique blend of lavender with her own fragrance. My heart ached because I knew I would never smell it again. But strangely, it comforted me to breathe in Ronnie's fragrance. She reminded me of the best parts of my mother, even though no one could take her place.

"Thank you," Ronnie said. She spoke softly, so that only I could hear, making it seem like we were having our own private conversation away from the boys. Maybe it was silly, but that made me feel special.

"Thank you for what?" I asked, the heat rising in my cheeks.

"For the message you sent me from the *Whirlwind*," she whispered. "The one telling me Kyler was all right." Her smile brimmed over with warmth that welled in her eyes. My own eyes blurred in response. "I was confused at first because the words didn't sound like him. Then when I saw you on the video transmission, it all made sense. I knew it was you."

I glanced at the floor. "It was no big deal."

"Oh, honey," she said, using two fingers to tip up my chin. "It was everything."

Tears spilled down my cheeks. She wiped them away with her thumb, but her soft touch only brought more tears to the surface. Soon my face was a waterfall, and she quit trying to dry the flow. It embarrassed me, losing control like that. I couldn't look at her, or at anyone else in the room. All I could do was sniffle and hope the boys weren't watching.

"You gave me a gift," she told me. "A gift that let me breathe for the first time in days, and I'm betting nobody asked you to do it. Am I right?"

I nodded.

"That's what I thought," she said. "Do you know what that says about you?"

Now she had my full attention. I wanted to know what my fake message said about me. So I focused on her eyes, even though it was like trying to stare at the sun. "What does it say?"

"That you're a compassionate and selfless young lady." She smoothed both hands over my tangled hair and added, "Your parents would be so proud of you."

That was too much.

My breathing hitched, and pressure wound so tightly behind my eyes that I got an instant headache. A jumble of emotions that I didn't understand rose up inside me, stealing words from my mind. I opened my mouth to say something—anything—but all I could do was gape like a fish out of water. I felt like I was choking on lavender, so I backed away until I could breathe again, and then I headed for the doorway and did what I did best.

I ran away.

I didn't stop until I reached my room on the third floor, where I slammed the door and threw myself onto the bed. I was so blinded by tears that I didn't realize I had company until a rustling sound drew my attention to the shadowy corner, and I gasped, sitting bolt upright as a man stepped forward.

The first thing I noticed was the name badge tacked to his shirt. It read *Guest of the Council: Lavar Jammeslot.* When I glanced at the man's face, my heart crashed, because I recognized the downward slashes of his mutation birthmarks. In that moment, I knew I didn't have an uncle. I didn't have anyone at all.

I was alone . . . worse than alone.

"Figerella Moonbeam," Captain Holyoake said as he pulled a coil of rope from his pocket. "I've come to take you home."

CHAPTER TWENTY-SIX

kyler centaurus

I knocked on Fig's door, but she didn't answer. Tilting an ear, I listened for noise coming from inside. "Nothing," I said to the Wanderer lady with the blue hair. I stepped out of her way and jerked a thumb at the door. "You should unlock it."

She puckered her mouth while she studied me and my brothers. I could tell she didn't know what to think of us, not that I blamed her. Five boys asking to invade a girl's bedroom sounded sketch. The fact that we'd left our parents in the pilothouse didn't help.

The lady bit her lip. "Maybe there's a reason Figerella's not answering."

"Yeah," Duke said. "Like she ate some bad food."

"And now she's passed out on the bathroom floor," Bonner added.

"Sick as a dog," Rylan continued.

"Choking on her own vomit!" Devin cried. "My God, woman! She could be dying in there!"

I hid a grin. My brothers were good.

"Okay, okay," the blue-haired lady said. "Wait here. I'll go in first."

She entered the key code, and the door slid open. A glance inside showed me nothing but darkness. I stood in the doorway and watched the woman turn on the lights and walk through the empty room. She peeked in the bathroom and shook her head.

Fig wasn't there.

"Huh," I muttered. "I wonder where she went. She couldn't have gone far. I mean, it's a big yacht, but not *that* big." I'd just begun to suggest checking the kitchen when a strange smell crossed my nose, and I inhaled again. I sniffed a few more times and noticed the smell growing stronger inside Fig's room. "Do you smell that?" I asked my brothers.

Bonner held up both hands. "Dude, it wasn't me."

"Not *that*," I said. "Something musky, like a vegetable."

Duke raised his nose in the air. "Garlic?"

"Scallions?" guessed Devin.

Rylan sniffed. "Chives?"

My stomach dropped. *No.* It was onions.

All of a sudden I knew what had happened to Fig.

"We have to get to the hangar," I told my brothers. "And fast."

The fact that I could still smell onions gave me hope, because it meant the person who'd eaten them had just been there moments ago. But there was no time to waste. I led the way out the door and jogged toward the stairwell, calling over my shoulder, "Follow me. We'll grab our supplies on the way."

CHAPTER TWENTY-SEVEN

figerella jammeslot

I dug in my heels, but it was no use. The soles of my boots skidded across the hangar floor as the captain dragged me to his shuttle. He opened the passenger door and shoved me into the seat. With my wrists bound behind my back, I couldn't stop him from fastening my safety harness and trapping me in place. I bucked forward, straining and grunting, but I was powerless to move more than a few inches in any direction.

He had won.

And he seemed to know it, too, because he wore a grin as he settled into the pilot's seat. It might've been the first time I'd seen him truly smile. "Someday you'll thank me for this," he said.

I huffed. "Don't hold your breath."

He ignored me, still smiling. But his grin flattened when he entered the code to open the hangar door and nothing happened. He punched in the code two more times, but the only response was a buzz and an error message that read INVALID ENTRY.

He growled and stepped out of the shuttle. "Stay here," he told me, as if I had any choice. "I'll have to open the hatch manually."

"Manually?" I asked. "Won't that blow you into space?" I nodded at his open door. "*And* suck all the oxygen out of the hangar?"

"There's a safety feature," he said. "It sets a countdown after I push the button. I'll have plenty of time to get back here before the hatch opens."

I didn't share the captain's confidence, so as soon as he walked away, I experimented with how far I could wriggle in my seat harness. I figured out that if I sucked in my belly and leaned to one side, I could stretch my hands to my hip. That wasn't far enough to unlatch my harness, but I might be able to reach the laser I kept tucked in my boot. All I needed was to raise my calf a few inches higher. . . .

I tried with all my might, stretching so hard I almost dislocated my shoulder. Just as my fingertips connected with the laser, I pulled it free from my boot.

And dropped it on the floor.

"No," I hissed.

I used my feet to try and pick up the laser, but I knew there wasn't much time before the captain returned. I listened through his open door while I worked. But instead of his footsteps, I heard a grunt and a scuffle, followed by a loud "What the—" and "Oof." I tried looking over my shoulders to see what was going on, but I couldn't twist far enough. Then my door opened, and Kyler appeared, holding a finger to his lips in a signal to be quiet.

"Captain Holyoake is in the hangar," I whispered. "You need to watch out."

Kyler chuckled as he unbuckled my safety harness. He used the fallen laser to cut the ropes from my hands. "The captain's about to meet my brothers. Trust me when I say he's the one who needs to watch out."

Ky motioned for me to follow, and we crept along the wall toward the airlock that led to the main part of the yacht. Captain Holyoake was standing at the control panel . . . or trying to, anyway. His feet kept slipping and sliding on the floor, so he could barely stay upright.

"Mega Über Lube," Ky whispered to me. "I squirted it on that one tiny spot. I knew he would have to come to the control panel after we disabled the hangar hatch."

"That was you?" I asked.

"Devin and Rylan, actually," Ky said, pointing at the airlock room. "They're on the other side of that door, getting ready to unlock it. Watch."

Right on cue, the airlock door opened. I spotted the twins and Bonner standing on the other side. The captain barely had time to glance at them when Duke, who had been hiding behind a smaller shuttle, ran toward the captain and body-checked him.

What happened next could only be described as poetic. In perfect synch, the captain went flying into the airlock chamber while Bonner and the twins leaped over the patch of Mega Über Lube on the floor and landed safely in the hangar. At once, the twins hacked the control panel and closed the airlock door, trapping the captain inside. The best part was that right before the door shut, Bonner stuck his rear end in the airlock and farted. There was a tiny window built into the door, just big enough for me to see the disgust on the captain's face.

I couldn't help laughing.

Kyler walked up to the airlock chamber and jabbed a finger at the captain. "The Centaurus brothers have something to say to you, Holyoake!" He hooked a thumb at me. "You can't mess with our sister."

While I blinked in confusion, Duke flexed his arms and delivered a dirty look through the window. "Yeah," he said. "Only *we* can mess with our sister."

"What are you talking about?" I asked.

Kyler reached in his pocket and produced a small data tablet. He held it between us and pulled up a document for me to read.

SUPERIOR COURT OF THE FIRST DISTRICT OF EARTH
FAMILY COURT, DOMESTIC RELATIONS BRANCH

The petition of Francis Roman Centaurus and Ronalda Smith Centaurus for adoption of the minor child:

Figerella Moonbeam Jammeslot

I had to reread the text heading twice before I believed what my eyes were trying to show me. Kyler's mom and dad wanted to adopt me?

That couldn't be right.

"What is this?" I glanced through the airlock window for Frank and Ronnie. If they wanted to adopt me, why hadn't they told me themselves? "Where are your parents?"

"Talking to their lawyer," Kyler told me. "A lot of people had to pull a lot of strings to make this happen on the quick, but it's happening. That's why we came here—to take you home with us. My parents are your parents, too, if that's what you want."

My mom and dad, whispered a tiny voice inside my head. But I was afraid to believe the voice, so I pushed it aside.

"Boom," said Bonner, mimicking an explosion with his hand. "You're one of us now, Fig."

"Well, not yet," Kyler said. "She has to agree to it first."

I scrolled through the rest of the document, whizzing past a bunch of legal terms I didn't understand, and a list of statements promising that Frank and Ronnie would provide for my care and give me a proper home and an education. I reached the last page, where Frank and Ronnie had already signed their names. There was only one blank signature line left, and it belonged to me. Below it read *Figerella Moonbeam Jammeslot Centaurus.*

"Centaurus," I whispered under my breath.

My heart swelled to the size of a melon. They wanted me in their family, so much that Kyler and his brothers had fought for me.

My brothers, the same voice whispered, but now I didn't try to silence it. I wanted this too badly to run away from it. Every cell in my body hummed with energy; nothing had ever felt so right. I knew that somewhere out there, my parents were smiling down at me. Maybe they'd even had a hand in making this happen—they loved me enough to do just that.

Kyler wrapped an arm around my shoulders. "So what do you say, Fig? Are you ready to join our crew?" He added behind his hand, "My folks are crazy about you. Plus, my mom's always wanted a daughter."

I tried to hold back my tears, but they spilled down my cheeks in waves. I smiled wide enough to split my face in half. "Here's what I say," I told him. "I want my brothers to show me what a NWARF is."

Bonner's mouth formed an O of excitement.

That should have been my first warning.

"Uh, Fig," Kyler said, wildly shaking his head. "You might not want to—"

Duke silenced him with a lifted hand. "Now, now, Kyler, don't spoil the moment. Our little sister wants a NWARF. Who are we to deny her request?"

"Yeah," Rylan said. "We aim to please, don't we?"

"Totally." Devin chuckled, rubbing his palms together. "Her wish is our command."

Bonner extended an index finger and told me to pull it.

I shouldn't have done that. A cloud of noxious gas surrounded me, and the next thing I knew, someone had me in a sweaty headlock while a pair of knuckles scrubbed my scalp. Then a voice cried, "Wedgie!" and I reached behind my back just in time to block the waistband of my undershorts. After that, I was done playing around. I grabbed the wrist that was holding me down and twisted it in a defensive move my father had taught me years ago. Moments later, Duke was on his knees begging me for mercy while Rylan, Devin, and Bonner held up their palms in surrender.

I released Duke's hand. "I'll go easy on you," I told him, "seeing as it's our first day as siblings and all. But next time I won't hold back."

Even as he rubbed his wrist, Duke smiled at me in admiration. "Dang, our little sister is fierce!"

A grin sprang to my lips. I found myself standing taller with pride.

"Heck yeah, she is," Bonner added. "Totally savage!"

"You guys haven't seen anything yet," Kyler said.

His laughter led my gaze to him, to the spoiled brat I had hoped to con out of his spaceship a few days ago. He had become my best friend when I'd least expected it, and now he would be my brother. Nothing could have made me happier. In fact, there was too much joy inside me. I almost couldn't hold it in.

"Welcome to the family, Weirdo," Kyler said. He gave my arm a playful slug. "You're going to fit right in."

ACKNOWLEDGMENTS

Maybe it only takes one person to write a book, but to *publish* a book requires a group effort, and that's something I don't take for granted. I'm very lucky to have a team of talented, passionate book lovers who work behind the scenes to bring my stories to life. Without them, you wouldn't be holding *Blastaway* in your hands.

To editors Laura Schreiber and Mary Mudd, thank you for guiding me through the revision process with suggestions that took Kyler's and Fig's adventures to infinity and beyond. You guys are brilliant, and working with you is a blast! (See what I did there?) To my agent, Nicole Resciniti, thank you for being my biggest fan and my champion. Your encouragement has carried me through a dozen books. Here's to a dozen more!

Big hugs to my critique partner, Lorie Langdon, who is a talented author and a wonderful friend. If I ever need to brainstorm a plot, or simply to talk about life, I always feel better after chatting with you. Much love to my hubby, Kevin Kreisa, for helping me invent ways to punish pirates and lasso the sun. You have a great mind for shenanigans!

As always, I'm grateful to my family and friends for their endless support in spreading the word about my books. You guys are the best! And finally, to my kids, thank you for asking me to write a book that you could read. I'm so glad I listened. Your lovable quirks and goofy antics gave me lots of inspiration for Kyler and his siblings. The Centaurus family is more real because of you. But even though writing *Blastaway* was fun, it's being your mom that's the ultimate adventure!